CELEBRATING THOMAS HARDY

Celebrating Thomas Hardy

Insights and Appreciations

Edited by

Charles P. C. Pettit

First published in Great Britain 1996 by
MACMILLAN PRESS LTD
Houndmills, Basingstoke, Hampshire RG21 6XS
and London
Companies and representatives
throughout the world

A catalogue record for this book is available
from the British Library.

ISBN 0–333–65651–2

First published in the United States of America 1996 by
ST. MARTIN'S PRESS, INC.,
Scholarly and Reference Division,
175 Fifth Avenue,
New York, N.Y. 10010

ISBN 0–312–15974–9

Library of Congress Cataloging-in-Publication Data
Celebrating Thomas Hardy : insights and appreciations / edited by
Charles P. C. Pettit.
p. cm.
Includes bibliographical references and index.
ISBN 0–312–15974–9
1. Thomas Hardy, 1840–1928—Criticism and interpretation.
2. Pastoral literature, English—History and criticism.   3. Wessex
(England)—In literature.   4. Country life in literature.
I. Pettit, Charles P. C.
PR4754.C33   1996
823'.8—dc20
96–3598
CIP

Editorial matter and selection © Charles P. C. Pettit 1996
Foreword © Furse Swann 1996; Chapter 1 © James Gibson 1996; Chapter 2 ©
Laurence Lerner 1996; Chapter 3 © Lance St John Butler 1996; Chapter 4 ©
Ronald Blythe 1996; Chapter 5 © Peter Levi 1996; Chapter 6 © Gillian Beer 1996;
Chapter 7 © Simon Curtis 1996; Chapter 8 © Michael Millgate 1996; Chapter 9 ©
Rosemarie Morgan 1996; Chapter 10 © Peter Rothermel 1996; Chapter 11 ©
Edward Blishen 1996.

10   9   8   7   6   5   4   3   2   1
05   04   03   02   01   00   99   98   97   96

Printed and bound in Great Britain by
Antony Rowe Ltd, Chippenham, Wiltshire

Contents

Foreword

Language makes it possible to define and share experience. Each one of us uses language in his or her own way but each language, from whatever part of the globe, is what holds us together as people. Language is what both unites and divides. Each voice too, is unique. Yet we all know, like Stephano's 'most delicate monster' – part Trinculo, part Caliban – that we have more than one voice; indeed, we are a veritable orchestra of potentially harmonious or conflicting voices. Hardy recognised this very clearly. In his poem 'So Various' he enumerates a succession of conflicting thumb-nail sketches of individuals totally contradictory in their apparent natures, yet all

> Were *one* man. Yea,
> I was all they.

This recognition of the immense, often contradictory, variety of voices which we all possess seems a useful starting point for introducing a volume of essays such as this.

For in Hardy's writings we find the voices of both realist and dreamer, conservative and radical, the nostalgic and the avant-garde, the comfortable and comforting and the uncomfortable and discomforting. It is not surprising, therefore, that he constantly disclaimed having any single philosophy which might be abstracted or deduced from his writings. Rather they were to be viewed as a series of 'seemings', 'impressions', ascertained through a life-time of enquiry, reading, observation, experience and conscious artistry.

Thus, when some 250 people gathered together in Dorchester from all over the world in the last week of July 1994 for the 11th International Thomas Hardy Conference, there was assembled a multitude of voices, each in its own way unique, yet all had come together because they recognised something of their own voice or voices in the voice or voices of Hardy. It was my intention, through the variety of lectures, seminars, poetry readings, recitals, concerts, music workshops, services, plays, exhibitions and dances which made up the eight-day conference, to mirror something of this multiplicity of voices.

This volume records the key lectures, ranging, as always, over wide aspects of Hardy's life and work, and of his relationship to other writers and to his readers today in far-flung areas of the world. It was important to me that, taking Hardy as the centre, we should cast our minds both back and forward from his time, to seek out his roots and inspiration, his links with writers such as John Clare and William Barnes, as well as his relationship to our own time. Parallels were drawn, between the Dorset agricultural worker in Hardy's day and now; between his social background and concerns and those of the recent Nobel Prizewinner for Literature Toni Morrison; between the class-conscious upwardly mobile young man of the 1870s and of the 1950s; between the experience of Tess at Flintcomb-Ash and the personal experience of a Chinese academic sent out to work in the rotten potato fields on the edge of the Gobi Desert during the Chinese Cultural Revolution. Throughout, the lecturers were invoking Hardy's voices and comparing them with their own in their own situation today.

And Hardy's voices are legion. Not only is he able, with Keats's 'camelion Poet', to enter into the lives and thoughts of other people – real or imagined – but he also enters into the imagined thoughts and 'voices' of such improbable 'Bodies' as sundials, tables, old newspapers, innumerable species of birds and trees, individual musical instruments, winds, skies, rabbits, dogs, old psalm tunes, the Elgin Marbles, the family face, ghosts galore, sun, moon and star – and, not infrequently, the Prime Mover himself. This Keatsian and Shakespearian capacity whereby the poet is 'continually in [forming] and filling some other Body' is also quintessentially Hardyan.

As Gillian Beer pointed out in her masterly lecture, such voices are not isolated for Hardy. In that great little poem 'In a Museum', which she quoted and discussed in her lecture, Hardy records the momentary but momentous illumination that the 'coo' of the now fossilised prehistoric 'musical bird' he sees in a glass case 'is blent, or will be blending' with the 'contralto voice I heard last night' in – and I believe it is one of the great lines of Hardy's poetry –

In the full-fugued song of the universe unending.

No voice is lost ultimately. All voices play their part in the totality of 'the full-fugued song of the universe'. The image of the fugue is important: the repetition of a theme by different voices, different instruments, at different pitches, in often subtly different variations

– this is at the heart of the West Gallery music which Hardy loved as well as that of the great classical Western tradition.

It is a theme which Hardy returns to on a number of occasions. In 'To Meet, or Otherwise' we find it. Here Hardy contemplates the importance of meeting – ultimately it will make no difference:

> ... Yet this same sun will slant its beams
> At no far day
> On our two mounds

But no, they should 'make the most . . . of what remains':

> By briefest meeting something sure is won

Each moment adds something to the great saga of history. And this, in its way, was as true of that week in Dorchester as of the projected meeting of Hardy and Florence Dugdale:

> So, to the one long-sweeping symphony
> From times remote
> Till now, of human tenderness, shall we
> Supply one note,
> Small and untraced, yet that will ever be
> Somewhere afloat
> Amid the spheres, as part of sick Life's antidote.

As T. E. Lawrence said in a letter to Robert Graves, after visiting Hardy at Max Gate, in September 1923: 'They used to call this man a pessimist. While really he is full of fancy expectations.' This volume, I hope, bears witness to the vitality and optimism and 'fancy expectations' which Hardy, three-quarters of a century on, is still able to inspire.

Furse Swann

Director, 11th International Thomas Hardy Conference

Preface

Furse Swann has in his Foreword given an elegant account of the genesis of this book in the Thomas Hardy Society's Eleventh International Conference, and has described his concept of the Conference programme as a whole, centred on the voices of Hardy and of his readers. It is a pleasure to acknowledge in writing Furse's role as 'onlie begetter' of this book through his creation of the Conference programme, and to thank him for his help when he handed on the torch to me for my task, which was to effect the metamorphosis of Conference lectures into book.

In his 'Apology' to *Late Lyrics and Earlier* Hardy alerted his readers to the 'chance little shocks that may be caused over a book of various character like the present . . . by the juxtaposition of unrelated, even discordant, effusions', and his words may aptly be applied to the present book, which includes significant variations in approach and tone, as well as in subject. As the sub-title *Insights and Appreciations* indicates, some papers are stringent and searching literary criticism of specific aspects of Hardy's achievement, while others are simply personal appreciation of Hardy's achievement as a whole. However, all these 'voices' have their own validity, and, crucially, all contribute to the overall concept of the variety both of Hardy himself and of readers' responses to him. In more pragmatic terms, any reader with an interest in Hardy, whatever his or her critical sophistication, will be sure to find something of interest here.

As in *New Perspectives on Thomas Hardy* (which was based on the previous Hardy Conference), a conscious editorial decision has been made not to require the contributors to re-write their lectures in the style of formal academic papers. It is hoped that the resulting vitality and relatively informal idiom, which stem from the papers' original oral delivery, will enhance the appeal of the book to Hardy enthusiasts and students.

For their appearance in volume form, the order of the papers has been changed to create a shape which emphasises the underlying concept for the reader. The book opens with papers concentrating directly on Hardy, and then moves out to begin the exploration of Hardy's relationships with other writers. These explorations are arranged in a basic chronological sequence (so far as possible, bearing in mind inevitable overlaps), beginning with Hardy and John Clare and leading up to Hardy and Toni Morrison, by way of William Barnes, the Decadent writers of the 1880s and 1890s, and George Moore. Michael Millgate's paper on Emma and Florence Hardy sits appropriately here. The volume concludes with personal appreciations by Peter Rothermel and contemporary writer Edward Blishen.

The notes at the end of each chapter identify the edition of Hardy used in quotations by each contributor, but chapter references (rather than page references to one particular edition) are given for all quotations from Hardy's novels throughout the book in view of the number of editions now available and the difficulty many people will experience in obtaining any one edition.

In conclusion, I would like to thank James Gibson for his helpful advice, and my wife Judith and my children Richard and Claire for their understanding and forbearance during the editing of this book.

CHARLES P. C. PETTIT

Notes on the Contributors

Gillian Beer is Professor of English and President of Clare Hall at the University of Cambridge. She is an Honorary Fellow of both St Anne's College, Oxford, and Girton College, Cambridge. She is Vice-President of the British Academy, and Chair of the Poetry Book Society. Her publications include: *Meredith: a Change of Masks* (1970), *The Romance* (1970), *Darwin's Plots* (1983), *George Eliot* (1986), *Arguing with the Past* (1989) and *Forging the Missing Link* (1994).

Edward Blishen became a full-time writer and broadcaster in 1959 after a long flirtation with teaching. His thirteen volumes of autobiography began with *Roaring Boys* in 1955; the latest, *The Penny World*, was published in 1990, and he is now working on what he fears might be the last, *Everything Must Go*. He was awarded the J. R. Ackerley Prize for Autobiography in 1981 for *Shaky Relations*. He compiled the *Oxford Book of Poetry for Children*, and with Leon Garfield wrote *The God Beneath the Sea*, which won the Carnegie Medal in 1970. For thirteen years he conducted a programme for African writers on the BBC's African Service, and lately has been presenting Radio 4's *A Good Read*. He is a Fellow of the Royal Society of Literature.

Ronald Blythe introduced and edited *A Pair of Blue Eyes* for Macmillan's New Wessex Edition (1975) and *Far from the Madding Crowd* for the Penguin English Library (1978). His works include: *The Age of Illusion* (1963), *Akenfield* (1969), *From the Headlands* (1982) and *Divine Landscapes* (1986). He is the editor of *William Hazlitt: Selected Writings* (1970). He is a poet, and has also published collections of short stories.

Lance St John Butler is Senior Lecturer in English Studies at the University of Stirling. His publications include: *Thomas Hardy after Fifty Years* (edited); *Thomas Hardy; Samuel Beckett and the Meaning of Being; Studying Thomas Hardy; Alternative Hardy* (edited) and *Victorian Doubt*. He was a contributor to *New Perspectives on Thomas Hardy*.

Simon Curtis taught at the University of Manchester. He has written on John Stuart Mill as Botanist in the Midi, the Vizetelly Publishing

Company and the reception of Zola in Britain, and, more briefly, on Charles Cotton, fisherman-poet, and the Australian poet Douglas Stewart. He is working on a piece on the minor Scots dialect poet James Nicol of Traquair, and on Hardy's *Late Lyrics and Earlier* for the Ryburn edition. He was Visiting Fellow at the University of New South Wales, Sydney, in 1989; has had three books of poetry published; and edits *The Thomas Hardy Journal*.

James Gibson is an Honorary Vice-President of the Thomas Hardy Society, of which he is a former Chairman; as creator and first editor of *The Thomas Hardy Journal* and Academic Director of two of the Society's Conferences he has played a leading role in Society affairs. He was formerly Principal Lecturer in English at Christ Church College, Canterbury. He has written or edited some fifty books, with total sales of some two million copies. His major Hardy works include his editions of *The Complete Poems* and *The Variorum Edition of the Complete Poems*, and various Hardy novels. He is editor of *A Casebook: The Poems of Thomas Hardy* (with Trevor Johnson) and both *Chosen Poems* and *Chosen Short Stories*. He has recently completed work on a short life of Hardy in the Macmillan 'Literary Lives' series, and is working on a volume of interviews and recollections of Hardy. He was a contributor to *New Perspectives on Thomas Hardy*.

Laurence Lerner is Edwin Mims Professor of English at Vanderbilt University, Nashville, Tennessee. His critical books include: *The Truest Poetry: an Essay on the Question, 'What is Literature?'* (1960), *The Truthtellers: Jane Austen, George Eliot, Lawrence* (1967), *The Uses of Nostalgia: Studies in Pastoral* (1972), *Love and Marriage: Literature in its Social Context* (1979), *The Literary Imagination: Essays on Literature and Society* (1982) and *The Frontiers of Literature* (1988). With John Holmstrom he edited a selection of contemporary reviews of Hardy under the title *Thomas Hardy and his Readers* (1968). He is also the author of nine volumes of poetry, including his *Selected Poems* (1984), and of three novels, the most recent being *My Grandfather's Grandfather* (1985).

Peter Levi is a Fellow Emeritus of St Catherine's College, Oxford, and a former Professor of Poetry at Oxford. He has published numerous volumes of poetry, and also thrillers, translations and *A History of Greek Literature* (1985). His biographical writings include: *Life and Times of William Shakespeare* (1988), *Boris Pasternak* (1989),

Tennyson (1993) and *Edward Lear* (1995). He has been devoted to William Barnes for forty-five years, and to Hardy for more than fifty.

Michael Millgate is University Professor of English Emeritus of the University of Toronto. Although most of his early work was on William Faulkner, his principal contributions in more recent years have been to the study of Hardy – among them: *Thomas Hardy: His Career as a Novelist* (1971, 1994), *The Collected Letters of Thomas Hardy* (7 volumes, co-edited, 1978–88), *Thomas Hardy: A Biography* (1982), *Thomas Hardy: Selected Letters* (edited, 1990), *Thomas Hardy's 'Studies, Specimens &c.' Notebook* (co-edited, 1994) and *The Letters of Emma and Florence Hardy* (edited, 1996). His editing for Macmillan of Hardy's ghost-written *The Life and Work of Thomas Hardy* (1984) led to the wider exploration of authorial deaths and literary estates which formed the subject of his *Testamentary Acts: Browning, Tennyson, James, Hardy* (1992). He is an Honorary Vice-President of the Thomas Hardy Society.

Rosemarie Morgan is a lecturer in English at Yale University. Her major works on Hardy are *Women and Sexuality in the Novels of Thomas Hardy* (1988) and *Cancelled Words: Rediscovering Thomas Hardy* (1992), and she has edited the manuscript of *Far from the Madding Crowd* for Penguin Classics (1996). She has contributed papers to many books and periodicals, including 'Inscriptions of Self: Thomas Hardy and Autobiography' (in *Thomas Hardy Annual*, 5, 1987), 'Mothering the Text: Hardy's Vanishing Maternal Abode' (in *A Spacious Vision*, 1994) and 'Touching the Body: Critical Approaches to the Body in Victorian Literature' (in *Victorian Literature and Culture*, 1996). She is an Honorary Vice-President of the Thomas Hardy Society.

Peter Rothermel taught English and German in grammar schools for many years, and worked for a spell for the BBC German Service. While teaching at his own former Grammar School in Stuttgart he also took seminars on American literature at Stuttgart University. From 1968 to 1984 he followed the call of the 'Pädagogische Hochschule Ludwigsburg' as Professor of English Literature and Language, until his recent retirement. His publications include papers on writers as diverse as Matthew Arnold, Conrad, Thackeray, E. M. Forster, Graham Greene, William Golding, Hawthorne, Faulkner and Kingsley Amis.

1

Thomas Hardy's Poetry: Poetic Apprehension and Poetic Method

JAMES GIBSON

There is an immediate difficulty in considering Middleton Murry's reference to Hardy's poetic apprehension and poetic method in that the word apprehension is capable of several meanings.[1] We might at first think that 'poetic apprehension' means Hardy's superb gift of observation. He was, as he told us, 'The man with the watching eye', 'a man who used to notice such things', and we remember J. M. Barrie's comment 'That man couldn't look out of a window without seeing something that had never been seen before.' Recently I met a man in his eighties who as a young boy had been taken on several visits to Max Gate by the then Vicar of Winterborne Monkton. He told me that on one of these visits Hardy turned to him and said 'Boy, what can you remember of the roofs you saw on your way here today?' He replied in some embarrassment that he could remember nothing. A week later, on another visit to Max Gate, he studied all the roofs on the journey there in case he was asked again. Eventually Hardy turned to him and said, 'Boy, tell me about the trees you saw on the way here today.' Again he had to confess ignorance and Hardy then said to him, 'Boy, you see but you do not observe!' It is a shrewd piece of discrimination. Hardy himself both saw and observed, and one of the strengths of his writing is his ability to choose significant evocative detail – the 'dry, empty, and white' road stretching across the heath 'like the parting-line on a head of black hair', the primaeval rocks forming the road's steep border, the gutters and spouts babbling 'unchecked in the busy way of witless things', the flag-rope gibbering hoarse and the shy hares printing long paces. Such descriptions are certainly part of Hardy's apprehension if we use that word in its dictionary definition of 'to be conscious of through the senses'.

That his senses were extraordinarily well-developed would have been obvious to any perceptive reader as early as 1872 when, at the very beginning of *Under the Greenwood Tree*, we read:

> To dwellers in a wood almost every species of tree has its voice as well as its feature. At the passing of the breeze the fir-trees sob and moan no less distinctly than they rock; the holly whistles as it battles with itself; the ash hisses amid its quiverings; the beech rustles while its flat boughs rise and fall.[2]

and Gillian Beer in her excellent essay 'Can the Native Return?' describes how Hardy in *The Return of the Native* 'makes us aware of the native inhabitants' power of making sensory discriminations lost to the town-dweller, what he calls "acoustic pictures" . . .'. 'He makes the ear', she tells us, 'attentive to the particular character of the heath, and builds a landscape derived not from the eye alone but from all the senses, and above all from sound and touch.'[3]

It is in *The Return of the Native*, too, that we read:

> The whole secret of following these incipient paths, when there was not light enough in the atmosphere to show a turnpike-road, lay in the development of the sense of touch in the feet. . . . To a walker practised in such places a difference between impact on maiden herbage, and on the crippled stalks of a slight footway, is perceptible through the thickest boot or shoe.[4]

So here we have the tactile sense, the sense of touch, as another indication of Hardy's apprehension, and here is richness indeed, a richness which is an important part both of the novels and of the poems. Hardy himself said that his aim was to make his novels as much like poetry as possible.

I have not yet mentioned the pre-eminent sense, the visual, but the examples of this both in novels and poems are everywhere. The visual sense is, of course, the most powerful, and Hardy has enriched our own visual memories enormously. There are a few uses of smell and taste, and I never cease to be impressed by his ability to convey muscularity, the kinetic sense, in his verse. Thus in 'Domicilium' we have 'High beeches, bending' where the muscularity of 'bending' is emphasised by the trochaic foot. And in 'The Darkling Thrush' the line 'At once a voice arose among' with its iambic feet and rising rhythm, makes us feel the upward flight of the bird.

Hardy's powerful sensory apprehension was complemented by an astonishing retentive memory. Usually the most modest of men, he acknowledges this when in his *Life* he says:

I believe it would be said by people who knew me well that I have a faculty (possibly not uncommon) for burying an emotion in my heart or brain for forty years, and exhuming it at the end of that time as fresh as when interred. For instance, the poem entitled 'The Breaking of Nations' contains a feeling that moved me in 1870, during the Franco-Prussian war, when I chanced to be looking at such an agricultural incident in Cornwall. But I did not write the verses till during the war with Germany of 1914, and onwards.[5]

Again, only a few months before he died, he told John Galsworthy that he could remember clearly stories his mother had told him eighty years before.[6]

Three poems which richly illustrate Hardy's poetic apprehension in its primary sense of observation are 'Domicilium', 'An August Midnight' and 'During Wind and Rain'.[7] In all these poems we have closely observed and carefully chosen detail. In 'Domicilium', which Hardy tells us was written when he was just eighteen, he begins with a straightforward piece of description.

Domicilium

It faces west, and round the back and sides
High beeches, bending, hang a veil of boughs,
And sweep against the roof. Wild honeysucks
Climb on the walls, and seem to sprout a wish
(If we may fancy wish of trees and plants)
To overtop the apple-trees hard by.

Red roses, lilacs, variegated box
Are there in plenty, and such hardy flowers
As flourish best untrained. Adjoining these
Are herbs and esculents; and farther still
A field; then cottages with trees, and last
The distant hills and sky.

Behind, the scene is wilder. Heath and furze
Are everything that seems to grow and thrive

Upon the uneven ground. A stunted thorn
Stands here and there, indeed; and from a pit
An oak uprises, springing from a seed
Dropped by some bird a hundred years ago.

                          In days bygone –
Long gone – my father's mother, who is now
Blest with the blest, would take me out to walk.
At such a time I once inquired of her
How looked the spot when first she settled here.
The answer I remember. 'Fifty years
Have passed since then, my child, and change has marked
The face of all things. Yonder garden-plots
And orchards were uncultivated slopes
O'ergrown with bramble bushes, furze and thorn:
That road a narrow path shut in by ferns,
Which, almost trees, obscured the passer-by.

'Our house stood quite alone, and those tall firs
And beeches were not planted. Snakes and efts
Swarmed in the summer days, and nightly bats
Would fly about our bedrooms. Heathcroppers
Lived on the hills, and were our only friends;
So wild it was when first we settled here.'

The first few words might have come out of an estate-agent's blurb, 'It faces west', and this is followed by a matter-of-fact description of the trees and plants which surround the cottage. Young poets tend to go for ornamental adjectives, but Hardy is already showing his dislike of the 'decorated line' as he once called it, and the adjectives are bare and economic. He cannot resist a little joke about the 'hardy flowers'. One can see his methodical architect's mind turning from the western view to the scene behind, and we notice his 'wild, wilder, wild' and the effect it conveys of the untamed and uncultivated surroundings. We have the first of several stunted thorns – Hardy could empathise with plants and animals as well as with suffering human beings – and an indication of the uncompromising reality with which he looks on nature. And he finishes his painting of the scene with the introduction of the animal world – the snakes and efts, the bats and ponies which would have been such a common feature of their lives.

The descriptive element in 'An August Midnight' is at a different level and is made to feel more intense by the powerful rhythm and the sheer economy with which the scene is depicted.

An August Midnight

I

A shaded lamp and a waving blind,
And the beat of a clock from a distant floor:
On this scene enter – winged, horned, and spined –
A longlegs, a moth, and a dumbledore;
While 'mid my page there idly stands
A sleepy fly that rubs its hands. . . .

II

Thus meet we five, in this still place,
At this point of time, at this point in space.
– My guests besmear my new-penned line,
Or bang at the lamp and fall supine.
'God's humblest, they!' I muse. Yet why?
They know Earth-secrets that know not I.

Max Gate, 1899

The first two lines are wholly descriptive with the visual lamp and blind supported by the sound of the clock, a sound made more vivid by the clock-like rhythm. There is a hint here of stage directions, and that Hardy may have been thinking the same is clear in line 3: 'On this scene enter . . .' where, as Ian Gregor has pointed out,[8] we might expect to hear a Shakespearian 'Henry IV and his nobles', and we have instead 'a longlegs, a moth, and a dumbledore' (i.e. a bumble-bee), and a fly brought to vivid life by the imaginative adjective 'sleepy' and that beautifully observed 'rubs its hands'. In the second stanza the scene is made even more vivid and real by the antics of the 'guests' in besmearing his 'new-penned line' and banging 'at the lamp' and falling 'supine'. What is so impressive about this poem, as it is about so much of Hardy's writing, is its authenticity. This, we feel, really did happen and his descriptive ability is largely responsible here. In a very real sense we are with Hardy in his study on that August midnight.

'During Wind and Rain' was first published in 1917.

During Wind and Rain

They sing their dearest songs –
He, she, all of them – yea,
Treble and tenor and bass,
   And one to play;
With the candles mooning each face. . . .
   Ah, no; the years O!
How the sick leaves reel down in throngs!

They clear the creeping moss –
Elders and juniors – aye,
Making the pathways neat
   And the garden gay;
And they build a shady seat. . . .
   Ah, no; the years, the years;
See, the white storm-birds wing across!

They are blithely breakfasting all –
Men and maidens – yea,
Under the summer tree,
   With a glimpse of the bay,
While pet fowl come to the knee. . . .
   Ah, no; the years O!
And the rotten rose is ript from the wall.

They change to a high new house,
He, she, all of them – aye,
Clocks and carpets and chairs
   On the lawn all day,
And brightest things that are theirs. . . .
   Ah, no; the years, the years;
Down their carved names the rain-drop ploughs.

We know that this poem is very much influenced by the death of Emma, his first wife, and by his reading of the book which she had written secretly a year before she died and called 'Some Recollections'. After her death Hardy would have read of Emma's childhood in Plymouth and of the garden there with the 'shady seat'.

She writes of her 'elders' and of a 'mania at that time for keeping handsome fowls', of her family singing around the piano, and of the high new house they moved to in Bedford Terrace. Perhaps most strikingly of all she uses the words 'all has been changed with the oncoming years'. Here we see Hardy's poetic apprehension working not on material items around him but on something he has read. Her nostalgia and his blend together and her descriptive pictures of her Plymouth life in the 1850s and 1860s provide an imaginative stimulus which results in one of his finest poems. The memories of past time move him so powerfully that he adds his own descriptive details and paints images of that Plymouth life which are both particular and universal. Some of us will still remember how singing together around a piano was such an important and enjoyable part of family and community life before the arrival of television.

Other common family activities are described in stanzas 2 and 3, the family gardening together and then breakfasting in the garden with its glimpse of the bay. The creeping moss (how precise is 'creeping'), and the neat pathways, the shady seat, the breakfast, the summer tree and the pet fowl, all give the poem richness. The final stanza significantly gives us a picture which suggests that the stability of the opening lines of the previous stanzas may be threatened by the move. We are back to 'change', and the second word in the stanza is 'change'. The very first word in the very first poem of Hardy's *Collected Poems* was 'Change' and, of course, we have been told in 'Domicilium' that 'change has marked / The face of all things'. Many of Hardy's greatest poems grow out of his sensitive apprehension of the passing of time and the inevitability of change.

But by 'poetic apprehension' Middleton Murry means far more than just an ability to write good descriptive poetry by imaginative observation, and here we must look at Hardy's own comments on the nature of poetry. We know that he saw it as sharing something with religion because the best poetry was concerned with the universal, with those aspects of our lives which unite all human beings -- birth and love and death and the emotional qualities which are an inescapable part of them. As Trevor Johnson so well puts it in his *Critical Introduction to the Poems of Thomas Hardy*:

> Most of us experience times when life is lived more intensely than usual, with heightened awareness of the significance of the material world, and such 'epiphanies' enable poets to make poetry out of the flotsam and jetsam of experience.[9]

One could say about Hardy what Candida Lycett-Green (John Betjeman's daughter) said recently about her father's poetry, 'his greatest gift was his ability to see the divine in the ordinary'. Such 'epiphanies', moments when our humdrum lives suddenly acquire a new significance and we see more deeply into the heart of things, make us aware of our common humanity, and that the universals which unite us are more important than the particulars which divide us. Hardy was talking about this in his 1919 letter to Amy Lowell when he wrote, 'Though of course in divine poesy there is no such thing as old fashion or new. What made poetry 2000 years ago makes poetry now.'[10] It is the particulars which become dated. When Hardy writes in the *Life* 'The Realities to be the true realities of life, hitherto called abstractions',[11] it is to this that he is referring. The great poems written after the death of Emma owe part of their greatness to his becoming more aware of the greater universal reality behind the closer particular reality. Again, in the *Life* we find

> . . . Consider the Wordsworthian dictum (the more perfectly the natural object is reproduced, the more truly poetic the picture). This reproduction is achieved by seeing into the *heart of a thing* (as rain, wind, for instance) and is realism, in fact . . .[12]

We know of Hardy's interest in the later works of Turner, and what he seems to be saying in that quotation is that a painting like Turner's *Rain, Steam and Speed* is in one very important sense far more real than any very detailed painting of the steam engine crossing the bridge in a rainstorm could ever be. Hardy's definition of literary realism was 'artificiality distilled from the fruits of closest observation'.

Emotions are inseparable from the universal – the sadness of death, the joy of love and birth – and for Hardy emotion was inseparable from poetry. There is no better definition of poetry than Hardy's simple 'emotion put into measure'.[13] Philip Larkin was to echo this in his 'And poetry is matter of emotion . . . one writes really to reproduce in other people the particular sensations or thoughts or emotions that you've had yourself.'[14] Again, in the *Life*, Hardy quotes approvingly from Leslie Stephen, 'The ultimate aim of the poet should be to touch our hearts by showing his own, and not to exhibit his learning, or his fine taste, or his skill in mimicking the notes of his predecessors.'[15] This postulates a very personal kind of poetry with the risk that it will be self-centred and self-conscious, narrow and egoistic, over-emotional, even sentimental. More than 150 of the 947 poems in *Complete Poems* begin with 'I', many of them are obviously autobiographical, and it is Hardy's continual aware-ness of the universal and of his insignificance as a person when seen *sub specie aeternitatis* that makes his poems wide rather than narrow. I like John Piper's 'Hardy taught us how to be nostalgic without being sentimental.'

I have spent some time looking at Hardy and the universal and emotion because it will help us to understand what I believe Middleton Murry meant by poetic apprehension. He himself writes about 'the apprehension of truth', and how 'In a "moment of vision" the poet recognises in a single separate incident of life, life's essen-tial quality,' and 'His reaction to an episode has behind and within it a reaction to the universe.' This is true of all of Hardy's greatest poems. I remember, too, Middleton Murry's

> But the great poet remembers both rose and thorn; and it is beyond his power to remember them otherwise than together.[16]

'Domicilium' is an interesting poem and extremely accomplished for the poem of an eighteen-year-old, but it lacks poetic apprehen-sion in its deeper sense. The Latin title is pretentious but forgivable in the young Hardy so painfully conscious of his humble back-ground. It can be regarded as a kind of overture in which two of his recurring themes – change, and the passing of time – appear like Wagnerian leitmotifs. We are made conscious of time by the refer-ence to the bird which dropped an acorn a hundred years ago and by the grandmother, now 'Blest with the blest', who begins what she has to say with 'Fifty years / Have passed since then, my child, and change has marked / The face of all things.' You can see the beginnings of that deeper apprehension here, as you can in the second stanza of 'An August Midnight' where Hardy elevates what in the first paragraph appears to be merely a descriptive poem into something of greater significance. In adding himself to the four insects and talking about 'we five' who meet here, significantly, 'in this still place, / At this point of time, at this point in space' and then describing them as his 'guests' he brings up post-Darwinian questions of our relationship with animals, and there is a thought-provoking end to the poem in which Hardy modestly points out that these insects may appear to be 'God's humblest' but he respects them because they have an instinctual knowledge about certain areas of existence which we lack.

What is so remarkable about Hardy is his ability to write good poems about such a wide range of human experience, some of which would seem to be anything but poetic. In his *Thomas Hardy: A Biography* Michael Millgate sums it up so well when he talks about 'the trenchant simplicity of his assumption that poetry was an entirely natural medium of human expression and, as such, entirely appropriate to almost any human situation . . .'.[17] In writing his 'General Preface' to the Wessex Edition of his work published in 1912 Hardy wrote, 'I had wished that those [poems] in dramatic, ballad, and narrative form should include most of the cardinal situations which occur in social and public life, and those in lyric form a round of emotional experiences of some completeness.' He was to publish five more books of verse after 1912 and the *Complete Poems* covers a quite remarkable number of human situations and does include a round of emotional experiences of some completeness. It constitutes a great Wessex and human epic. Hardy seems to have responded immediately when something triggered his poetic apprehension. Thus, here we have Florence writing to Lady Hoare at Stourhead to tell her how Hardy wrote the poem 'Song of the Soldiers' (later entitled 'Men Who March Away') within a few days of the beginning of the 1914–18 war:

> He asks me to tell you that he scribbled it hastily upon his return from church on Sunday last (where we had an awful sermon from a drivelling curate). Indeed he wrote the main part of the poem while we were at dinner. Bad for his digestion doubtless![18]

'During Wind and Rain' is written by a maturer Hardy than the one who wrote 'Domicilium' and 'An August Midnight'. Like almost all great writers, and like Shakespeare or Chekhov in particular, Hardy is so painfully aware of time passing, of the tears of things, of the regret for opportunities missed, and moments of joy and happiness not recognised as such until they are but memories. Its title echoes the closing song of the clown in Shakespeare's *Twelfth Night* with its melancholy refrain of 'the rain it raineth every day' and with the clown looking back to when he was 'a little tiny boy'. 'During Wind and Rain' is built up like so many of his poems on a contrast between the past and the present, between life and death. Here again we see Hardy's poetic apprehension at its best. Out of Emma's memories, written in 1911 about her childhood of so many years earlier, he makes a moving poem. 'A book', said Franz

Kafka, 'should be an axe for the frozen sea within us', and here Hardy is touching our heart by showing his own and also Emma's. The last line of each stanza provides a powerful image of decay and death:

> How the sick leaves reel down in throngs!

> See, the white storm-birds wing across!

> And the rotten rose is ript from the wall.

and

> Down their carved names the rain-drop ploughs.

The leaves are sick and dying, the white birds presage a storm, the rose is rotten and even the names on the gravestones will soon be eroded by the rain. There is an economy of statement but a richness of suggestion here which is truly impressive and memorable; the feeling is so intense, the choice of detail so right, that it becomes universal.

Poetic apprehension requires honesty and courage, a readiness to face and accept the true reality. Most of us who have met death, in war or in our families, know that the basis for wisdom is an acceptance of the fact that the world was not made for our delight, that Nature does not have a holy plan, and that all that humankind can do is to learn to live together with a tolerance and loving-kindness (one of Hardy's favourite words) which will help to assuage what may be harsh realities. Clough wrote 'It is the wisdom of man to accept and love the real.' Loving the real may be difficult but it is wise to accept it. Hardy did and that may be one of the reasons why F. R. Leavis once suggested as an examination question: 'Hardy is Wordsworth a hundred years older and wiser.' Certainly if Hardy were alive today he would be writing poems about our modern craze for escapism, our worship of false gods, and he would have been particularly worried by the way in which so many people are more interested in the TV serial 'Neighbours' than they are in their neighbours.

Middleton Murry sees the poetic process as twofold. 'The one part, the discovery of symbol, the establishment of an equivalence, is what we may call poetic method. . . . The other part is an aesthetic apprehension of significance, the recognition of the all in the one.'[19] It may be over-simplifying what is said there to treat 'poetic method' as the technique a poet uses to express his ideas and feelings but that is how I intend to consider it. Hardy uses the word 'expression' for it. For both Murry and Hardy the subject was more important than the technique and Murry tells us that 'Poetic method frequently exists without poetic apprehension' while Hardy tells us that his weakness 'has always been to prefer the large intention of an un-skilful artist to the trivial intention of an accomplished one'.[20] What must surely strike any informed reader of Hardy's verse is that he is a supreme master of technique. Dennis Taylor in his valuable books on the poetry has shown us how wide was his reading of the works of earlier poets and how varied were the many forms of rhyme, stanza and metre he used. Ralph Elliott and Raymond Chapman[21] have done a great deal to make us aware of his large and diverse vocabulary and what William Archer calls his ability to see 'all the words in the dictionary on one plane so to speak' and to regard 'them all as equally available and appropriate for any and every literary response'.[22]

'Domicilium' is in blank verse and is a good pastiche of Words-worth; 'An August Midnight' is in six-line stanzas with a rhyme scheme A B A B C C in the first stanza and C C D D E E in the second, and the line lengths vary between eight and eleven syllables. The change of rhyme pattern in the second stanza may be because each of the three couplets is complete in itself, while the final one very neatly contains the important point Hardy wants to make. It has the clinching effect of the final couplet of a Shakespearian sonnet.

The stanzas in 'During Wind and Rain' are extremely unusual as are so many of Hardy's. They have seven lines of lengths vary-ing from four to ten syllables and a rhyming scheme A B C B C D A, but, as so often, Hardy links the stanzas together and pleases the ear by having one rhyming sound 'aye' which is heard twice in every stanza, eight times altogether, and two lines which are repeated 'Ah, no; the years O!' and 'Ah, no; the years, the years.' In earlier versions of the poem all four lines read 'Ah, no; the years O!' and the change illustrates one of Hardy's favourite poetic devices. In the *Life* he talks about how he had learnt the value of what he calls 'cunning irregularity' in Gothic architecture and how he had carried this principle into his poetry.[23] After hearing 'Ah, no; the years O!' in stanza 1, we expect the line to be repeated when in stanza 2 we hear 'Ah, no; the years', but instead of 'O' we hear the repeated 'the years' and there is a pleasing change in the line which Hardy uses as a kind of refrain. The vowel sound of 'years' is a long drawn-out one and the repeated 'the years, the years' supports the sense. It is worth noticing, too, how the first and last lines of each stanza have the same rhyme – 'songs', 'throngs', for example – and how by this device Hardy links past and present, life and death.

As in so many of his poems, Hardy makes a great deal of use of pronouns. All four stanzas begin with 'They' (which incidentally rhymes in each stanza with 'yea' or 'aye' and provides throughout the poem a rich assonantal 'ay' sound) and we have also, in the second line, 'He, she'. Who these people are we don't know, these pronouns have no antecedents, but by this kind of impersonality Hardy emphasises the universality of the situation. 'He' and 'she' could be you or me or any one of us. We may no longer sing together around a piano but many of us do assuredly work and play in the garden, and most of us have experienced the emotional disturbance of a removal from one house to another. There are other technical features which deserve mention, but I will just point out how powerful are the last lines of each stanza with their largely monosyllabic utterance and their powerful imagery. In 'And the rotten rose is ript from the wall' Hardy is able to use the alliteration he so loves, and the repeated 'r' sound is a guide by Hardy to the words he wants emphasised: 'rotten rose . . . ript'. This is uncompromising acceptance of the reality that all life ends in death, and it is far removed from the language of Herrick's 'Fair daffodils, we weep to see / You haste away so soon' and Tennyson's 'petals from blown roses on the grass'. 'Hardy is Tennyson fifty years older and wiser and more realistic.' Consider!

Turning now very briefly to our other two poems, we should note how 'Domicilium' shows that Hardy is already technically proficient. It is written mainly in an iambic rhythm with subtle variations. Thus trochaic feet are used at the beginning of several lines where emphasis is required – 'Climb', 'Dropped', 'Blest' and 'Swarmed', for example. There is already an attempt to use alliteration, as in line 2 with its 'beeches', 'bending' and 'boughs' and the last line with its 'wild', 'was', 'when' and 'we'. Hardy's poems are built up on repetition – of sounds, words, rhythms – and the reader assimilates the repetition and enjoys it. Technical features worth mentioning in 'An August Midnight' are that clever second line which rhythmically imitates the beat of a clock:

And the beat/ of a clock/ from a dis/ tant floor

Then there is the awkwardness and harshness of consonants in 'winged, horned, and spined'; the closely observed 'bang at the lamp', and the falling supine, which is, of course, what insects do; and finally Hardy's use of what in the eighteenth century was a rhetorical feature of style – the triplet. There was felt to be something very pleasing about a combination of three words, three phrases or three clauses: a, b and c was felt to be more euphonious than a and b. Hardy had made a thorough study of the eighteenth-century prose writers and frequently uses the triplet or rule of three in his novels. In this poem it is used three times in the first stanza and twice in the second.

The continuing appeal of Hardy's poems must surely be in part because they are immediately readable and understandable. Edward Thomas described the chief characteristics of Hardy's poetry as 'simplicity and intensity' and there is a sense in which his poetic method looks so simple and yet, as he said himself, his is an art that conceals art.

I now want to look at the poem 'Beyond the Last Lamp'[24] because it is a perfect example of poetic apprehension and method:

Beyond the Last Lamp

(Near Tooting Common)

I

While rain, with eve in partnership,
Descended darkly, drip, drip, drip,
Beyond the last lone lamp I passed
    Walking slowly, whispering sadly,
    Two linked loiterers, wan, downcast:
Some heavy thought constrained each face,
And blinded them to time and place.

II

The pair seemed lovers, yet absorbed
In mental scenes no longer orbed
By love's young rays. Each countenance
    As it slowly, as it sadly

Caught the lamplight's yellow glance
Held in suspense a misery
At things which had been or might be.

III

When I retrod that watery way
Some hours beyond the droop of day,
Still I found pacing there the twain
    Just as slowly, just as sadly,
     Heedless of the night and rain.
One could but wonder who they were
And what wild woe detained them there.

IV

Though thirty years of blur and blot
Have slid since I beheld that spot,
And saw in curious converse there
    Moving slowly, moving sadly
     That mysterious tragic pair,
Its olden look may linger on –
All but the couple; they have gone.

V

Whither? Who knows, indeed. . . . And yet
To me, when nights are weird and wet,
Without those comrades there at tryst
    Creeping slowly, creeping sadly,
     That lone lane does not exist.
There they seem brooding on their pain,
And will, while such a lane remain.

  Hardy gave a great deal of attention to his titles, and his first title, 'Night in a Suburb', is far less suggestive than the later 'Beyond the Last Lamp' with its obvious metaphorical connotations. The information that the scene is '(Near Tooting Common)' is typical of Hardy, who likes his readers whenever possible and desirable to know the time and place. Such details often give his poems authenticity and we do, of course, know that Hardy was living in Tooting in 1881. The poem was published in *Harper's Monthly Magazine* in

December 1911, exactly thirty years later, and I was told by one of the Macmillan family that Hardy had sent a manuscript to George Macmillan in 1925 with an accompanying letter explaining how 'the poem had been suggested by an incident Hardy saw when visiting Alexander Macmillan at his home in Upper Tooting'.[25] Here we have another example of an incident lying fallow in Hardy's memory for many years, and the emotions stirred up then are 'recollected' perhaps not in tranquillity but in something like it. But did Hardy have that incident in mind when, writing *Tess* in 1890, he makes a passer-by observe Angel and Tess on that painful wedding night 'walking very slowly, without converse . . .' looking 'anxious and sad', and then returning later 'he passed them again in the same field, progressing just as slowly, and as regardless of the hour and of the cheerless night as before'?[26] And did he happen to see Atkinson Grimshaw's painting of a man and a woman walking under the lamplight in a setting so like the poem and exhibited at the Royal Academy not long before he began to write *Tess*? We know how powerful Hardy's visual memory was and we know of his life-long interest in art.

We can see poetic apprehension at work here and one of the great attractions of Hardy's poetry is that so much of it grows out of life and human contact. How right Hardy is when he talks about 'art's subsidiary relation to existence' and records in the *Life* his feeling 'that the beauty of association is entirely superior to the beauty of aspect, and a beloved relative's old battered tankard to the finest Greek vase. . . . An object or mark raised or made by man on a scene is worth ten times any such formed by unconscious Nature. Hence clouds, mists, and mountains are unimportant beside the wear on a threshold, or the print of a hand.'[27] Hardy had his values right.

It takes a very human-oriented person to see life in this way and to be able to make a memorable and moving poem out of a simple incident such as any one of us might have witnessed and passed by with hardly a pause. It is a poem about love and the passing of time, as so many of Hardy's poems are, and even if we did not know that Hardy had said it began with an incident which he actually witnessed we might have guessed from the intensity with which it is written that this began in real life. Poetic apprehension is there in that he has seen poetry in the misery which the two lovers are experiencing, and made that particular experience at that dark and rainy place, at that point of time, at that point in space, into something we can all share nearly a hundred years later. But a great deal is deliberately left uncertain because Hardy doesn't know what causes their grief and it is better left to the imagination. Misery is misery no matter what the cause, and the shadowiness about the couple seems to make them a symbol of unhappy lovers everywhere. They are beyond the last lone lamp and going into darkness, not knowing that a great poet will universalise their sadness and produce in us pity. There is so much pity in Hardy's writing, pity for the suffering and the deprived, for the disappointed, the bereaved and cruelly treated. Hardy would have agreed with Galsworthy that 'pity is like the pearl in a diseased oyster'.

And this incident, described in the first three stanzas as if it has just happened, is then revealed in stanza 4 as having taken place thirty years ago. By this kind of double vision, by which he sees the past as if it were the present, and then distances it as if he were taking a telescope away from his eye – he uses the same device in 'Beeny Cliff' – he puts our sufferings against the massive background of time which he sees as the enemy of us all, as it is. How often his theme is that of time passing, how often we hear in his poetry 'the beat of a clock'. And place is just as important, and his final thought in this poem is that it was those tragic figures in that street which gave the place its meaning. To return to one's old school, or college, or home-town when those you knew there have gone away is to know what Hardy means. It is the same place and yet different because the people you knew there who gave the place a meaning for you are no longer there. It is people and human relationships which matter. 'Still in all its chasmal beauty bulks old Beeny to the sky', but what is important for Hardy is that the woman now is 'elsewhere'.

Because of the nature of the incident and the lapse of thirty years Hardy has few details to use in his poem and this may be why the vocabulary may seem to some readers too poetical in the worst sense – 'rain, with eve in partnership', 'absorbed / In mental scenes no longer orbed / By love's young rays', 'droop of day'. Yet the style he adopts seems to me very suitable to the situation he is describing, which is shadowy and anything but clear-cut, and almost always examination of the phrase will reveal more meaning than may at first appear. The darkness and the rain combine to aggravate the plight of the unhappy pair; the 'drip, drip, drip' is powerfully acoustic and may remind some of us of the 'Drip, drip, drip' of Alec's blood in *Tess*. 'Linked loiterers' is an unusual combination of words and we may think that this is Hardy just trying to be alliterative, but its very unusualness should make us think about it and, as so often in Hardy, it becomes clear that it is dense with meaning. 'Linked' has physical associations – the lovers have their arms entwined – and it has the metaphorical meaning of two people joined together by their love for each other, possibly even joined together in their troubles, like the links of a chain. And 'loiterers' has the sense of their aimless movement backward and forward under the lamplight as they talk in their grief and find it difficult to separate. People in distress do find it difficult to stay still. Similarly 'blur and blot' at first sight looks too facile but how well it describes how time blurs our recollections of the past and then blots them out. It is a very accomplished poem revealing what a master of poetic method Hardy was. He said himself that there was a natural music in the sincere language of the emotions, and we hear this music throughout his verse. 'Beyond the Last Lamp' is full of music if read aloud, as all Hardy's poems should be, and though its rhythm is basically iambic there are shrewdly placed variations in the beat which remove any possibility of monotony. For example, after the first three iambic lines of each stanza, the fourth line begins with a trochee. The refrain '. . . slowly . . . sadly' is cleverly used to convey the mood, but Hardy keeps changing the wording of the line to obtain the subtle irregularity he is seeking. At the same time the words 'slowly' and 'sadly' act as rhymes joining all the stanzas together and emphasising the unity of the poem and of the experience, even though thirty years separate the two parts of the poem.

A final example of Hardy's poetic apprehension and poetic technique working together to create a moving elegy is 'The Last Signal'.[28]

The Last Signal

(11 Oct. 1886)

A Memory of William Barnes

Silently I footed by an uphill road
    That led from my abode to a spot yew-boughed;
Yellowly the sun sloped low down to westward,
      And dark was the east with cloud.

Then, amid the shadow of that livid sad east,
    Where the light was least, and a gate stood wide,

Something flashed the fire of the sun that was facing it,
    Like a brief blaze on that side.

Looking hard and harder I knew what it meant –
The sudden shine sent from the livid east scene;
It meant the west mirrored by the coffin of my friend there,
    Turning to the road from his green,

To take his last journey forth – he who in his prime
Trudged so many a time from that gate athwart the land!
Thus a farewell to me he signalled on his grave-way,
    As with a wave of his hand.

Winterborne-Came Path

William Barnes, the Dorset schoolmaster, clergyman, linguist, engraver, and, above all, writer of Dorset dialect verse, was well-known to Hardy, and when Hardy moved to Max Gate in 1885 he was very close to Barnes's home at Came Rectory. Barnes died in October 1886 and as Hardy left Max Gate and began to walk across the fields to Came Church where the burial was to take place he saw the sun flash on the coffin, which was being carried out of the Rectory. To Hardy it became a last signal of farewell from a man he had known for nearly thirty years, admired, and regarded as a friend. The poetic apprehension which makes a moving poem out of so slight an incident is superb and the poetic method immensely interesting. Hardy had a great respect for Barnes as a poet, linguist and student of languages and he cleverly shows this respect and incidentally his own technical virtuosity by using technical features favoured by Barnes. Thus he uses the Welsh device called 'union' where an end-of-line rhyme is repeated in the middle of the next line, 'road', 'abode'; 'east', 'least'; 'meant', 'sent'; and 'prime', 'time'; also the Welsh cynghanedd, which is an involved, repetitive consonantal passage. In the third line, for example, we have L L S N S L L N S together with a strong assonance on the 'oh' sound:

Yellowly the sun sloped low down to westward
    L L   S N S L L   N   S

Barnes, too, preferred Anglo-Saxon English to the Latinised and here again Hardy has deliberately gone for Anglo-Saxon words: 'footed' and 'grave-way', for example. This method of paying tribute to Barnes could have misfired by being too clever, but the authenticity and integrity of feeling, and a poetic apprehension and poetic method which perfectly balance each other, make this one of the finest poems by one poet about another in the English language. The imagery of light flashing out of the darkness is brilliant in conveying Hardy's feelings about Barnes and what Barnes had meant to him. In all Hardy's greatest poems poetic apprehension and poetic method achieve this kind of fusion.

Notes

Quotations from Hardy's novels are taken from Macmillan's New Wessex Edition (London: Macmillan, 1974–6).

1. James Gibson and Trevor Johnson (eds), *A Casebook: Thomas Hardy: Poems* (London: Macmillan, 1979) p. 90. Hereafter cited as *Casebook*. Middleton Murry's essay first published as 'The Poetry of Mr Hardy', in *The Athenaeum*, November 1919.
2. *Under the Greenwood Tree*, Pt First, Ch. 1.
3. Gillian Beer, *Can the Native Return?* (The Hilda Hulme Lecture, 1988) (London: University of London, 1989) p. 18.
4. *The Return of the Native*, Bk First, Ch. 6.
5. *The Life and Work of Thomas Hardy, by Thomas Hardy*, ed. Michael Millgate (London: Macmillan, 1984) p. 408. Hereafter cited as *Life*.
6. *Life*, pp. 474/5.
7. *The Complete Poems of Thomas Hardy*, ed. James Gibson (London: Macmillan, 1976). Hereafter cited as *Complete Poems*. 'Domicilium' is poem no. 1, 'An August Midnight' no. 113, 'During Wind and Rain' no. 441.
8. Ian Gregor, *Poems of Thomas Hardy* (cassette produced by A. V. for Schools, no date).
9. Trevor Johnson, *A Critical Introduction to the Poems of Thomas Hardy* (London: Macmillan, 1991) p. 164.
10. R. L. Purdy and Michael Millgate (eds), *The Collected Letters of Thomas Hardy*, vol. 5 (Oxford: Clarendon Press, 1985) p. 293.
11. *Life*, p. 183.
12. *Life*, p. 151.
13. *Life*, p. 322.
14. Philip Larkin, extract from *The Beverlonian* (Beverley Grammar School), vol. 19, no. 75, February 1976.
15. *Life*, p. 131.
16. *Casebook*, p. 91.

17. Michael Millgate, *Thomas Hardy: A Biography* (Oxford: Oxford University Press, 1985) p. 474.
18. Letter from Florence Hardy to Lady Alda Hoare, dated 10 September 1914 (Stourhead House Library).
19. *Casebook*, p. 89.
20. *Life*, p. 333.
21. Ralph Elliott, *Thomas Hardy's English* (Oxford: Blackwell, 1984); Raymond Chapman, *The Language of Thomas Hardy* (Basingstoke: Macmillan, 1990).
22. William Archer, Review of *Wessex Poems* in the *Daily Chronicle*, 21 December 1898.
23. *Life*, p. 323.
24. *Complete Poems*, no. 257.
25. Letter from William Macmillan to James Gibson, dated 17 September 1973.
26. *Tess of the d'Urbervilles*, Ch. 35.
27. *Life*, pp. 120, 124.
28. *Complete Poems*, no. 412.

2

Moments of Vision – and After

LAURENCE LERNER

A man and a woman fell in love, married, were happy; then the marriage turned sour, and for long years they had little to say to each other; the woman died, and the man found he had fallen in love with her again. Stricken with grief, he felt the pain of parting with astonishing intensity, and in memory he revisited the scenes of their courtship, reliving their early happiness. It was as if the years of estrangement had sealed up their youthful love in amber, and her death had suddenly shone a bright light on it.

This could be fact or fiction, the plot of a novel or the theme of a poem or series of poems. Readers of Hardy know of course that it is fact, and that it is the theme of Hardy's one coherent sequence of poems, the 'Poems of 1912–13'. We know that Hardy and Emma were estranged, and that death mysteriously overcame that estrangement. You probably know the story that when the maid came to tell Hardy that Emma was dying, he stared at her, remarked 'Your collar is crooked', and paused to straighten his papers before going to her room and crying 'Em, Em, don't you know me?'[1] You may know that one of the first things he did after Emma's death was to send for Florence Dugdale, who may well have been his mistress by then. Whether this is true, and if true whether it was cause or effect of the estrangement, is the sort of question biographers set themselves, and to a biographer everything – including the poems – is biographical evidence. And so the use to which the distinguished biographer Robert Gittings puts the poems is to 'examine' their 'full meaning' by relating them to what is known of Hardy's actual behaviour towards Emma before and after her death: this behaviour 'explains the profound remorse which gives these remarkable poems their secret, unspoken intensity'.[2]

I begin by mentioning this biographical approach in order to detach myself from it. I am not going to treat the poems as material for Hardy's biography, because I am not a biographer, and also because I think this procedure is damaging to poetry. A poem turns the often shabby material of private life into something of lasting interest: it mingles fact and invention in whatever way best suits the poem. The biographer who then unpicks this, in order to rescue the bits that are fact, is unwriting the poem. But we are only interested in Hardy's life because of what he wrote, and to unwrite his works in order to come at the underlying facts seems to me a curious reversal of priorities. I propose therefore to look at these poems *as poems*, to ask what they are saying and how they say it, and if I find any contradictions it will not be between poetic assertion and fact, but only the contradictions that form part of the poetic experience.

Hardy called one of his volumes *Moments of Vision*, and the phrase seems to point to the main subject of lyric poetry:

> Lalage's come; aye,
> Come is she now, O! . . .
> Does Heaven allow, O,
> A meeting to be?
> Yes, she is here now,
> Here now, here now,
> Nothing to fear now,
> Here's Lalage!³

– not Hardy at his most subtle or most polished, but pleasant enough in a poem 'written to an old folk-tune'; and – this is why I've quoted it – one of the archetypal lyric subjects, the delight of the lover as the girl comes to meet him: it belongs to the same species as the love poems of Dante or Donne or Yeats. Not all love poems announce themselves as being about a particular moment, but it is striking how many draw on a moment of vision in the writing. In what is probably the greatest love poem of the nineteenth century, 'Two in the Campagna', Browning describes the splendour and limitations of human love, most conscious of imperfections at the moment when it seems most perfect; and allows this general reflection to emerge from the capturing of a moment:

> I wonder do you feel to-day
>   As I have felt since, hand in hand,

> We sat down on the grass, to stray
>   In spirit better through the land,
> This morn of Rome and May?
>
>   . . .
>
> No. I yearn upward, touch you close,
>   Then stand away. I kiss your cheek,
> Catch your soul's warmth, – I pluck the rose
>   And love it more than tongue can speak –
> Then the good minute goes.

And not only moments of love: the greatest attempt to build a long poem out of lyric intensity is Wordsworth's *Prelude*, which announces its method explicitly in the twelfth book:

> There are in our existence spots of time,
> That with distinct pre-eminence retain
> A renovating virtue . . .
>   Such moments
> Are scattered everywhere, taking their date
> From our first childhood.[4]

Most readers of Wordsworth find that his rendering of these spots of time (clinging to a mountain cliff during a storm, rowing on the lake at night in a stolen boat and turning back in terror, hearing of the death of Robespierre from a passing traveller) constitute the high moments of the poem, and that Wordsworth's attempts to integrate them into a larger structure produce some rather laboured theorising, along with the ponderous lists of abstract nouns that Wordsworth is all too liable to fall back on. This points surely to the power and also the limitation of this idea of lyric poetry. You can make a short, intense, powerful poem out of the capturing of a moment of vision, but will that be the only kind of poem you can write?

Moments of vision: the title is Hardy's, but the phrase is perfectly appropriate as a description of Wordsworth's spots of time. We must remind ourselves of the ambiguity of 'vision': vision is what your oculist treats, and it is what the mystic experiences, it means both what comes through the eye and what transcends ordinary sight. So when Wordsworth, writing of the spot of time in his childhood when he was terrified by the lonely common where a murderer had once been hanged, tells us that

> I should need
> Colours and words that are unknown to man,
> To paint the visionary dreariness,[5]
> . . .

his expression wonderfully captures the ambivalence of the experience. 'Visionary dreariness' can mean that the eye beheld only dreariness, or that it was dreariness transfigured by imaginative vision.

A visionary moment seems to exist outside time; so one way of integrating it into a longer poem would be to reinsert it into time. Browning wrote another and much longer love poem, called 'By the Fire-Side', which does just this. In this poem the speaker looks forward to 'life's November' in which he'll sit reading Greek and daydreaming about the moment by the little Italian chapel when all barriers dropped between the lovers and they met in the 'moment, one and infinite'. That was clearly a moment of vision, and that part of the poem belongs to the tradition of love's uniqueness, the concentrating of experience into a single intense moment, transcending the everyday: the mysterious powers 'had mingled us so, for once and good'. But what gives 'By the Fire-Side' its special quality is the temporal framework. It deals with three points in the speaker's life, the perfect moment by the chapel, the old age from which he'll be looking back at it, and the moment in between when the poem takes place. By joining them together, the poem reintroduces the moment of vision into time, and transforms a poem of romantic love into a poem of married love:

> When, if I think but deep enough,
> You are wont to answer, prompt as rhyme . . .

The word that would be impossible in a Petrarchan love poem is 'wont': only in married love can habit be praised. The simile makes the point neatly: rhyme is not an isolated moment, but part of a pattern. The intimacy of the married is like a rhyme-scheme.

I have lingered on Browning because the way he reinserts the moment of vision into time compares structurally to what Hardy does in the 'Poems of 1912–13'. It does not of course compare emotionally, for Hardy is not writing poems of happy marriage, but what he is doing is to recall moments of early happiness with great intensity, and then reinsert them into a context of changing experience, the fading of early hope, and the grief of loss – quite different

from Browning's poem as human experience, but leading to the same structural strategy, the placing of the moment in a context of the changes wrought by time. The best example of this is 'At Castle Boterel':

At Castle Boterel

As I drive to the junction of lane and highway,
　　And the drizzle bedrenches the waggonette,
I look behind at the fading byway,
　　And see on its slope, now glistening wet,
　　　　Distinctly yet

Myself and a girlish form benighted
　　In dry March weather. We climb the road
Beside a chaise. We had just alighted
　　To ease the sturdy pony's load
　　　　When he sighed and slowed.

What we did as we climbed, and what we talked of
　　Matters not much, nor to what it led, –
Something that life will not be balked of
　　Without rude reason till hope is dead,
　　　　And feeling fled.

It filled but a minute. But was there ever
　　A time of such quality, since or before,
In that hill's story? To one mind never,
　　Though it has been climbed, foot-swift, foot-sore,
　　　　By thousands more.

Primaeval rocks form the road's steep border,
　　And much have they faced there, first and last,
Of the transitory in Earth's long order;
　　But what they record in colour and cast
　　　　Is – that we two passed.

And to me, though Time's unflinching rigour,
　　In mindless rote, has ruled from sight
The substance now, one phantom figure
　　Remains on the slope, as when that night
　　　　Saw us alight.

> I look and see it there, shrinking, shrinking,
>   I look back at it amid the rain
> For the very last time; for my sand is sinking,
>   And I shall traverse old love's domain
>   Never again.

March 1913

This poem says three things. First, it records the moment of vision, with wonderful particularity, including the detail of the sturdy pony who 'sighed and slowed'; then it places that moment in a general context, and finally in the particular context of his subsequent life. Let me say a word about all of these.

What tense should a poem use to recall a moment of vision? Normally, this should obviously be the narrative past tense, but if we are completely transported back into the moment it could use the present – as is done in 'Timing Her' ('Lalage's coming . . .'), or in many of Wordsworth's sonnets. 'Two in the Campagna' moves with great skill between past and present, and in the crucial stanzas 5 and 6 it captures the moment by not using verbs at all, replacing them with nouns ('Such letting nature have her way'). 'At Castle Boterel' does drop into the present once ('We climb the road') but that is only in passing, for narrative vividness, and the pluperfect that immediately follows ('we had just alighted') makes it clear that we are not really in the present, for the act of placing the memory in context clearly supposes that we are no longer inhabiting that memory. For that reason, the past tense is essential.

The first context in which that moment is placed is that of the primaeval rocks that have seen so many couples pass, and that will outlive them all. Seen in this context, the passing of the lovers is unimportant, but we know that it was supremely important.

> But was there ever
> A time of such quality, since or before,
> In that hill's story?

The answer, of course, is yes and no. There was nothing special about the moment, and the cliffs had seen many such; but to them – to him – it was indeed special. Hence the statement that what the cliffs record, 'in colour and cast / Is – that we two passed'. This is objectively nonsense, but subjectively he is convinced of it; and the ambiguity, the hesitation between the true and the false meaning, is represented by the dash.

And then, in the last two stanzas, the poem places the moment in a particular context, that of his subsequent life. Here we are not told, as we are in some of the other poems, that the love had turned sour; we are not even told explicitly that she is dead, simply that

> Time's unflinching rigour,
> In mindless rote, has ruled from sight
> The substance now.

This could mean that the memory, like all memories, no longer exists in the physical world (in 'substance'); or that the woman is dead (though that would be straining the meaning of 'substance'); or that the validity of what the memory represents has gone (a rather more plausible meaning for 'substance'), and this could then be a reference to the spoiling of the marriage. We are not meant to choose between these meanings, because the poem relies for its power more on the structural effect of placing the memory in context than on the narrative element, the question of what had happened to their love. That is why I find it helpful to compare it to the emotionally very different 'By the Fire-Side'.

'Beeny Cliff' is a simpler poem, which uses the same strategy. It too invokes a distant and vivid memory:

> O the opal and the sapphire of that wandering western sea,
> And the woman riding high above with bright hair flapping
>   free –

– and then sets it only very briefly in context, telling us in the last stanza

> The woman now is – elsewhere – whom the ambling pony bore,
> And nor knows nor cares for Beeny, and will laugh there
>   nevermore.

– a fairly strong hint that she is dead, though you might notice that we have the same device of a dash to produce ambiguity before the word 'elsewhere'. This is indeed an ambiguity, though that may only become clear when we look at another poem:

I Found Her Out There

I found her out there
On a slope few see,
That falls westwardly
To the salt-edged air,
Where the ocean breaks
On the purple strand,
And the hurricane shakes
The solid land.

I brought her here,
And have laid her to rest
In a noiseless nest
No sea beats near.
She will never be stirred
In her loamy cell
By the waves long heard
And loved so well.

So she does not sleep
By those haunted heights
The Atlantic smites
And the blind gales sweep,
Whence she often would gaze
At Dundagel's famed head,
While the dipping blaze
Dyed her face fire-red;

And would sigh at the tale
Of sunk Lyonnesse,
As a wind-tugged tress
Flapped her cheek like a flail;
Or listen at whiles
With a thought-bound brow
To the murmuring miles
She is far from now.

Yet her shade, maybe,
Will creep underground
Till it catch the sound

> Of that western sea
> As it swells and sobs
> Where she once domiciled,
> And joy in its throbs
> With the heart of a child.

Gittings speaks of remorse and guilt in the 'Poems of 1912–13', and this poem is perhaps the profoundest – and the most indirect – expression of guilt. It does not contain a word of explicit self-reproach: the guilt is expressed entirely through the strange narrative strategy. The poem pities Emma because she is not buried in Cornwall, and cannot therefore sleep

> By those haunted heights
> The Atlantic smites
> And the blind gales sweep,

and it ends touchingly with the glimpse of 'her shade, maybe', creeping underground to relive her youthful joy in the Cornish coast. Now the reason she is not buried in Cornwall is of course that Hardy married her and brought her to Dorset, but there is no mention of marriage in the poem. The only thing the speaker of the poem did was to prevent her lying in the grave in Cornwall, and this opens up the possibility of a shadow poem running underneath the commonsense reading. For there is nothing to prevent it from telling us that he removed Emma from Cornwall with the purpose of preventing her from being buried there – even, if we want a rather gruesome reading, that he dug up a dead body with the malicious purpose of laying it to rest far from its youthful home. What profounder expression of guilt could there be than to write a poem with that shadow meaning?

That is why I invoked this poem when speaking of the penultimate line of 'Beeny Cliff':

The woman now is – elsewhere – whom the ambling pony bore,

'Elsewhere' is not just a euphemism, a way of not saying that she is dead; it is a deliberate ambiguity, meaning either that she is dead, or that she is no longer in Cornwall. For this poem, they come to the same thing.

And now, back to 'I Found Her Out There': it too has an ambiguity in its last stanza which can be fully glossed by other poems in the sequence. How seriously does the poem mean its supernatural touch at the end, its suggestion that 'her shade, maybe, / Will creep underground' to get back to Cornwall? Has Emma become a ghost?

Poem after poem in the series hints that she has, and then (sometimes) tells us that she hasn't. This uncertainty is the central subject of 'The Voice':

The Voice

Woman much missed, how you call to me, call to me,
Saying that now you are not as you were
When you had changed from the one who was all to me,
But as at first, when our day was fair.

Can it be you that I hear? Let me view you, then,
Standing as when I drew near to the town
Where you would wait for me: yes, as I knew you then,
Even to the original air-blue gown!

Or is it only the breeze, in its listlessness
Travelling across the wet mead to me here,
You being ever dissolved to wan wistlessness,
Heard no more again far or near?

    Thus I; faltering forward,
    Leaves around me falling,
Wind oozing thin through the thorn from norward,
    And the woman calling.

December 1912

Like most of Hardy's ghosts, this one hovers on the edge of existence, vividly present in a poem that allows us to deny it any real presence. For that reason I am disappointed at the linguistic timidity which led Hardy to offer the rather laboured phrase 'wan wistlessness' in the third stanza, instead of what he originally wrote, 'You being ever dissolved to existlessness', a word coinage that fits exactly into the theme of the poem. But the theme of existlessness did not, fortunately, depend only or even mainly on that coinage, since it is sustained by the very striking metrical change in the last stanza.

Three stanzas describe the woman much missed calling to him, in a regular dactylic scheme, and then suggest, in the same lilting rhythm, that it might be only the breeze; and then the final stanza changes its metre so sharply that it reads more like a footnote than part of the poem, pointing to the scene, telling us that the poem is over, that we've stepped outside the canvas – and, interestingly, including 'the woman calling' as an item in the composition; but the sense of sad reality in this prosaic gloss enables us (the effect is subtle but, surely, unmistakable) to read that last flat statement at one remove: 'the woman calling' was part of my version of the scene, not part of the scene.

We have now encountered what is probably the most striking poetic device in the whole sequence, the introduction of the woman as a ghost. Sometimes this leads to ambiguity about the existence or existlessness of the ghost, as in the lines in 'After a Journey'

> I see what you are doing: you are leading me on
>   To the spots we knew when we haunted here together,

where the carefully chosen 'haunted here together' is poised between two meanings: the perfectly natural sense of 'haunt' meaning 'frequent' (already indicated in 'your olden haunts' a stanza earlier), and the supernatural sense, which would give us a piece of wordplay: what we used to do together could be seen as what your ghost is doing now.

The device of introducing Emma as a ghost occurs in at least two other poems: in the first place in 'The Haunter', which depends for its effect on changing the point of view. The poem is spoken by the woman's ghost, lamenting that she cannot get through to her widower to let him know how devoted she now is ('what a good haunter'), how glad she is that he feels such remorse. We read this poem, of course, knowing that it is by Thomas Hardy: that is, by the man who felt, now that his wife was dead, that he had neglected her. But suppose we read it in ignorance of this fact, not knowing whether it was by a man or a woman. We would feel, surely, that we wanted to know, that it is very difficult to judge the moral posture of the poem without knowing. For if the poem is written by a woman it is an act of self-justification: 'he may have behaved badly but I behave better, even as a ghost'; and 'I am the victim, even as a ghost, because I can't comfort him'. Even by telling us how sad it is *for him* not to be able to receive her reassurance, the poem presents *her* as the one who exercises charity, whose sole desire is to comfort him.

But if the poem is by a man, then it is an act of self-reproach. It presents the woman as behaving better than he did, and the description of her as a faithful one, a good haunter, is an expression of her forgiveness and so (if he is the author) of his awareness that he needs forgiving. This is a case where we need to know the sex of the author, not for biographical reasons, but to guide us in our choice between different readings. The crucial question about this poem is, 'Who invents the ghost?'.

The other wonderful ghost poem is 'The Phantom Horsewoman':

The Phantom Horsewoman

I

Queer are the ways of a man I know:
    He comes and stands
    In a careworn craze,
    And looks at the sands
    And the seaward haze
    With moveless hands
    And face and gaze,
    Then turns to go . . .
And what does he see when he gazes so?

II

They say he sees as an instant thing
    More clear than to-day,
    A sweet soft scene
    That was once in play
    By that briny green;
    Yes, notes alway
    Warm, real, and keen,
    What his back years bring –
A phantom of his own figuring.

III

Of this vision of his they might say more:
    Not only there

> Does he see this sight,
>   But everywhere
>   In his brain – day, night,
>   As if on the air
>   It were drawn rose-bright –
>   Yea, far from that shore
> Does he carry this vision of heretofore:

IV

> A ghost-girl-rider. And though, toil-tried,
>   He withers daily,
>   Time touches her not,
>   But she still rides gaily
>   In his rapt thought
>   On that shagged and shaly
>   Atlantic spot,
>   And as when first eyed
> Draws rein and sings to the swing of the tide.

1913

Here there is no doubt that the phantom is 'of his own figuring', and it belongs not to the present, as in 'The Haunter', but to the past: it is the young and beautiful Emma, undamaged by time and marriage, and still in Cornwall – and once again, there is one detail that takes on richness from being placed in the whole series.

This poem too has its ambiguity: who is speaking? Here are three answers: that of Hillis Miller, for whom the speaker is Hardy, observing himself; that of J. O. Bailey, for whom it is an observant gossip; and that of Tom Paulin, for whom it is Emma, in dialogue with Hardy.[6] The question 'Who is speaking?' is not of course the same as our previous question, 'Who wrote the poem?' – i.e. 'Who invented the speaker?', and this time there are not such clear moral implications to the question, but once we've asked it it's difficult to resist the wish to answer it. Hillis Miller's suggestion, typical of that critic in its quest for self-division and self-reflexiveness, is attractive but surely wrong: if Hardy is talking to himself it is very clumsy of him to write '*They say* he sees as an instant thing', as if he does not know his own thoughts but other people do. The poem is clearly giving us Hardy as viewed from the outside. Paulin's suggestion is more convincing, and would fit the shifts of identity that characterise the whole sequence, in which Hardy sometimes pretends to be Emma. But to refer to her husband as 'a man I know' seems wilfully misleading; the device of having Emma's ghost chat to the neighbours to find out about her husband ('They say he sees . . .') is clumsy and implausible; and I wonder too why she should so resolutely see herself in the third person, dropping no hint that the girl rider is herself. So I conclude that Bailey must be right, that this is not a deliberate ambiguity, but that the poem is spoken by an observant neighbour, and offers as hearsay the thoughts which the poet knows perfectly well to be truth.

Finally, 'The Going': the first poem in the sequence, and one of the best:

The Going

Why did you give no hint that night
That quickly after the morrow's dawn,
And calmly, as if indifferent quite,
You would close your term here, up and be gone
    Where I could not follow
    With wing of swallow
To gain one glimpse of you ever anon!

    Never to bid good-bye,
    Or lip me the softest call,
Or utter a wish for a word, while I
Saw morning harden upon the wall,
    Unmoved, unknowing
    That your great going
Had place that moment, and altered all.

Why do you make me leave the house
And think for a breath it is you I see
At the end of the alley of bending boughs
Where so often at dusk you used to be;
    Till in darkening dankness
    The yawning blankness
Of the perspective sickens me!

> You were she who abode
> By those red-veined rocks far West,
> You were the swan-necked one who rode
> Along the beetling Beeny Crest,
>   And, reining nigh me,
>   Would muse and eye me,
> While Life unrolled us its very best.
>
> Why, then, latterly did we not speak,
> Did we not think of those days long dead,
> And ere your vanishing strive to seek
> That time's renewal? We might have said,
>   'In this bright spring weather
>   We'll visit together
> Those places that once we visited.'
>
>   Well, well! All's past amend,
>   Unchangeable. It must go.
> I seem but a dead man held on end
> To sink down soon. . . . O you could not know
>   That such swift fleeing
>   No soul foreseeing –
> Not even I – would undo me so!

December 1912

It contains much of the material we have seen recurring through-out: the admission that the marriage had gone wrong ('Why, then, latterly did we not speak?'), and the calling up of the early, happy memory of Emma in Cornwall ('the swan-necked one who rode'). It contains, too, a good deal of typically Hardyesque diction – '*lip* me the softest call', or 'darkening dankness': small verbal details that may not be particularly felicitous, but are Hardy's way of putting his fingerprint on a poem, like a trademark, so that for readers who already know his poetry it will clearly be recognised as the genuine article.

This poem too has a central strategy, and one that has clear moral implications: it blames Emma for dying. Dying is presented as some-thing she did on purpose, almost as if to spite him; as something she planned, and whose full effect she was able to foresee:

> Why do you make me leave the house
> And think for a breath it is you I see . . .

This enables the poem to end by telling her that she got it wrong, that the result was much more distressing to him than she had calculated:

> O you could not know
> That such swift fleeing
> No soul foreseeing –
> Not even I – would undo me so!

There is of course something a wife could do to which these reproaches would be wholly appropriate: to leave her husband. Here again is a shadow poem attached to the surface poem. That is why the poem is called – ambiguously – 'The Going', and why the word 'dead' is used twice but never to refer to Emma: there are the 'days long dead', and the fact that the speaker now seems like a 'dead man held on end'.

I said this affects the moral posture of the poem, but we must not oversimplify: the reproach is not a sign of harshness but of love. To *blame* a spouse for dying is emotionally a very logical thing to do: it expresses the pain of loss by seeing it as desertion, it postulates a relationship so close that if one of the partners is hurt it must be the responsibility of the other. More than any other poem in this strange sequence, 'The Going' must be seen as a love poem.

Let me end by returning, briefly, to the biographical approach I began by rejecting. Robert Gittings insists that Hardy was lying when he claimed that Emma's death was sudden and unexpected. Listing the reasons that should have made him perfectly well aware that she was dying, Gittings asserts: 'the terrible conclusion is that Hardy shut his own eyes to his wife's state, and tried to shut the eyes of others after her death'. He therefore says of 'The Going': 'the whole truth is not revealed in this apparently all-revealing poem'.[7] Michael Millgate is less censorious. He does suggest some adverse judgements on Hardy's conduct, but then adds: 'it is not necessary, however, to judge him more harshly than he did himself'. He realises that 'what gave Hardy pain was precisely what provided the fuel for his art', and since his concern is biography he deals with the pain rather than the fuel, aiming to understand Hardy's feelings about Emma rather than to read the poems. In fact he makes less use of the poems than Gittings does, which may be a relief to those whose interest lies in the poems themselves.[8]

How Hardy behaved – and felt – over his wife's death is not an easy matter for the biographers: that little episode of his telling the maid that her collar was crooked could be callousness or deep emotion, and it is easy to imagine it occurring at a moment of high tension in a novel by James, as a glimpse of how a trivial act can possess a deep meaning to which outsiders are blind. But how Thomas Hardy behaved in real life is not the subject of these poems, which draw on autobiographical material, not to give clues to the biographers, but to make art out of life, to create a world in which the truest poetry is the most feigning.

Notes

Quotations from Hardy's poems are taken from *The Complete Poems of Thomas Hardy*, ed. James Gibson (London: Macmillan, 1976), and variant readings from the same editor's *The Variorum Edition of the Complete Poems of Thomas Hardy* (London: Macmillan, 1979).

1. Robert Gittings, *The Older Hardy* (London: Heinemann, 1978) p. 149.
2. Ibid., pp. 152/3.
3. 'Timing Her'.
4. William Wordsworth, *The Prelude* (1850) Bk XII, ll. 208–10, 223–5.
5. Ibid., ll. 254–6.
6. J. Hillis Miller, *Thomas Hardy: Distance and Desire* (Cambridge, Massachusetts: Harvard University Press; London: Oxford University Press, 1970) p. 251; J. O. Bailey, *The Poetry of Thomas Hardy* (Chapel Hill: University of North Carolina Press, 1970) p. 305; Tom Paulin, *Thomas Hardy: The Poetry of Perception* (London: Macmillan, 1975) p. 133.
7. Gittings, *The Older Hardy*, pp. 150, 153.
8. Michael Millgate, *Thomas Hardy: A Biography* (Oxford: Oxford University Press, 1982) pp. 480/1, 488.

3

Stability and Subversion: Thomas Hardy's Voices

LANCE ST JOHN BUTLER

Studying and working at a British university in the last thirty years it has struck me, though it is no very difficult insight to achieve, that the primary intellectual concern of modern times is political. A majority, perhaps, of all students everywhere have been inclined to set aside their books for the other pursuits of youth, of course – in late eighteenth-century Cambridge the estimate was made that for every reading Man there were a hundred Men *tout court* – but in every age there is the thing that moves people to seriousness and action, that is the dominant metaphor, the current Grand Narrative to live by. And for most students and other intellectuals the serious matter in our age has become politics. An argument can be generated more quickly on this topic than on most others, feelings more quickly aroused. Solemnity and a sharp drop in the sense-of-humour quotient are the likely result of prolonged discussion of political matters in university, as in other circles. The Left look sharply about them for evidence of a sinister and designing Right; the Right keep their heads down; the Centre, the liberally-minded well-disposed ordinary men and women of the campus or the Clapham omnibus, likely themselves to be accused of fascism if they speak up for anything as mildly non-Left as the Right-to-Life campaign or against anything as sacred as the single-parent family, remain the way they prefer to be – quiet.

This situation is perhaps changing – things are now, in the post-Thatcher 1990s, not as they were in the anti-American sixties or the pro-feminist seventies, but it has been reserved for us, nonetheless, to be the period of the Politically Correct movement, a movement notably moral and even sanctimonious in tone. I stress all this in order to invite you to consider what the equivalent situation must have been a hundred and a hundred-and-fifty years ago, during the lifetime of Thomas Hardy. I suggest that then the serious matter, the

39

thing which would provoke argument, the basic *point critique* of intellectual life, was not politics but religion. Earnest young men at the universities joined religious not political groups and put energy and money into praying, preaching, reading, and arguing the religious questions of the day. No doubt more money and energy was invested in dinners, drinking, sports and the pursuit of the fair sex, but I take that to be a pretty constant ground-bass with which we need not at present be concerned.

If we cast our minds back over what we can remember casually of Hardy's life this situation seems to be confirmed in some measure. Looking at the young Hardy, not of course at university but getting himself an education nonetheless in Dorchester and London, we can probably remember his arguments with fellow architectural apprentices over infant baptism (rehearsed later in *A Laodicean*) or his efforts at studying the New Testament in Greek (reflected in Jude's studies at the end of Hardy's career as a novelist). We are unlikely to be able to bring to mind very many similar instances of his involvement in political questions. Equally, if we glance through his poems we can find a dozen concerned with things religious for every one devoted to political matters.

And yet. The first 'And yet' could be the position favoured by the more radical critics of our time, under the influence of Michel Foucault and others. For such as Terry Eagleton and John Goode there is no question – all criticism must be political because all writing, willy-nilly, takes up a political position; even the most scrupulous avoidance of anything political is itself a political gesture. I have some sympathy with this view but I am not sure how useful it is as an approach to Hardy; his extraordinary breadth of vision makes it extremely hard to pin him down even at the most unconscious level of performance. Thus, for example, the feminist critique of Hardy is fascinating and convincing and puts a big question mark over his attitudes towards women, but when we raise our heads for a moment and consider what Hardy was doing and when he was doing it, it remains obvious that his credentials as a non-sexist somehow remain untouched. And then perhaps this insistence on the omnipresence of the political is only evidence of our current way of seeing the world; no doubt an ardent Victorian struggling with religious questions would also have been able to see the writing of his day according to a single yardstick – did it make for or against religion? We wear the spectacles we have.

The second 'And yet' is a more traditional one and more directly concerned with Hardy himself. How *could* so sensitive a man, with his capacity for indignation against injustice and his extraordinary sense of what is due to every one of God's creatures, great and small, how *could* he have been unpolitical? Pursuing this line we would want to insist that a specific political attitude just *can* be found in Hardy if we only look carefully enough. This leads inexorably to the further question: if Hardy did have some politics, what were they? Which way, for instance, did he vote? And we can put his texts to an old and telling test – are they on the side of stability or on the side of subversion? Where would he have stood if the Revolution had come, or, to ask the question in a more calmly British and probable manner, was he a Reformer or not? What can we learn by trying to find the answers to questions like these?

The materials to hand for trying to provide answers are numerous; everything written by and about Hardy could be read in the light suggested, and of course, as has been inevitable in our political age, there are critics who have made Hardy into a political animal: John Goode, Patricia Ingham, Roger Ebbatson and others, also of course the feminist critics such as Rosemarie Morgan. The three recent biographers have had their opinions, explicit and implicit, on the topic, and there are the letters, the notebooks and so on, not to mention the novels and stories themselves. We could start trying to see how strong a case emerges for Hardy as a political animal from three basic sources. One is the first two volumes of the letters (this takes us up to 1901 by which time I think we might assume *a priori* that Hardy's political opinions, if he had any, were fairly fully formed); the second is the most recent biography – that by Martin Seymour-Smith; the third is the most extended attempt yet produced to make Hardy a Marxist – the perhaps not very widely-known study by G. W. Sherman entitled *The Pessimism of Thomas Hardy* of 1976.

Putting these three sources together we could probably tell a story somewhat as follows about Hardy the politician, a word I use in the rather unusual sense that Hardy himself gave it in a letter to his sister Mary during his very first years in London, 'You are not a politician' he tells her in explanation of why he is sending obituaries of Palmerston to their father but not to her.[1] The implication could be that Hardy at this time saw himself as 'a politician' at least in contrast to Mary.

The big political issue of Hardy's young manhood was the question of manhood suffrage (just as the big question of his later adulthood would be that of female suffrage). This matter of which men should be allowed the vote was particularly vehemently canvassed during the 1860s, culminating in the Second Reform Bill of 1867 when Disraeli 'dished the Whigs', stole their liberal clothes and extended manhood suffrage some small way beyond the propertied class. We are inclined to read the short poem '1967' as a characteristically depressed lyric about death, all-conquering Time and the unique value of love:

> In five-score summers! All new eyes,
> New minds, new modes, new fools, new wise;
> New woes to weep, new joys to prize;
>
> With nothing left of me and you
> In that live century's vivid view
> Beyond a pinch of dust or two;
>
> A century which, if not sublime,
> Will show, I doubt not, at its prime,
> A scope above this blinkered time.
>
> – Yet what to me how far above?
> For I would only ask thereof
> That thy worm should be my worm, Love!

The poem is dated '16 Westbourne Park Villas, 1867' and it represents well enough the experiments in gloom that its author then favoured, but it should not be taken precisely *au pied de la lettre*. The exclamation mark with which it ends confirms the slightly 'dramatic or personative' nature of the thought-process involved. And we could pay a little more attention to the third stanza where the sentiment expressed is out of keeping with the rest of the poem as it is usually read; after all, if the poem is only about the poet's future indifference to the doings of succeeding generations, what is the point of stressing the limitations of the present?

If the poem is read as a more tentative document, the striking of a pose of pessimism (though the feelings may be genuine for all that), then there is some room left for a real concern on Hardy's part for what is currently amiss in 1867. And the 'blinkers' of the time could well include, *inter alia*, resistance to political change, such as the blocking tactics employed by diehard Tories against the earlier versions of suffrage reform legislation in 1867. There are other candidates too, of a more general nature, such as the whole of mainstream Victorian morality, but Hardy had not yet come into collision with Mrs Grundy nor had he suffered, it would seem, from too harsh an application of Victorian ideas about pre-marital sex or class origins. And, after all, when he took the omnibus from Westbourne Park Villas to work it was to go to Arthur Blomfield's offices, which were in the same building as those of the Reform League.

Now, the Reform League bore about the same relation to conservative opinion in 1867 as Tony Benn and Red Robbo bore to the same venerable object a century later; the League had been in part organised by Karl Marx and by the nascent Trade Union movement; it was the 1867 equivalent of a body 'financed by Moscow' in the 1960s. Hardy and his fellow apprentices at Blomfield's are recorded as having assailed the Reformers with some equivalent of that venerable schoolboy weapon the paper dart, and they could hardly have failed to notice the upheaval the passage of the Reform Bill was making – Carlyle called the reformist proposals 'Shooting Niagara' and Matthew Arnold reacted negatively to the riots that were sparked off by the initial failure of the bill, as witness the directly political and rather reactionary outpourings of *Culture and Anarchy* of 1869. Hardy threw paper down at the reformers from Blomfield's office window as a joke but also, presumably, as a staunch Church of England man and here, suddenly, we come to the apparent contradiction at the heart of Hardy's thinking, and, indeed, at the heart of most discussion of Hardy's opinions on any serious subject. For he seems to be what he always said he was, inconsistent.

On the one hand there are the paper missiles hurled at the representatives of radicalism, which sounds Tory and goes along with his bible-reading and carol-singing. On the other hand, at the very same moment, he was commenting on the 'blinkered time' he lived in, and indeed not long after his attendance at Palmerston's funeral in Westminster Abbey he was starting to pen *The Poor Man and the Lady*, of which he says to Alexander Macmillan in a letter of 1868 that it has a 'strong feeling against . . . the upper classes of society'.[2] As we know, the novel was never published, partly because Macmillan decided that Hardy 'meant mischief'.

So on the side of stability there is church-restoration, laughing at the Lefties of the time, attending the funeral of the man who had, as

Hardy himself observed, been around in politics for sixty years. But on the side of subversion there is Will Strong, the 'Poor Man', apparently addressing a crowd of workers in Trafalgar Square, the very place where the Reform League held its meetings, having been banned from Hyde Park after the serious disturbances there. This at a time when a politician such as Robert Lowe – not a man of the left – was predicting that Revolution was 24 hours away.

Hardy had always had a streak of radicalism. His mother had brought him up on the story of the Tolpuddle Martyrs, which is not very surprising when one remembers the short distance between Bockhampton and Tolpuddle. There is the story in the *Life* of young Tom, aged four, brandishing a wooden sword dipped in pig's blood and marching round the garden crying 'Free Trade or blood!' As that story would have to be dated around 1844 it sounds about right. His father took him, at about this time, to an anti-corn-law demonstration in Dorchester and in 1850 he was present at a no-popery riot in the town.[3] The *Life* also records Tom's memory of the shepherd boy starved to death of whom he heard in his child-hood; the autopsy showed that the boy had nothing in his stomach but some raw turnip. This sort of thing must surely be connected to Hardy's interest in the Utopian socialism of Fourier; as early as 1863 he was copying out a diagram of Fourier's scheme; he kept the diagram and pasted it into the front of the *Literary Notebooks*, which start in 1876. Martin Seymour-Smith remarks that Tom was 'markedly idealistic' in the 1860s and 'was deeply interested in the reasons for human misery'.[4] He was still thinking about Fourier in 1880, but in 1877 he had copied this from the *Fortnightly Review*:

> French thinkers 'fall, as regards society & government, into the error against which Bacon warned physical investigators, of sup-posing in nature a greater simplicity than is to be found there'.[5]

Seymour-Smith wants to restrict the scope of Hardy's agreement with this to Comte and his Positivism, but I see no reason at all to exclude Fourier from the stricture. Naturally, it seems to me, Hardy was attracted to but also doubtful about political schemes – anything must be better than *this*, but what could possibly *work*?

Hardy's family, according to the biographers, seem to have been Liberal in inclination, but one does not have to read far in his works, or indeed in the biographies, to see that he was also attracted to the aristocratic and traditional and to such Tory institutions as the

Church of England. Seymour-Smith catches some of the dichotomy of Hardy's thinking when he tells us, on the same page, both that Hardy's family were Liberal and that he was 'no believer in "progress".'[6] Hardy himself noted in 1881 that 'Conservatism is not estimable in itself, or Radicalism.' Some critics referred to *The Poor Man and the Lady* as a Socialist novel, but Hardy himself called it 'socialistic', characteristically marking a distance from full commitment to a position. In 1872 he must have been aware of the formation by Joseph Arch of the first Agricultural Union since Tolpuddle days. The Union met with considerable resistance but it attracted a lot of members, including many in Dorset. At its height it had 100,000 nationwide, although economic and other forces brought on a sharp decline so that by 1889 its membership was a mere 4,500.

In these circumstances it is not surprising that Hardy responded positively to a request from Mrs Oliphant for a piece on the 'labouring poor' of Dorset, though pressure of work on 'the less substantial productions that editors demand of me' meant that there was a delay of a year between the original request and the eventual publication of 'The Dorsetshire Labourer' in the July 1883 issue of *Longman's Magazine*.[7] He wrote, shortly after its publication, to John Morley explaining that, although he was a Liberal, he had 'endeavoured to describe the state of things without political bias'.[8] And the essay is, indeed, a masterpiece of thoughtful commentary on the lot of the work-folk that does not descend to political specifics. The result of reading it is sympathy with the labourers discussed and perhaps a feeling that it is as well not to judge and not to indulge in snobbery at the expense of others, but the piece is not a call to arms or to the barricades.

When Hardy was invited later the same year to contribute an article to the *Contemporary Review* on 'Labourers' his initial response was that he would write the article 'should I have any special opportunity of observing the labourers in their political aspect' – he obviously knew what was wanted. This was on 12 October. On 5 November he writes again, this time declining to do the article for a specific and new reason: such a topic is unacceptable to him because it is 'such a purely political subject'.[9] This wavering is very interesting; as we would have expected from the evidence of 'The Dorsetshire Labourer' it certainly isn't an excuse concealing lack of ideas; on the contrary, the 5 November letter continues with a fairly extensive analysis of the work-folk who have no rights to or permanence in their houses or even their jobs; he suggests 'a personal interest in a particular piece of land' as a remedy. Under the old order labour was associated with place; now a kind of 'dis-association' has set in and we need a new system. This perfectly captures the two sides of Hardy's thought: he regrets the passing of the old, he is aware of the misery of the new and he wants to go backwards and forwards at the same time, trying to find something as good as the old to replace the new. It is almost impossible to say whether this is conservative nostalgia or utopian socialism; we might compare William Morris. But what is even more interesting is his refusal to write the article; from this point on he will repeat again and again that he cannot get involved in politics; it is not that he is neutral, far from it; it is rather that he sees, perhaps for the first time, when asked to write a second article about the work-folk he knew so well, that it is the artist's role to see life steadily and see it whole and not to be sucked into the practical, daily political tasks concerning short-term ends and the means to achieve them. A few years earlier, while writing *The Return of the Native*, Hardy had come as close as he ever came to an expression of political activism: 'Literature is the written expression of revolt against accepted things' he noted; this opinion, which is strangely reminiscent of Terry Eagleton's notion that the humanities are *always* in 'crisis' because they constitute *ipso facto* a re-examination of current ideas, and which therefore sounds very radical indeed, must be matched by the November 1883 detachment of the artist, a mixed position from which Hardy would rarely be moved for the rest of his life. Perhaps we might say that it depends what you mean by 'political'.

Thus in 1885, when the disestablishment of the Church of England was a major topic in the General Election of that year, he has his proposal to make: the Church might 'modulate by degrees . . . into an undogmatic, non-theological establishment'.[10] But the proposal is couched in an interrogative mode and made as part of a 'dream' that is quite the opposite of a call for action.

The most practically political that Hardy ever became in action rather than expression may have been in connection with his friendship with Robert Pearce Edgcumbe, the Gladstonian Liberal candidate who came within forty votes of unseating the Conservative candidate in the by-election in Dorchester on 7 May 1891. Hardy offered, by letter, to leave London and return to his native heath exclusively in order to cast his vote for his friend, but added, revealingly, 'I do not take any active part in politics as you know, & even if I did I have of late so many doubts about the situation our politicians have led us into that I can hardly write myself as of either party', but he meant to vote for Edgcumbe as 'the candidate ... most likely to act wisely as events reveal themselves ... & also ... for friendship's sake'.[11] If I did not have such an immense respect for Hardy's intellect and his steady view of the world I might be tempted to say here that he is trying to have his cake and to eat it; he obviously knows the political situation well and has thought about it enough to know that he cannot choose between the parties, but he also wants to make clear that he will vote on personal grounds only; it isn't an illogical position but it is equally determined to be humane and detached and simultaneously to keep its distance while still making its points. The key word perhaps is 'active' ('active politics'), a word he repeated often in similar anti-political disclaimers; it implies that he has indeed *thought* about political issues but finds them so complex and undecidable that he will not enter the arena. Above all, the job of the artist is to stay outwith the arena and to do what Hardy always claimed he did best – observe. What 'absolutely forbids political action' is 'the pursuit of what people are pleased to call Art'; artists must eschew politics 'to win unbiassed attention to it [art] as such'; 'this may be unfortunate, but it is true'.[12]

Offering to stand by and rush to Dorchester to vote as soon as a telegram from Edgcumbe summoned him, strong evidence of friendship in someone of Hardy's habits, he removes any suspicion of political activism by quoting Marcus Aurelius to his friend: 'Be not perturbed; for all things are according to the nature of the universal.' This quotation, one of Hardy's favourites,[13] is an implicit rebuke to politicians and, although in this case intended as comfort, tends to devalue activism of all kinds. Here as elsewhere we come close to the quasi-Buddhist Hardy of Jagdish Dave's excellent book.[14]

To the editor of the *Daily News* on 14 December 1891 Hardy sent a proof page from *Tess*, after the paper had published Gladstone's speech on the migration of country labourers to the towns, commenting: 'As I am not a politician the opinion I print has at least the merit of impartiality.'[15] Detachment, non-perturbation, impartiality, these are the hallmarks of the artist. They explain Hardy's lowish estimate of Zola, whom he considered would have done just as well writing political pamphlets or sociological treatises; he believed him to be 'no artist, but at bottom a man of affairs, who would just as soon have written twenty volumes of, say, the statistics of crime, or commerce, as of fiction – a passionate reformer, who has latterly found his vocation'[16] – the reference at the end of this is to Zola's involvement in the detail of the Dreyfus case. Martin Seymour-Smith sees this sort of comment as evidence that Hardy had an 'elevated notion of the poet's calling'[17] and that is surely right, but there is something more too: it also implies a self-denying ordinance on Hardy's part – he himself is interested in Reform but he must only treat it at long distance, not merely to preserve his artistic integrity but perhaps for the very sake of Reform itself, as witness his comment of 1889, defending himself, not for the last time, against the charge of pessimism: 'The first step towards cure of, or even relief from, any disease being to understand it, the study of tragedy in fiction may possibly . . . be the means of showing how to escape the worst forms of it, at least, in real life.'[18] As one might say, if way to the Better there be, it exacts a full look at the Worst. Even more explicitly he told Maude Hadden, Secretary of the Humane Diet Department of the Humanitarian League, 'I think that a writer of fiction (unlike other people) is more likely to exercise an influence for humanity in any given direction by belonging to no Committee pledged to a course, as he then escapes the charge of exaggerating for a purpose.'[19] As I say, it depends what you mean by politics.

The theory of artistic detachment was put to a pretty severe test by the reception of *Tess* and *Jude*. A good deal of the criticism, particularly of the latter book, had a political edge to it. The obscenities were bad enough but they were made far worse by not being gratuitous – they seemed to be part of a programme, a subversive activity aimed at the destruction of marriage as an institution, a programme for Free Love or for the destruction of the Oxbridge system. But Hardy was careful to point out (and this time to Florence Henniker so we can presume that he meant it) that *Jude* was 'not a novel with a purpose' and that 'I think it turns out to be a novel which "makes for" humanity – more than any other I have written.'[20] The formula was altered in other letters to read 'makes for morality', which gives us an interesting opposition: novels could have a *purpose* – that would be politics and Zola-ism – or they could *make for* something – that would be broader, more general, not specifically political but something to do with humanity or morality. Similarly, on Free Love, Hardy tells Florence, perhaps surprisingly to those who have only read *Jude* superficially, 'I hold no theory whatever on the subject . . . & seriously I don't see any possible scheme for the union of the sexes that w[oul]d be satisfactory.'[21] So he is not in the business of *schemes* but this does not lead him simply to avoid or abandon topics such as Free Love, his novels indeed are made of

little else, it's just that he won't be labelled or pinned down, he wants absolute freedom to discuss the matter 'impartially'. He refused systematically to join organisations for the promotion of political purposes, turning down not only Maude Hadden but also George Bedborough of the Legitimation League, founded in 1893 with the aim of promoting responsible Free Love and equal rights for all offspring, because 'as a mere observer & recorder I am personally limited to the representation of these tragedies as faithfully as possible, without bias, or what is called "purpose"'.[22]

We should not think, however, that Hardy actually imagined that even with the strongest possible commitment to detachment, the artist would ever be able to avoid his confinement in time and space and achieve a sort of Olympian universal overview (like Buddha he saw that Nirvana was not to be had just for the asking). To William Harvey and others at the Press Club, who had presented him with an address on his birthday in 1899, he wrote:

> Even in the best instances, what one man can exhibit of life . . . is no more than a single thread of a rich tapestry hanging in the gloom, whose complete pattern will never be shown by mortal hand.[23]

But his ambition, while employing an intensely localised realistic surface, was always to exhibit as much of the weaving as possible. He called himself 'constitutionally uncritical' when asked for an opinion on another writer, and I think we can apply this idea to him in the broadest sense. There are no villains in Hardy, no individuals culpably responsible for evil; the rich tapestry just has too many threads for us to single out one for blame; it is as if he made a bid to *transcend* political action. Politics is necessarily too confined just as Victorian religion was perhaps too confined for the broad canvas on which he set himself to paint. But then perhaps even Reason was too narrow. Writing to the Rationalist Joseph McCabe he declined being included in his *A Biographical Dictionary of Modern Rationalists* because 'no man is a rationalist . . . human actions are not ruled by reason at all in the last resort' and he is 'rather an irrationalist than a rationalist'.[24]

I hope what emerges from this sketch of some of Hardy's political thoughts is a picture of a writer who had strong political ideas, some of them directly practical, to do with divorce for instance, and some of them originating in a degree of socialistic idealism. This made him a Liberal *faute de mieux* (he told Morley that he was a Liberal but that he did not wish 'to declare himself publicly') though not an Anarchist – as Seymour-Smith observes, 'it would be absurd to depict him as a man who wanted the boat to be rocked by riots or revolution'.[25] He may have thought that things were getting worse rather than better, as some critics maintain, or the exact opposite, as other critics maintain. In all these matters he presents us with the two sides of each question in a manner unsatisfactory for those with a political *parti pris*. It is evident for instance that he had very considerable sympathy with the plight of Victorian women caught on the horns of the double moral standard of the time, but Rosemarie Morgan and others have shown us another side to his handling of the issue of control over women's lives and he himself in 1892, a year after the publication of *Tess*, refused to become a Vice-president of the Women's Progressive Society because he did not believe in their main aim, namely women's suffrage, as he explicitly told the lady who invited him. This sends a frisson down our politically-correct backs but it shows his extraordinary honesty, subtlety and ability to ignore current hobby-horses. Though a Liberal, he twice refused to stand as the Liberal candidate for the Rectorship of Glasgow University. This two-sidedness he was happy, with his usual modesty, to call 'inconsistency' or 'irrationality' but it is really something nearer to impartiality, to the imperturbability of Marcus Aurelius; it has something Buddhist in its refusal to be disturbed by the passing moment.

The great Russian theorist of the novel, Mikhail Bakhtin, proposed that the novel was a form, above all others, that could accommodate more than one voice. For him the novel is not a monologue by the writer or narrator but a dialogue between a number of conflicting or contrasting voices that themselves represent the different groups in society with their different claims. Usually a subversive voice can be heard in a novel, satirising, overturning or, as Bakhtin put it, 'carnivalising' the mainstream discourse of the time. He has some fascinating analyses of passages in Dickens where Dickens's narrator, by a form of Free Indirect Speech, presents us with the pompous or cliché-ridden voice of middle-Victorian opinion without so much as beginning a new sentence. I cannot go into all that here but I would like to conclude by suggesting that Hardy must inevitably be seen, if I am right about his uncommitted but profoundly interested two-sidedness, as having voices too, that he manages a Bakhtinian polyphony and that, if we want to decide how or whether he is political, the best way to analyse his fiction (and indeed his poems) might be with Bakhtin's help.

In 'The Dorsetshire Labourer' we have a lovely example of an apparent 'inconsistency' that can serve as an introduction to this way of thinking. The essay opens with a claim that all humanity is the same, that the 'few features' that distinguish Hodge from his fellows have been seized on and exaggerated by caricaturists 'while the incomparably more numerous features common to all humanity have been ignored'.[26] Two pages later he is making the opposite claim: six months' acquaintance with the country would enable the observer to distinguish among the types of work-folk; Hodge is 'disintegrated into a number of dissimilar fellow-creatures, men of many minds, infinite in difference'.[27] The Bakhtinian point is that Hardy is aware that there is a vast number of voices ('many minds') available in society; the Hodges (now plural) 'have private views of each other . . . applaud or condemn each other, amuse or sadden themselves by the contemplation of each other's foibles or vices'. Of course what they have in common is that each 'walks in his own way the road to dusty death'.[28] But meantime they are, primordially, *voices*: they possess not 'a vile corruption of cultivated speech' but 'a tongue with grammatical inflection rarely disregarded' although when they have 'attended the National School they would mix the printed tongue as taught therein with the unwritten, dying, Wessex English that they had learnt of their parents . . .'.[29]

The sensitivity expressed here cannot much surprise those acquainted with Hardy's fiction. Few other novelists have included so much dialogue in their novels and Hardy is an expert at the rendering of differing voices. His English, and the English of his characters, is of multiple origin and considerable ingenuity. As a narrator he has at his command a dozen shades of irony and seriousness which have proved to be pitfalls for the more solemn style of criticism. He doesn't use much Free Indirect Speech because he doesn't need to, instead he specialises in revelatory dialogue. I would suggest that it is in the careful analysis of this dialogue that we will find his deepest political opinions expressed. These turn out finally to be immensely complex, quite unable to be divorced from questions of morality, religion, science, history and chance, 'irrational' for the hard-pressed politician and, ultimately, anthropomorphic, man-shaped, individualised, subjective, personal; each voice has its turn, each voice is shown to be the appropriate one for that individual during his or her brief sojourn on earth, each is to be listened to and pitied. As Hardy wrote to Joseph Eldridge of the South Dorset Liberal Association on 8 June 1892, he could not openly declare his Liberalism because, once labelled, he 'could not approach all classes of thinkers from an absolutely unpledged point – the point of "men, not measures" – exactly the reverse of a true politician's'.[30]

Notes

1. *The Collected Letters of Thomas Hardy*, ed. Richard Little Purdy and Michael Millgate (Oxford: Clarendon Press, 1978–88) vol. I, p. 6. Letter dated 28 October 1865. Hereafter cited as *Collected Letters*.
2. Ibid., p. 7. Letter dated 25 July 1868.
3. Florence Emily Hardy, *The Life of Thomas Hardy, 1840–1928* (London: Macmillan, 1962) p. 21. Hereafter cited as *Life*.
4. Martin Seymour-Smith, *Hardy* (London: Bloomsbury, 1994) p. 72. Hereafter cited as Seymour-Smith.
5. *The Literary Notebooks of Thomas Hardy*, ed. Lennart A. Björk (London: Macmillan, 1985) vol. 1, p. 115. Quoted by Seymour-Smith, p. 72.
6. Seymour-Smith, p. 20.
7. *Collected Letters*, vol. I, p. 107. Letter dated 22 July 1882 to Margaret Oliphant.
8. Ibid., pp. 118–19. Letter dated 25 June 1883. Quoted in Seymour-Smith, p. 299.
9. *Collected Letters*, vol. I, pp. 121, 123. Letters to Percy Bunting dated 12 October and 5 November 1883.
10. Ibid., p. 136. Letter dated 20 November 1885.
11. Ibid. Various letters dated April and May 1891.
12. Ibid., p. 234. Letter to Edgcumbe dated 23 April 1891.
13. Quoted in letter to Edgcumbe dated 8 May 1891, in *Collected Letters*, vol. I, p. 236. For significance to Hardy see also *Life*, p. 176.
14. Jagdish Dave, *The Human Predicament in Hardy's Novels* (London: Macmillan, 1985).
15. *Collected Letters*, vol. I, p. 248.
16. *Collected Letters*, vol. II, p. 231. Letter dated 1 October 1899 to Edmund Gosse.
17. Seymour-Smith, p. 299.
18. *Collected Letters*, vol. I, p. 190. Letter dated 14 April 1889 to John Addington Symonds.
19. *Collected Letters*, vol. II, pp. 135/6. Letter dated 18 October 1896.

20.   Ibid., p. 94. Letter dated 10 November 1895.
21.   Ibid., p. 122. Letter dated 1 June 1896.
22.   Ibid., p. 160. Letter dated 12 April 1897.
23.   Ibid., p. 220. Letter of early June 1899.
24.   *Life*, p. 403. Quoted in Seymour-Smith, p. 319.
25.   Seymour-Smith, p. 303.
26.   'The Dorsetshire Labourer', *Longman's Magazine*, vol. 2, 1883. Reprinted in Harold Orel (ed.), *Thomas Hardy's Personal Writings* (Lawrence: University of Kansas Press, 1966; London: Macmillan, 1967) p. 168.
27.   Ibid., pp. 170/1.
28.   Ibid., p. 171.
29.   Ibid., p. 170.
30.   *Collected Letters*, vol. I, p. 272.

4

Thomas Hardy and John Clare: A Soil Observed, a Soil Ploughed

RONALD BLYTHE

Every now and then the philosopher-historian stands back from the continual cycle of wars and trade to wonder why, throughout the centuries, it is the warrior who receives the honours, and the man who grows the corn little or no honour at all. The customary reason given for this imbalance is that he who protects the tribe must govern it, and he who feeds it must, well, get on with his work. Both know that springtime and harvest wait for no man, and whoever's task it is to turn with the turning year must abide in his 'condition'. Yet why, persists the philosopher-historian, has this so-called 'condition' to be so low in men's esteem that 'peasant', a word which derives from the old French for a countryman, and which in consequence should have the ring of beauty about it, has instead a ring of what is ignoble? Peasant, says the *Oxford English Dictionary*, is 'a member of a class of low social status that depends on agricultural labour as a means of subsistence'. Yet who, in a society which devours bread and meat and milk and fruit and wine and beer and fish, does *not* depend on agricultural labour as a means, not of subsistence, but of existence? So why has Hodge had to stumble his way through history, the living image of all that is considered crude and uncultured, when he himself is the cultivator of everything which sustains life, not to mention the creator of landscapes which inspire poets and painters, and which all of us now venerate?

In the nineteenth century two great English poets spoke for this 'condition' in a language which disturbed their readers. John Clare actually spoke directly from it. Thomas Hardy daringly elevated its so-called simple dramas to what he called 'Sophoclean' heights. John Clare, like Robert Burns, had touched the degrading soil. Thomas

Hardy, although closely related to those who ploughed and sowed, did not.

Recent biographers and literary critics have had to face up to both Clare's and Hardy's 'peasant' dilemma in order to make sense of both their genius and their predicament. Robert Gittings reminds us of the large number of labouring folk who were Hardy's relations, and whom he passed by. But I have frequently seen such apparently either snobbish or uncaring attitudes during funerals in our village church. One of the 'old people' dies and, behold, the church is, for half an hour, filled with the indigenous population, many of whom I learn only now belong to the dead person's family. 'Oh, yes, didn't you know, I am his cousin. She is my wife's aunt. That is his nephew, the one who went away . . .'. And I have to tell myself that I have witnessed little or no acknowledgement of such relationships during the lifetime of the deceased. Weddings and funerals apart, closely related village people often have a way of living apart although they share the same few miles. In Clare's and Hardy's day, families were vast and full of secrets regarding blood relationships. They were also rather 'cool' – which was due, maybe, to the unmanageability of sustaining true family feeling on such a scale. And there was, too, that other reason, which I shall come to, for why John Clare and Thomas Hardy behaved as they did towards their roots – that local earth out of which sprang their greatness. To be any kind of writer where one was so deeply rooted could be an awkward business – still can. To be one who needed as much environmental nourishment as the crops themselves could be both a godsend and a disaster. John Clare and Thomas Hardy had everything they required for their inspiration to hand, and they knew it. Yet to translate such common stuff into the finest rural poetry and the finest rural novels in the language carried with it a personal exposure which was hard to bear. As we know to this very day, there is a fugitive aspect to every village. The indigenous writer or artist of any kind blows his own and his neighbours' cover, often injuring both himself and his background in the process. No one will ever know where Hardy and Clare 'got it from'. They are sports: odd, strange individuals who are at one and the same time 'one of us' – and yet clearly not one of us. They see what we refuse to see, or cannot see until it is pointed out to us. They are both reporters or chroniclers, and visionaries.

The conventional nineteenth-century reader was puzzled by what was then called 'peasant poetry'; they allowed for its novelty but nothing more. John Clare's publishers – who had published John Keats – promoted Clare as a second Robert Bloomfield. Bloomfield's long poem *The Farmer's Boy* appeared when Clare was a child – a real farmer's boy, a gardener's boy, pot-boy, a little working lad. It sold 26,000 copies. And Clare himself was always to feel a tender affinity with the Suffolk poet whose origins, single burst of literary success and long years of subsequent neglect pitifully reflected his own background and experience. At the same time Clare, the next generation after Bloomfield, was not like him in any way except in his peasantry. He was more learned, more a naturalist, more a poet and, sadly, more grandly tragic. Robert Bloomfield did not work the soil but was exiled from it. In his famous poem he was a London shoemaker remembering his distant village, and who had become literate by reading the London newspapers. Because of his living in London, his ability to write poetry was less amazing than John Clare's ability to write his. There were no crushing village eyes to dodge. All the same, it was more Bloomfield's novelty value than being a writer in the usual sense which made his work sell. The literary establishment abused Keats for his 'cockney' nerve at daring to invade a classic territory, but it gave Bloomfield a condescending pat on the head. And it did much the same twenty years later when Clare's startling collection *Poems Descriptive of Rural Life and Scenery* appeared in 1820 under the publishers' description of him as 'a Northamptonshire Peasant' – the kind of description which initially crippled Robert Burns.

John Clare was twenty-seven when he met his first and only fame. Not for the next century and a half would his rightful standing as the most direct voice of rural England be acknowledged. 'Where did he get it from?' was the question most asked in his own time. They knew where Mr Wordsworth and Mr Coleridge and Lord Byron got it from – and almost where poor young Keats got it from (not the best source) – but where did this little ploughman get it from? Clare's readers were both genuinely and sensationally interested. His reply to a question which dogged him all his life was, 'I kicked it out of the clods.' The poetry, he meant. The rudeness of the questioning received a rough answer which was no answer at all. It reminds us of Christ's first sermon in his local church, given when he was thirty – late in those days for such a debut. He had unrolled Isaiah and spoken so eloquently that those who had known him all his life were bewildered. 'Where does he get it from? Isn't he the carpenter's son?' They meant that he was not a graduate of the rabbinical schools and that neither until this moment had he shown any gift for language.

Both John Clare and Thomas Hardy were recognised by their mothers as being 'different' or special – or indeed odd. As we know, Hardy's mother (aided by his paternal grandmother) nourished the difference with her stream of dreadful tales about Napoleonic War soldiers, ferocious assize justice, rural melodramas, gossip and scandal. Mrs Clare could neither read nor write and, in her son's words, thought 'that the higher part of learning were the blackest arts of witchcraft'. Inadvertently she fed him with those insecurities which were to haunt the cottages right up to the Second World War. He added, however, that his mother's ambition 'ran high of being able to make me a good scholar as she had experienced enough in her own case to avoid bringing up her children in ignorance'. To make him literate, no more. But not to make him a poet – steer him clear of that, please God. Hardy's mother, on the other hand, was determined to give her son as excellent an education as possible and she offended those who charitably provided what they thought was sufficient learning for such a boy. Mrs Clare – 'God help her', wrote her son – had her 'hopeful and tender kindness crossed with difficulty, for there was often enough to do to "keep cart upon wheels", as the saying is, without incurring an extra expense of pulling me to school, though she never lost the opportunity when she was able to send me . . .'.[1] A penny a week could not always be found. But child-labour could. Jemima would have none of this. Hardy seems never to have done anything manual, not even a bit of gardening. John Clare carried sacks of flour from the mill, toiled at The Blue Bell, the pub next to his parents' cottage, gardened for Lord Exeter, planted the quickset hedges around the village after it had been enclosed, and *ploughed*.

What the two poets did have in common was a physical slightness which could have been due to their difficult births. Clare was the weakest baby of twins – his sister died – and Hardy was thrown into a basket as stillborn until the midwife noticed that there was life in him. Clare was a small handsome man of five foot two – the same height as Keats. Hardy was taller and with the disproportionate head and body which one often sees in Victorian photographs. Both writers possessed a kind of watchfulness of expression which made them unusual, even beautiful at times. Both adored women. Each suffered and yet was made great because he could only 'breathe' his native air. This air was both vital – and tainted.

Although it is fanciful to dwell on possible meetings between writers, in Clare's case he would never have heard of Thomas Hardy, who was twenty-four when Clare died and had published nothing. The poor, everlastingly scribbling old man in the Northampton Asylum would not have known of Hardy's existence. Many years before, when Clare was in the Epping Asylum, young Alfred Tennyson was living next door and they might well have glimpsed each other, Clare toiling in the rascally Dr Allen's garden and Tennyson writing *In Memoriam*. Each would have heard the bells of 'Ring out, wild bells!' for they were those of Waltham Abbey. So, Tennyson in mourning, and Clare digging. Being a peasant, it was the policy of nearly all those who tried to help John Clare to set him to manual work.

But it came in handy. Throughout the splendid *The Shepherd's Calendar* we can see the literary strengths of Clare's agricultural skills and expertise. The hand which wrote 'The Nightingales Nest' stacked the sheaves. If Hardy knew of Clare's poems he never mentioned them. His 'Clare' was, of course, William Barnes. Barnes and Clare once wrote with a marvellously similar emotional quality on the same theme – the being forced to leave the old home. Barnes's poem is the unforgettable 'Woak Hill' of which E. M. Forster once said that 'if one has not tears in one's eyes at the end of "Woak Hill", one has not read it'.[2] John Clare's poem on this subject is 'The Flitting', written after a kind but uncomprehending patron set the poet up in a cottage in a village which was not his own village:

. . .

Strange scenes mere shadows are to me
Vague unpersonifying things
I love with my old hants to be
By quiet woods and gravel springs
Where little pebbles wear as smooth
As hermits beads by gentle floods
Whose noises doth my spirits sooth
And warms them into singing moods

Here every tree is strange to me
All foreign things where ere I go
Theres none where boyhood made a swee
Or clambered up to rob a crow

No hollow tree or woodland bower
Well known when joy was beating high
Where beauty ran to shun a shower
And love took pains to keep her dry . . .

William Barnes is still accused of inaccessibility because of his use of dialect, which astonished me, as it did E. M. Forster and countless other readers who knew nothing of Dorset's local language. Barnes was born eight years after Clare and outlived him by almost a quarter of a century. In the social terms of their day, Barnes the farmer's son, the schoolmaster and clergyman, would have belonged to a quite dizzily aloft realm to that of the country-folk which he wrote about. And yet he articulates their very souls.

Clare's poetry is the English field given voice. There was no kicking it out of the clods but a profound drawing of it from both the cultivated and uncultivated land of his birthplace. If our farms and wildernesses could utter it would be in his words. His is a uniquely informed utterance. A huge reading as well as a constant contemplation of his native scenery, between them, produced in him a kind of rural scholarship which causes the modern student to alter his or her perception of what it was like to be a farm labourer in late-Georgian Britain. Simply because a shepherd or ploughman could not, or did not, write, we have no reason to believe that he did not feel or see the things which a realistic poet such as John Clare felt and saw. Or indeed, did not share William Barnes's knowledge of the innermost tenderness of humanity. John Clare's gradual collapse of health (exacerbated, as is so often the case, by 'helping hands' and pressures of all kinds) robbed us of what surely would have been one of the most remarkable rural works of all time, a 'peasant' naturalist's version of Gilbert White's classic *The Natural History of Selborne*. Fractions of this wonderful book appear in Margaret Grainger's *The Natural History Prose Writings of John Clare*.[3]

The land and its workers also speak through Thomas Hardy with an authentic but different voice. It is the voice of the trapped, of men and women who are hedged in as much by what we now call the environment as by their parish boundaries. Not by any other writer is an indigenous group so fatally blown about by localised storms. *Far from the Madding Crowd*, published in 1874 when Hardy was 34, heralded his arrival as a great novelist. In this tale he spreads a few fields and pastures, a few houses, a few short travels in that humdrum direction or this, and a few villagers in stances which have been ordained by local tradition or by classical myths. So far, so familiar. But then Hardy does something not seen before. He gives his characters a double dimension, the one which they recognise and the one by which a Greek playwright would have recognised them. They work incessantly, and time for such business as making love or sightseeing or gossiping has to be snatched. Talk takes place during tasks and if you wanted to do something extraordinary in the improving line, you hoped for a little accident or a brief illness. I once read of a nineteenth-century parson who, walking by a cottage about 9.30 p.m., heard a family singing Wesley's hymns and reproached it for not getting enough sleep to do its fieldwork efficiently. It was not uncommon for labourers to be given very small gardens so that all their energies went into their master's farm. ''Twas a bad leg allowed me to read the *Pilgrim's Progress'*, says Joseph Poorgrass. Cain Ball managed a visit to Bath due to a respite from toil caused by having 'a felon upon his finger'.[4] The plot of *Far from the Madding Crowd* is so firmly tied in to the implacable demands of work that an element of its comedy insists that, by right, there should be neither the strength nor the opportunity to do anything else. In Hardy leisure frequently breeds disaster. In *Far from the Madding Crowd*, and like John Clare, he saturates all the common knowledge of his home place with his reading. Hardy's intention, brilliantly realised, was a stylised actuality, the style being that of the classic pastoral, the actuality that of standard farming practice during the time of his mother's youth. He said that he meant to complete this novel 'within a walk of the district in which the incidents are supposed to occur', and that he found it 'a great advantage to be actually among the people described at the time of describing them'.[5]

An advantage, yes, a comfort, no. They were too close for that. A few years later Hardy was to explain what he believed was the purpose of fiction. It was, he said, 'To give pleasure by gratifying the love of the uncommon in human experience, mental or corporeal', this succeeding most when the reader was made to feel that the characters were 'true and real like himself'.[6] The critics were upset. How could farm-labourers ('peasant' was going out by the 1870s) think and hope and behave, well, like *us*? Whilst admitting that Mr Hardy had 'hit upon a new vein of rich metal for his fictitious scenes', a contemporary critic viewed Hardy's treatment of farm-labourers with some irony: 'Ordinary men's notions of the farm-labourer of the Southern counties have all been blurred and confused.

It has been the habit of an ignorant and unwisely philanthropic age to look upon him as an untaught, unreflecting, badly paid, and badly fed animal, ground down by hard and avaricious farmers, and very little, if at all, raised by intelligence above the brutes and beasts to whom he ministers.'[7]

Such remarks in a review of *Far from the Madding Crowd*, in the *Saturday Review*, shockingly illuminate the predicament of John Clare half a century earlier. In 1823 he was at the pinnacle of his brief celebrity. Here was a peasant writing books! Here was a peasant who had been to London and who had hobnobbed with men of letters, Coleridge, Lamb, Hazlitt. Taylor the publisher, still with the once bestselling Robert Bloomfield in mind, exulted in this phenomenon and he worked hard to polish up Clare's grammar in order that ladies and gentlemen would be able to read his work. In vain the poet protested. The miracle – or novelty – was that he could write verse. It need only be made readable. His publisher promoted Clare but wrecked his poetry, and there was little he could do about it. He was a peasant and had to be guided. The restoration of Clare's text during the post-war years (plus our ever-increasing interest in the countryside) has uncovered a Clare as fresh and captivating as a landscape from which the varnish and dirt of ages have been skilfully removed.

Far from the Madding Crowd is set between two long stretches of agricultural depression and in what historians like to dub 'a golden age'. In his later novels, Hardy would be accused of darkening the English countryside for his own melodramatic purposes. The truth of the matter was that towards the close of the nineteenth century, and a whole hundred years after the birth of John Clare, the lives of Britain's farmworkers had become so poverty-stricken and tragic that the Norfolk novelist Mary Mann, herself a farmer's wife, could look at their lot and presume that only some grim purpose known to God could justify it. In Hardy's essay 'The Dorsetshire Labourer', written in 1883, we have a direct piece of rural sociology which reveals how much he knew of what was going on all around him. And yet he could say, quite truthfully in certain respects, 'that happiness will find her last refuge on earth [among those who till the soil], since it is among them that a perfect insight into the conditions of existence will be longest postponed'.[8] Where ignorance is bliss, in other words.

Impertinent questions drew Clare's response that he kicked his poems out of the clods. Does Thomas Hardy celebrate the life of the (human) clod? Never. This slur on village England he refutes from the very beginning. For one thing, it was too near home. Yet the problem of animating what had, until he began to write, been ignored as being below the level of polite interest, or as being simply lumpen, would have been insuperable had he tried to work it out. But he did not. What he *did* was to write so superbly about his own people that it made it pointless to ask, 'Why these poor toilers?' Behind him lay the harsh facts of Jemima's youth. All around him lay a mass of inherited material of every kind: the best, the worst. In a poem called 'Spectres that Grieve', one of many which are threnodies for the ordinary country folk, Hardy makes the dead who have been denied a proper history by their so-called betters, protest from the grave:

> 'We are stript of rights; our shames lie unredressed,
> Our deeds in full anatomy are not shown,
> Our words in morsels merely are expressed
> On the scriptured page, our motives blurred, unknown.'

Much of Hardy's work defends the dispossessed. But it has to do so from a height. Being what he was, he could not be what he had come from. Similarly John Clare. This is the dilemma of the great writer or artist who stays at home. Hardy's actual touching-the-soil poems are few and far between. One is 'The Farm-Woman's Winter':

I

> If seasons all were summers,
>   And leaves would never fall,
> And hopping casement-comers
>   Were foodless not at all,
> And fragile folk might be here
>   That white winds bid depart;
> Then one I used to see here
>   Would warm my wasted heart!

II

> One frail, who, bravely tilling
>   Long hours in gripping gusts,
> Was mastered by their chilling,

And now his ploughshare rusts.
So savage winter catches
The breath of limber things,
And what I love he snatches,
And what I love not, brings.

Hardy is unusual as a writer in that he lets characters from his novels have an extra life in his poems. There is 'Tess's Lament', and in 'The Pine Planters' we have Marty South, the heroine of *The Woodlanders*, having to fell trees alongside the lover who refuses to look at her. Their actions are mechanical:

We work here together
    In blast and breeze;
He fills the earth in,
    I hold the trees.

He does not notice
    That what I do
Keeps me from moving
    And chills me through.

He has seen one fairer
    I feel by his eye,
Which skims me as though
    I were not by.

And since she passed here
    He scarce has known
But that the woodland
    Holds him alone.

I have worked here with him
    Since morning shine,
He busy with his thoughts
    And I with mine. . . .

But it was for Hardy the desolate fields of Flintcomb-Ash which represented the nadir of farm toil. It is where poor Tess ends up when she is reduced, as so many women were, to near-slavery. In 'We Field-Women' Hardy shows this place in varying degrees of weather:

How it rained
When we worked at Flintcomb-Ash,
And could not stand upon the hill
Trimming swedes for the slicing-mill.
The wet washed through us – plash, plash, plash:
    How it rained!

How it snowed
When we crossed from Flintcomb-Ash
To the Great Barn for drawing reed,
Since we could nowise chop a swede. –
Flakes in each doorway and casement-sash:
    How it snowed!

How it shone
When we went from Flintcomb-Ash
To start at dairywork once more
In the laughing meads, with cows three-score,
And pails, and songs, and love – too rash:
    How it shone!

But of course it is in his magnificent set pieces of the farming
year, such as the famous scene in chapter 22 of *Far from the Madding
Crowd* in which shearing is given a sumptuous treatment unlike
anything previously seen in literature, that Thomas Hardy reveals
the closeness of his eye, if not his hand, to his local earth. Similarly,
the patriarchal splendours about dairying in *Tess* where a Dorset
farmer controls a world like that of Abraham. In such scenes Hardy
challenges every previous concept of the 'simple task' and directs
the reader's vision to a view of labour which holds within it those
satisfactions which are usually found in poetry and religion. His
story-telling is filled with meditation. One is made aware of his
divided intelligence as he sees life as the shearers see it, and then
as he himself sees it. Joseph Poorgrass sums up the whole business
of farming with his, ''Tis the gospel of the body, without which we
perish, so to speak it.'[9]

John Clare would have agreed. But his position was a complex
one. When a man ploughs, it is with one foot in the furrow and
one on the level. It makes a rough progress, up and down, up and
down. He was the peasant; he was the supreme English poet of
the countryman's experience. Eventually – one could say inevitably –

the unevenness tripped him into Northampton General Lunatic Asylum where, far from insane most of the time, he wrote. With little else to do, the output was enormous – and uneven. This cache of sometimes earthbound, often soaring rural poetry lay mostly buried until the 1920s onwards, when writers such as Edmund Blunden, the Tibbles, Geoffrey Grigson, Geoffrey Summerfield and Eric Robinson brought it into the sunlight.

The progress of agriculture is a kind of Alps, all peaks and plunges. For so natural an activity, it is strangely precarious and easily ruinous. Clare and Hardy sang its heights and charted its depths. Clare lived through the trauma of Enclosure, cursing its evils, and then through the bitter years of Chartism. Hardy was just at the beginning of his career when a biblical spell of rain washed away all the brief farming prosperity of the 1850s and brought in the long years of depression. By the 1890s, when he renounced novel-writing for poetry, there began what they called 'the flight from the land' as the labourers fled from agricultural misery. At this moment another young writer, Henry Rider Haggard, who had made a name with exciting adventure stories about Africa and who in his thirties was now farming in Norfolk, tried to halt the exodus. He employed fifteen labourers. They worked twelve hours a day in summer and every hour of daylight in winter, and had no holidays. And for a few shillings a week. Their brute strength astounded Haggard. In January he watched them bush-draining a huge clay field. It took them ten weeks and at the end he observed, 'Such toilers betray not the least delight at the termination of their long labour.'[10] All this just a century after the birth of Clare and just when Hardy had abandoned fiction.

Clare was in continuous flight from the land as workplace, but only to find his true working place in the little hidden copses and dells and woods where he could write unseen and undisturbed – and especially un-noticed. His and Hardy's poetry differed because one touched and the other watched the soil. Each fully understood its majesty and its treachery. Clare's work is alternately a *Te Deum* and a *De profundis* to the cultivated and uncultivated acres of his native Helpston, the place of endless work and endless dreams. The accuracy of what he witnessed there can be judged in his bird-poems. Here to conclude is 'The Sky Lark':

The rolls and harrows lies at rest beside
The battered road and spreading far and wide

Above the russet clods the corn is seen
Sprouting its spirey points of tender green
Where squats the hare to terrors wide awake
Like some brown clod the harrows failed to break
While neath the warm hedge boys stray far from home
To crop the early blossoms as they come
Where buttercups will make them eager run
Opening their golden caskets to the sun
To see who shall be first to pluck the prize
And from their hurry up the sky lark flies
And oer her half formed nest with happy wings
Winnows the air – till in the clouds she sings
Then hangs a dust spot in the sunny skies
And drops and drops till in her nest she lies
Where boys unheeding past – neer dreaming then
That birds which flew so high – would drop agen
To nests upon the ground where any thing
May come at to destroy had they the wing
Like such a bird themselves would be too proud
And build on nothing but a passing cloud
As free from danger as the heavens are free
From pain and toil – there would they build and be
And sail about the world to scenes unheard
Of and unseen – O where they but a bird
So think they while they listen to its song
And smile and fancy and so pass along
While its low nest moist with the dews of morn
Lye safely with the leveret in the corn

Notes

Quotations from Hardy's poems are taken from *The Complete Poems of Thomas Hardy*, ed. James Gibson (London: Macmillan, 1976); those from his novels are taken from Macmillan's New Wessex Edition (London: Macmillan, 1974–6). Quotations from Clare's poems are taken from *Selected Poems and Prose of John Clare*, chosen and edited by Eric Robinson and Geoffrey Summerfield (Oxford: Oxford University Press, 1967), and *The Later Poems of John Clare*, same editors (Manchester: Manchester University Press, 1964).

1. Clare's comments on his mother are from *Sketches in the Life of John Clare, written by himself, March 1821*, ed. Edmund Blunden (London: Coblen-Sanderson, 1931).

2. E. M. Forster, *Two Cheers for Democracy* (New York: Harcourt, Brace, 1951) p. 204.

3. Oxford: Oxford University Press, 1983.

4. *Far from the Madding Crowd*, Ch. 33.

5. *The Life and Work of Thomas Hardy, by Thomas Hardy*, ed. Michael Millgate (London: Macmillan, 1984) p. 102.

6. Ibid., p. 154.

7. Review of *Far from the Madding Crowd* in *Saturday Review*, 9 January 1875. Reprinted in R. G. Cox (ed.), *Thomas Hardy: The Critical Heritage* (London: Routledge, 1970) pp. 40–1.

8. 'The Dorsetshire Labourer', *Longman's Magazine*, vol. 2, 1883. Reprinted in Harold Orel (ed.), *Thomas Hardy's Personal Writings* (Lawrence: University of Kansas Press, 1966; London: Macmillan, 1967) p. 169.

9. *Far from the Madding Crowd*, Ch. 22.

10. H. Rider Haggard, *A Farmer's Year*, introd. Ronald Blythe (London: Century Hutchinson (The Cresset Library), 1987) p. 79.

5

Hardy's Friend William Barnes

PETER LEVI

That Wessex which we call Hardy's Wessex is only an idea of course. There is something magical or fey about the maps of it that Hardy began to publish in 1895, but they do represent something real – a dialect, the boundaries of a way of life – and it was undoubtedly that deeply original, deeply provincial poet William Barnes who first established it as a literary province. Tennyson talked of Wessex dialect: he got some notes on it from Thomas Hughes of Uffington, and used them in the dialect scenes of his play *Becket*, where they make a preposterous impression, which the dialect poems of Barnes never did. I have argued in a life of Tennyson[1] for the virtual certainty that it was Barnes who inspired Tennyson in 1861 to the first of his own Lincolnshire dialect poems. Thomas Hardy grew up very conscious of his provincial origins, in the shadow of Barnes who was the monarch of literary Wessex and a successful poet, one of whom there was a cult when Hardy was born. Hardy, in his early poems, followed Barnes in dialect verse, and in his Welsh and Persian tricks also. And Hardy never lost a certain respect, admiration, affection for the old man, although there were some forty years between them, thirty-nine between Barnes's birth at Rushay in 1801 (or possibly 1800) and Hardy's in 1840, and forty-two between Barnes's death at Winterborne Came in 1886 and Hardy's at Max Gate in 1928. They were both antiquarians, both excited by the dialect, on which Barnes did serious work and which Hardy carefully observed, but Barnes's world was all but confined to the Blackmoor Vale, and Hardy's went further so that his limits had to be more deliberately defined. There is something entrenched about Hardy's idea of Wessex, whereas Barnes's Blackmoor Vale is even today rather unselfconscious and innocent.

It is not a moral or an intellectual matter; it is the luck of the generations. In 1847 the railway arrived at Dorchester, but Barnes's golden age was before Waterloo, and he remembered the coming of the first stage-coach at Sturminster Newton. Hardy heaved himself up by the bootlaces to become an architect and a writer, and middle class: in his writing nothing came easily to him, they say. His ancestors and his claim to be from what used to be called a county family were fantasies: his true lineage is from an honourable and interesting line of stone-masons. But Barnes was painted by Thorne of Sturminster for the Revd Mr Lane Fox, his ancestry goes back through farmers and landowners to a grant of land from Henry VIII in 1540, and perhaps to a servant of King John. His life was a struggle almost more titanic than Hardy's, because the land went in his grandfather's day. His father died in William's childhood; his uncle was a tenant farmer who crashed soon after Waterloo. He became a clergyman from being a schoolmaster by taking a degree at Cambridge as a 'ten year man', that is, keeping his name on the College books with a minimum of formalities for ten years. He went on after his BA to get a BD, and that was the key to Winterborne Came. They were both self-taught, though Barnes was more ferociously intellectually ambitious; that also was a matter of generation. Barnes's father had a small-holding on Bagber Common, near Sturminster Newton. Mr Lane Fox as the Vicar spotted young William, who was the fifth of six motherless children, and tutored him a little in Latin and Greek, and lent him books.[2] Barnes found a job at 13 under Mr Dashwood, the lawyer, but when Dashwood died he moved hopefully to Dorchester: he already had literary pretensions.

In 1821 when Alfred Tennyson was a boy being tutored by his father, young Barnes was printing his own poems in a book and in the local papers, studying French, playing duets with a friend, learning music from an organist, learning to engrave on copper and wood, reading the classics with the Revd H. J. Richman of Dorchester, and courting Julia Miles, whose father was dubious about his prospects. He sold drawings, engravings, visiting cards, and a narrative poem called 'Orra: a Lapland Tale', which he printed in 1822. At Christmas the two young people got secretly engaged, and William went to Mere, at the other end of the Blackmoor Vale, to take over as village schoolmaster in a loft above the Market House where the inscription now is, while Julia taught little girls in Dorchester. So far, the story is typical of the early nineteenth century: the poems were on the whole embarrassing, but the drawings and engravings were remarkably able. In 1825 the hostile Mr Miles

was transferred as a customs officer to Nailsea, where Julia hated
the smoke of the glassworks. William was paid for engraving by a
Blackmoor man in bookbinding and cheese: he thought of setting
up in Bath, and applied for a teaching post at Plymouth and a
clerkship in a Dorchester bank, then in 1827 he managed to rent the
Chantry at Mere for £20 a year and open a boarding school, and
with this prospect Mr Miles accepted him and he married Julia.
Their love letters from 1820 to 1827, with some poems, engravings
and drawings, were edited by Charlotte H. Lindgren for the Dorset
Record Society in 1986, and Barnes's lovely drawing of the fifteenth-
century stone Chantry house where the boarding school was, a
building put up by the royal architects and masons for the chantry
priests at Mere in 1425, has been printed at Wincanton for the friends
of that church.

In 1835 they moved back to Dorchester and opened a school in
Durngate Street. Two years later it was in South Street and in 1847
they were at number 40; by the time he was ordained (1847) they
had seven children, six of them alive; but in 1852 Julia died and
was buried in Dorchester. His *Poems of Rural Life in the Dorset Dialect*
came out in 1844, but more were to come. In 1862 his school had
its greatest success. A boy who was a natural linguist came first in
all England in an examination for the Indian Civil Service, and when
this news hit *The Times* Barnes got shoals of letters of application:
but he had just closed down his school, and retired to be Rector of
Winterborne Came. His strategy of being a clergyman headmaster
had indeed been a success, but very late in the day. He was now a
distinguished man of letters all the same. Hardy was 22 and proud
to know him. Barnes had written a great number of philological and
antiquarian books and a terrifying number of articles: and he had
translated The Song of Solomon into the Dorset dialect for the English
Dialect Society. He lived on at Winterborne Came for 24 years of
tranquil eccentricity. He complained of the word 'bicycle' for
example; he thought 'wheel-saddle' would have been better. For
'forceps' he proposed 'nipperlings', for 'bibulous' 'soaksome', for
'botany' 'wortlore', for 'meteor' 'welkin-fire', and for 'telegraph'
'spell-wire'. He was proud of the four Dorset demonstrative pronouns and the numerous Dorset words for the parts of a tree. Yet
his Dorset poetry was not a didactic exercise, it was not pedantic in
any way. He just wrote it, as he told Hardy, because he had to. His
last words spoken to Hardy were these: 'The sparrows are pulling
my thatch to pieces. I shall have to have it attended to I'm afraid.'

Old age and pallor overtook him, but here he is in Hardy's eyes in the vigour of his early eighties:

> Until within the last year or two there were few figures more familiar to the eye in the county town of Dorset on a market day than an aged clergyman, quaintly attired in caped cloak, knee-breeches, and buckled shoes, with a leather satchel swung over his shoulders, and a stout staff in his hand. He seemed usually to prefer the middle of the street to the pavement, and to be thinking of matters which had nothing to do with the scene before him. He plodded along with a broad, firm tread, notwithstanding the slight stoop occasioned by his years. Every Saturday morning he might have been seen thus trudging up the narrow South Street, his shoes coated with mud or dust according to the state of the roads between his rural home and Dorchester, and a little grey dog at his heels, till he reached the four cross ways in the centre of the town. Halting here, opposite the public clock, he would pull his old-fashioned watch from its deep fob, and set it with great precision to London time. This, the invariable first act of his market visit having been completed to his satisfaction, he turned round and proceeded about his other business.[3]

When he died he was 85, and that is the beginning of his obituary by Hardy. The splendidly mordant drawing of the portrait gives it a certain authority, though Leader Scott, the pen-name of Barnes's daughter Lucy Baxter, adds in her charming and informative life of the poet that his pockets would be stuffed with sweets to give children, 'or now and then a doll might be seen with its head peering out of the clerical pocket'.[4] As for the strange clothing, he adopted it only when the plum of the Rectory of Winterborne Came dropped in his lap (the advowson was Colonel Damer's, and his cousin had luckily resigned the parish), so that Barnes's teaching days were over: 'Cassock and wide-brimmed hat, knee breeches and large buckles on his shapely shoes. He had passed through many phases of costume before finally adopting this one, which he deemed enjoined by the ecclesiastical canons.' At one time he wore a poncho, at another a Scottish plaid. He liked a red cap: the first a Basque beret someone brought home from the Pyrenees, after that a Turkish fez, and finally something made by his daughters. 'Comfort or utility was always his object, united very often with a total disregard of appearance.'[5] He was the sweetest of men and of a ripe eccentricity.

It is not my purpose to expound his intellectual views, which were wide-ranging and quite as peculiar as his dress: but there is an analogy between his intransigent views of philology and Anglo-Saxon, entailing his opposition to Latin or Greek words in English, and his stunning originality as a Dorset poet. In 1831 he went to Wales, and it was his experience of Welsh literature and language that started him off as a philologist: he had a bit of Persian and Sanskrit, which he used for coaching pupils for the Indian army or civil service; then the Persian and Welsh came together to suggest new formal tricks or devices in his lyric poetry. He became extremely sensitive to the uses of alliteration and half-rhyme and internal rhyme within a tight stanza form. When this new and pleasing style was used in Dorset dialect it was very beautiful in the ear. In common English poems he used it more sparingly and it is less successful. It does not matter that we do not observe what rules he applied to his stanzas – he invented them and they were not written down; it matters even less to us where he got them. All that matters is how wonderfully they work: they are a rediscovered element in the sweet, traditional harmony of verse. They are often mistaken for some intrinsic quality of Dorset dialect: not so. That gleam of his language is invented and applied by him to the dialect, which in itself is no more musical than any other.

Barnes loved Dorset dialect and it set something free in him. When he read or heard Tennyson's Lincolnshire dialect verse he was horrified, because he felt in it a mockery of the people and a lack of that love which he himself so intensely felt, and which inspired him both as a priest and as a poet. He is wrong about Tennyson, or the difference is a class difference. William Barnes is much closer to the innocence, both as a poet and as a man, of Charles Tennyson, who was also a country vicar. His first use of Dorset dialect was because he thought it was like Doric, a pure and antique country speech such as he conceived Theocritus to have used.[6] He was not a great Hellenist but that was his impression, so that although the philologist in him was never absent in his Dorset poems, and although he issued them with a glossary and a dissertation on Anglo-Saxon, he remained true to his idea. Dorset dialect set him free in poetry to express his own golden age, his Blackmoor Vale world of before Waterloo, which it is true to say largely survived his lifetime and faintly echoes in ours. In the early Dorset poems he alludes to Virgil by calling them eclogues, and in his prose he quoted and imitated Virgil's eclogues more than once. 'The Common a took in' was called 'Rusticus dolens' in the *Dorset County Chronicle*, 'The Lotments' was 'Rusticus gaudens'; others were 'Rusticus Domi/ Emigrans/ Rixans/ Procus' ('A bit of sly courting') and 'Rusticus Res Agrestes animadvertens' ('Two Farms in Woone'). In 1833–4 they caused a small stir, and there was a little flurry of correspondence in the papers.

There is no doubt that he was a Blackmoor Vale man at heart. When he saw a marquee at Cambridge put up for a visit of the Prince Consort, he wrote home to say it was 'as large as the shed of our railway station'. He saw the whole congregation slipping out one by one to fight a rickfire, until the parson was left preaching alone. Indeed in Dorchester he saw the whole congregation gassed by underfloor heating, first the children, then the youths, then the adults, with only the preacher high in his pulpit left exhorting them. And however learned the circumstances of his dialect poetry were, it was still true that 'I wrote them so to say as if I could not help it. The writing of them was not work but like the playing of music'[7] – something which of course involves all kinds of trade secrets, which the listener need not notice. On the other hand it is as mistaken to say of him as it was of Shakespeare: 'Sweetest Shakespeare, Fancy's child / Warbles his native wood-notes wild'.[8] His poetry was intricate by skill, as Shakespeare's lyrics also are. Hardy was not far wrong in writing that Barnes 'really belonged to the literary school of such poets as Tennyson, Gray, and Collins'.[9] He was not quite right, because the intellectual force and research that went into Barnes's dialect poetry were not classical but entirely his own, and he was not as smooth as Gray or Collins. However that may be, Hardy feels and Tennyson suggests that he was recognised in 1844; Hopkins was crazy about him in his day (later), and Auden adored him. The high-minded Bridges disapproved, and when Eliot says of Kipling that people resent poetry they are unable to understand, and despise poetry they easily understand – alas, he hits Barnes with both barrels.

And yet one only needs to pick up a poem by Barnes to be bewitched. One does not need to have learnt the principle of Anglo-Saxon alliteration from Dasent's Rask's *Icelandic Grammar* to hear the particular music when William Barnes combines it with stanzaic verse and a faint undertone of the hymn tune, in a poem to an elm tree. It is just a little like the elm of dreams in the sixth book of the Aeneid:

But when the moonlight marks anew
Thy murky shadow on the dew,
So slowly o'er the sleeping flow'rs
Onsliding through the nightly hours,
While smokeless on the houses height
The higher chimney gleams in light
Above yon reedy roof . . .[10]

This is not Barnes at his best because it is in standard English, just
a little enlivened by a device that pleases him: moonlight, marks,
murky; slowly, sleeping, onsliding; houses, height, higher . . . and
so on. But the form is sentimental, it derives from middle-class
drawing-room poems and songs of the 1820s as early Tennyson
does; only with Barnes, he speaks middle-class poetic common
English as if it were a foreign language, as if it were stiff and not
native to him. The all-important tension between vernacular rhythm
and the demands of metre gets lost. So do his patterns and devices.
Lucy Baxter offers 'Clouds' as a good example of how his Dorset
poems translated into common English ones without loss. Yet in
the first stanza, for 'A-shiftèn oft as they did goo / Their sheäpes
vrom new ageän to new', he translates 'For ever changing as they
flew / Their shapes from new again to new'. But the alliteration of
'shiftèn sheäpes' has got lost, and 'oft' is better than 'for ever'. Yet
we must not exaggerate: of course nineteenth-century dialect is an
obstacle to many people, and fine translations of Barnes can still be
made into easier and excellent English. Pauline Tennant has done
it. Further, Barnes's own 'National English' poems, as they were
entitled, can be wonderful: or at least the music is wonderful though
the words may be less so. Take 'Melhill Feast':

Aye up at the feast, by Melhill's brow,
So softly below the clouds in flight,
There swept on the wood the shade and light,
Tree after tree, and bough by bough.

. . .

Then by the orchards dim and cool,
And then along Woodcombe's elmy side,
And then by the meads, where waters glide,
Shallow by shallow, pool by pool.

And then to the house, that stands alone,
With roses around the porch and wall,
Where up by the bridge the waters fall,
Rock under rock, and stone by stone . . .

The alliterations and near rhymes are intricate and subtle: I am not
sure that I can unravel them: 'Melhill's brow I softly below . . . clouds
in flight I swept wood shade bough . . . house I roses . . .' and so
on. It is easy to hear how the words run and I am very fond of
the 'meads, where waters glide', but it is wellnigh impossible to
reduce this beautiful behaviour of the commonplace language to a
set of rules.

I have chosen to discuss this kind of poem first because it is
easier to dissect than the Dorset dialect poems. There is one more
stage before we get to those: I have said that young Hardy imitated
the famous and elderly poet. One can observe it superficially in his
poem in Sapphics 'The Temporary the All', the first poem in his
first volume *Wessex Poems*, and again in 'Postponement' in the
same volume. In 'Valenciennes' he adopts the accent and dialect
of Dorset. In 'The Alarm', there are Barnes-like oddities of speech:
'skyway' for example:

In a ferny byway
Near the great South-Wessex Highway,
A homestead raised its breakfast-smoke aloft;
The dew-damps still lay steamless, for the sun had made no
skyway,
And twilight cloaked the croft.

Hardy clearly admired the strange knobbly quality of Barnes's language. In 'A Sign-Seeker', 'the nightfall shades subtrude', and in
'Friends Beyond' we have 'mothy curfew-tide', while the title of
another poem is 'In a Eweleaze near Weatherbury'. 'The Bride-
Night Fire' is in much solider dialect than 'The Alarm', so much so
that it needs a glossary. This poem is a short story, with touches of
humour, written in 1866 and first published in a magazine in 1875.
It is unique in Hardy's work, I believe, and most fully justifies the
title *Wessex Poems*. Barnes himself was not above the same kind of
poem, though they are not often reprinted. Hardy's *Select Poems of
William Barnes* (1908) sternly declares that dialect is not comic and
that the lyrics should be taken seriously, and that has set the tone

of how Barnes's lyrics have been treated: but it may be thought that the atmosphere of solemn sweetness has done no service to his reputation. Certainly Hardy's dialect poem is wonderfully lively and unsolemn, and the line 'Her cwold little figure half-naked he views' has been altered for publication. It should read 'Her cwold little buzzoms half-naked he views'. Barnes is equally a master of the vernacular, but less daring, I suppose.

In his dialect poems it is possible sometimes to see the banality of an idea through the disguise of reality that the dialect may give it. In 'The Woody Hollow' for example, he casts a wonderful garment over what is utterly simple, and one can hardly resist reading him in an uncritical frame of mind. In the end this poem records a frank attempt to become 'as little children', but it works truthfully enough: one must remember that essentially Barnes is an earlier poet than any Victorian: it would be easier if he were two hundred years earlier, because one feels there is something wilful about the sentiments of 1820 dressed up in a provincial past we never knew. We must try to know it, as we try to know Hardy's early days:

> When evenen's risèn moon did peep
> Down drough the hollow dark an' deep,
> Where gigglen sweethearts meäde their vows
> In whispers under waggen boughs;
> When whisslen bwoys, an rott'len ploughs
> Wer still, an' mothers, wi' their thin
> Shrill vaïces, call'd their daughters in,
>   From walken in the hollow . . .

Barnes was a perfectly genuine man and in his poetry the smaller the vignette he offers the sharper and more genuine it will be. 'Vellen o' the Tree' for example is a perfect poem that Edward Thomas or Charles Cotton might have written. It is quite unpretentious, like a watercolour by Peter De Wint.

'Evenen in the Village' has the same quality, yet in 'Evenen Twilight' the reader has to make a positive effort to see in what kind of world words so conventional were perfectly genuinely said: it is a poem that remembers older days than its own, but the refrain is not insistent and none of its moods is false:

> How sweet's the evenen dusk to rove
> Along wi' woone that we do love!

When light enough is in the sky
To sheäde the smile an' light the eye
'Tis all but heaven to be by;
   An' bid, in whispers soft an' light
   'S the russlen ov a leaf, 'Good night',
      At evenen in the twilight.

I think that, being in dialect, the poems are careless of conven-
tion as they are of dignity. The dancers 'hop about lik' vlees . . . An'
cows, in water to their knees / Do stan' a-whisken off the vlees',
and the conventional white road up the hill is just a fact of life.
His eclogues, and a poem like 'Whitsuntide an' Club Walken', which
he also wrote about in prose, can give a thrilling insight into an
age that is over, and institutions few alive can have known. I do
remember the club walk with the band and the church service in
Lancashire in 1959, but alas I never took part in the celebrations that
rocked the fells later in the day. Barnes disapproved of the drink
and the fighting in Dorset: 'Zoo in the dusk ov evenen, zome /
Went back to drink, an' zome went hwome'. Not that Barnes is
unrough. The smockfrocks chase the skirts, and there are fights and
poking of boys down holes:

      There I do vind it stir my heart
      To hear the frothen hosses snort,
      A-haulen on, we' sleek-heäir'd hides,
      The red-wheel'd waggon's deep-blue zides.
      Aye; let me have woone cup o' drink,
      An' hear the linky harness clink
      An' then my blood do run so warm . . .[11]

In all these poems, as in similar work by John Clare, it is the unexpected collocations of the simple observer that catch one and
make the poems very memorable. They may begin quite simply,
like Be'mi'ster with green woody hills around it, high hedges, 'a
thousan' vields o' zummer green' and elms and hedge-flowers:
that is memorable enough, but then:

      Where elder-blossoms be a-spread
      Above the eltrot's milk-white head,
      An' flow'rs o' blackberries do blow
      Upon the brembles, white as snow,

To be outdone avore my zight
By Jeäne's gaÿ frock o' dazzlen white.[12]

When we read in the 'Eclogues' about the new Poor Laws or
the Common taken in, we are perhaps less excited: because we
have heard all that before so many times, and we have ourselves
seen bad days, and had some taste of what Barnes's worse days
must have been like. It is as if he wrote just enough poems of that
kind to be politically correct: a concept of which his happy age of
the world was innocent. His instincts indeed were conservative,
he saw a role for the gentry and wished they fulfilled it. It is true
that of the two voices, John Clare is incomparably more plaintive.
Barnes's peasants see ruin coming, but Clare is really ruined. Virgil's
'Eclogues' lie at the back of Barnes's: in particular the first where
one of the herdsmen has lost his land and must go into exile. It is
not really at all a close analogy with anything Barnes suffered: and
I do not think he would be a better poet if he were unhappier or
less sweet-natured than he is. He carries, as only those with happy
childhoods can do, the sweetness of his nature in a kind of time
capsule that nothing can disturb. He is really a most remarkable
human being, of a kind that has almost never become a writer in
the last 350 years. Indeed I suspect we have all known people as
devoted, as sweet-natured (more usually women) and as undisturbed. One of their characteristics is that they express themselves
quite unselfconsciously in conventional terms. The difference with
Barnes is that his intimate vernacular was the Dorset dialect, and
that was in the time capsule that came from his early childhood,
when his father was a smallholder on Bagber common. He was
obsessed with the place, and bought two fields there himself when
he was a grown man. He just loved the business of having a tenant,
and arguing with him against the polling of elm trees.

I do not feel I have been able to characterise William Barnes
centrally: he is in his dialect verse more deeply what it appears he
was in life, and he is that by entering into a countryman's life both
his and not his, with a life-giving warmth. He gets out of his conventional poems what he consciously puts into them, but something more important emerges from his commerce with the dialect.
For one thing, he is really more rustic than he knows: he is not
rusticus dolens, he is deeply a nineteenth-century Blackmoor Vale
man, Christian only in the sense that the gravestones, with their stern-
ness, their Roman stoicism and their childish clarity, are Christian.

There is a restraint about his poems, but we feel strongly what he restrains. This queer kind of Christian rustic stoicism is present in the use he makes of the simplest conventions he adopts. Because he is more rustic than he realises the dialect is very revealing, not of him personally, but of meadows and lanes full of characters, a whole world that we have no other means of reaching. The dialect is a kind of fondling of once familiar things, eltrots and greggles (cow parsley and bluebells), and people. He is not a Virgilian poet, and not Theocritean: the only touch of Theocritus is a cage he made out of rushes as a child, and that may easily be coincidence: Theocritus had one for catching crickets. He is more like Horace trying to rewrite Virgil's 'Eclogues' in the style of the satires.

His longest political argument is in that able eclogue 'The Times' about the position of small farmers and labourers (one man of course could be both) in hard times, and it contains some zany arguments against the Corn Laws. We know there were country riots against those laws, which kept the price of bread high and kept out foreign grain; indeed I am told I had an ancestor hanged by a mob over the Corn Laws, and I certainly have a friend whose great-grandfather was burned in effigy on his own lawn by his own parishioners. Barnes is comparatively low-toned. One of his people says he would like to see England double the size; the other answers:

> But if they were a-zent to Parli'ment
> To meäke the laws, dost know, as I've a-zaid,
> They'd knock the corn-laws on the head;
> An' then the landlords must let down their rent,
> An' we should very soon have cheaper bread:
> Farmers would gi'e less money vor their lands.

It seems a highly unlikely series of conclusions, but no doubt it represents the level of real rustic arguments in Barnes's day about the market economy. The eclogue ends in a fable about the pig and the crow. It is Horatian and very well told, but I am not certain how it applies, except through a certain ominous and suspicious country wisdom. The poem ends:

> Ah! I do think you mid as well be quiet;
> You'll meäke things wo'se, i'-ma-be, by a riot.
> You'll get into a mess, Tom, I'm afeärd;
> You'll goo vor wool, an' then come hwome a-sheär'd.

Is this some suppressed memory of the Tolpuddle martyrs? There is a lot of shifting of blame onto agitators who come from elsewhere. The poem and its date and the precise local conditions are worth more study than I can offer.

But I had promised you a certain enchantment to be found in these poems. It is most obviously seen where Ralph Vaughan Williams spotted it, in 'My Orcha'd in Linden Lea':

> 'Ithin the woodlands, flow'ry gleäded,
>   By the woak tree's mossy moot,
> The sheenen grass-bleädes, timber-sheäded,
>   Now do quiver under voot;
> An' birds do whissle over head,
> An' water's bubblen in its bed,
> An' there vor me the apple tree
> Do leän down low in Linden Lea.
>
> When leaves that leätely wer a-springen
>   Now do feäde 'ithin the copse,
> An' painted birds do hush their zingen
>   Up upon the timber's tops;
> An' brown-leav'd fruit's a-turnen red,
> In cloudless zunsheen, over head,
> Wi' fruit vor me, the apple tree
> Do lean down low in Linden Lea.
>
> Let other vo'k meäke money vaster
>   In the aïr o' dark-room'd towns,
> I don't dread a peevish meäster;
>   Though noo man do heed my frowns,
> I be free to go abrode,
> Or teäke ageän my homeward road
> To where, vor me, the apple tree
> Do leän down low in Linden Lea.

They are not writing poems quite like that any more. The plot is so simple it hardly exists: a countryman, a free labourer who may wander if he chooses, is coming home at the end of summer through the woods (a mossy moot is the trunk of a felled tree), the leaves are changing colour, the birds have lost their voices, it is late September and the early apples are ripe. The technique of the poem is not a formal pattern of alliteration but there is a lot of stray alliteration, and even more half-rhyme and internal rhyme: 'dark-room'd towns ... don't dread', and 'vo'k ... dark-room'd towns ... don't ... noo man ... frowns'. These are not tricks applied to the language, they are not predictable, they are used instinctively, by a kind of second nature. Did Hopkins learn some of the philological oddities of his verse from habits that to Barnes were second nature?

> And flockbells off the aerial
> Downs' forefalls beat to the burial ...[13]

Barnes's habit of joining two words in a new word attracted notice in his lifetime, but Hardy inherits it, and as for Hopkins, what about 'baldbright' and 'hailropes', 'heavengravel' and 'wolfsnow', all in one stanza? The later poets lack Barnes's simplicity, which can seem almost like a riddle, as in 'A Brisk Wind':

> The burdock leaves upon the ledge,
> The leaves upon the poplar's height,
> A-blown by wind all up on edge,
> Did show their underzides o' white;
> An' withy trees bezide the rocks
> Did bend grey limbs, did swaÿ grey boughs,
> As there, on waggen heads, dark locks
> Bespread red cheäks, behung white brows.

The shock to the senses of these sharp, primary observations is like that of primary colours, with which the poem ends. It is all like a series of linked haiku.

There are poems by Barnes like a bucket of extremely cold water, but there are others with an exquisite and trailing kind of music where what the poem says seems determined by its metrical pattern. 'A Winter Night' for example is like that, and at first reading you might have sworn it was a poem by Thomas Hardy:

> It was a chilly winter's night;
>   And frost was glitt'ring on the ground,
> And evening stars were twinkling bright;
>   And from the gloomy plain around
>   Came no sound,
> But where, within the wood-girt tow'r,
> The churchbell slowly struck the hour;

As if that all of human birth
　Had risen to the final day,
And soaring from the wornout earth
　Were called in hurry and dismay,
　　Far away;
And I alone of all mankind
Were left in loneliness behind.

This scary but perfect little poem surprises one several times: first by not being about Christmas, then by the ghostly flitting rather than general resurrection, and then most of all by the single figure left alone in the empty graveyard. If Hardy had written it, there might have been more verses, as there are in 'Channel Firing'. I do not think it was influenced by that much younger master, but Barnes may have sown a seed in Hardy's mind. When Hardy, hardly above school age, read to better himself and kept word-lists, Barnes was one of the authors he studied; he even fancied an amour with Lucy Barnes, but she was too shy for him. That must have been when he was eighteen or so, since she was three years older than he was; it must have been in the last years of the school, before Barnes moved out to Winterborne Came in 1862, with his daughters acting as curates, and one of his sons in the end as Rector of Winterborne Monkton, which was the next parish.

The most famous poem of his last years was 'The Geäte a-Vallèn To', one of the last few poems he dictated, in October 1885, about a year before he died. It is a poem that melts in the mouth, neatly enough executed but not strongly enough incised to be by Horace. The openings of each stanza are in the same magical version of the vernacular as Thomas Moore's *Irish Melodies*, which must lie somewhere among his forgotten models. Moore himself lay buried not far from Barnes's youthful horizons in a country churchyard not far from Bath:

In the zunsheen ov our zummers
　Wi' the haÿ time now a-come,
How busy were we out a-vield
　Wi' vew a-left at hwome . . .

　　. . .

There's moon-sheen now in nights o' fall
　When leaves be brown vrom green . . .

and finally . . .

> To hear behind his last farewell
> The geäte a-vallèn to.

In the end he becomes a patriarchal figure, prophetic and so distant in his old age as to be terrifying, dressed in fur-lined crimson
to the waist, crouching in his chair over the fire and discussing
Tennyson. I prefer him in the days of his riper eccentricity. If you
want to recall that dead world, just remember how Tennyson was
planting out primulas when he met the Irish poet Allingham whom
he greatly liked, and swept him up to visit Winterborne Came. They
got to Lymington at once, and then sat through a long hot day in a
train while Tennyson smoked that filthy tobacco he liked, puffing out
smoke like the engine. A man got into their compartment who was
a professional clock regulator for the Great Western Railway, and
at every station (this train stopped at every station) he got out and
corrected the clock by his watch to London time. In the evening they
got to Dorchester and next day they walked to Lyme Regis sending
on their luggage by a coach, because Alfred wanted to carry out a
pilgrimage to Jane Austen. On the night they spent in Dorchester
they walked out to Winterborne Came, and saw old Barnes – a little
earlier Barnes had called on Tennyson at Farringford. (On that
occasion Barnes had gone to bed earlyish, as Tennyson was in full
cry after Darwinism and pantheism and so on, being a thorough
liberal: Barnes had little taste for 'speculation in matters theological'.) But the person in this rambling story who most embodies
the age is surely the railway company's regulator of clocks. There
was universal mechanical time, and we would never be free of
it again. As C. H. Sisson has written in words well applied by
Robert Nye to the poetry of Barnes: 'The man that was the same in
Neolithic and in Roman times, as now, is of more interest than
the freak of circumstances. This truth lies at the bottom of a well of
rhythm.'[14]

It is in the freedom of his rhythms that you immediately know
William Barnes for what he was: I mean their vernacular freedom,
as in 'Black and White':

> . . .
> When you stroll'd down the village at evening, bedight
> All in white, in the warm summer-tide,

The while *Towsy*, your loving old dog, with his back
Sleeky black, trotted on at your side:
Ah! the black and the white! Which was fairest to view?
Why the white became fairest on you.

At the end of the barton the granary stood,
Of black wood, with white geese at its side,
And the white-winged swans glided over the waves
By the cave's darksome shadows in pride:
Oh! the black and the white! Which was fairest to view?
Why the white became fairest on you.

There is something more spirited or more developed, more intricate
than a lilt in this poetry. The paradox is that where Tennyson places
every footstep faultlessly like a man crossing a marsh, Barnes, having
once digested his far-ranging examples and become able to produce
them by second nature, can be perfectly, easily fluent. One would be
wrong to say too fluent, because his easy voice, the easy sway of his
voice, is an essential element in the enchanting effect of his poetry.
Many things lay beyond his range, but he could do what was tradi-
tionally done and is not done now, and was not done in his time:

O spread ageän your leaves an' flow'rs,
    Lwonesome woodlands! zunny woodlands!
Here underneath the dewy show'rs
    O' warm-aïr'd spring-time, zunny woodlands! . . .

O let me rove ageän unspied,
    Lwonesome woodlands, zunny woodlands!
Along your green-bough'd hedges' zide,
    As then I rambled, zunny woodlands!
An' where the missen trees woonce stood,
Or tongues woonce rung among the wood,
My memory shall meäke em good,
    Though you've a-lost em, zunny woodlands![15]

One despairs in the attempt to construct a paper about anything so
fragile: it is like snow, it is only made of pure water and it runs
out of your hand. But Shakespeare would have recognised it as
poetry, Milton would have envied it as poetry, Chaucer would have
smiled at it, Donne would have been interested, no one would
have thought it uninteresting until after the Civil War. It may be the

Blackmoor Vale is in this sense prelapsarian, it has something about it continuous with the days before the Civil War. The world of Barnes's eclogues is not in the least timeless, but the time they belong to might as easily be before the Civil War, that great divide and loss of English innocence. They are the only world of poetry for more than a century that Charles Cotton and Izaak Walton could have entered into without a qualm.

His rhymes can be playful and his verse is never full-toned as Shakespeare's is, but it perfectly fits the world and the people it reveals. In 'Shaftesbury Feäir' he calls the place Paladore, not a new name in his day:

> As you did look, wi' eyes as blue
> As yonder southern hills in view,
> Vrom Paladore – O Polly dear,
> Wi' you up there,
> How merry then wer I at feäir.

Yet taken together his poems carry the weight of life in their good-natured and reticent way, and somehow of the life of whole villages, a whole way of life. They are not essentially poems about the past even though it helps to know that they arise from the genius of a little child before Waterloo. If they were not in some way frozen there, they would not be as powerful as they are; but they are not about their period, that is only their condition, which so long after-wards it is useful for us to notice. Their subject is life, which is surely the subject of all true poetry, and it is surprising how much they carry of the experience of life at their simple level. It is not a life that ever touches the newspapers, and history hardly touches it even at Waterloo: hardly touches it at all I suppose until 1914 when the whole rural youth of England were taken away to another country and shot. That disaster is the foundation of the modern world. But when William Barnes thinks at all about English history it is to tell his daughter on his death-bed after having dictated 'The Geäte a-Vallèn To', ' "Observe that word 'geäte'. That is how King Alfred would have pronounced it, and how it was called in the *Saxon Chronicle*, which tells us of King Edward, who was slain at Corfe's geäte." After a pause he continued, "Ah! if the Court had not been moved to London, then the speech of King Alfred of which our Dorset is the remnant – would have been – the Court language of today, and it would have been more like Anglo-Saxon than it is now".'[16] That is exactly how a scholar of Shakespeare's day would

have considered things, in just the same spirit. It is freakish enough
of course, but it rouses one's affection for the good old poet. His
vein of eccentricity was golden.

Twenty years ago I had the honour of reprinting his version of
the 'Song of Songs', published in 1859 with many others in various dialects by the English Dialect Society under the patronage of
Lucien Bonaparte.[17] The entire enterprise was rich in comedy, and
in the Bodleian Library the only way to find Barnes's contribution
used to be to look under SAL for Salamonis, as Biblical books in
whatever language were under their first authors in Latin. Yet the
effect, extremely queer as it undoubtedly is to most ears, is not
without beauty.

I be the rwose o' Sharon, an' the lily o' the valleys.
   Lik' a lily wi' thorns, is my love among maïdens.
   Lik' an apple-tree in wi' the trees o' the wood, is my love
among sons. I long'd vor his sheäde, an' zot down, an' his fruit
wer vull sweet to my teäste.
   He brought me into the feäst, an' his flag up above me wer
love.
   Refresh me wi' ceäkes, uphold me wi' apples: vor I be a-pinèn
vor love.
   His left hand wer under my head, an' his right a-cast round
me.

When it came to translating from the Old Friesian, Barnes was less
restrained. It is there he introduces the compound 'blowinggreen
lithebloom', which prefigures Hopkins. Yet as a young man in 1826,
thirty-three years before, he translated a sonnet of Petrarch with an
icy neoclassic perfection such as he never attained in his own poems
in common English. He was a man like Edward Lear in whom
translation or pastiche might set free powers that would surprise
him and still surprise the world. They are quite different in the
case of the dialect version of the 'Song of Songs', which is a beautiful
and most restrained piece of work, much better than the other dialect
versions, as far as I remember them, and in the case of Petrarch:

And those two lovely eyes that lit my track
Are gone, and reason in the waves is drowned.

One would not imagine they could have been written by the same
person.

Thomas Hardy said goodbye to them both. It was after a walk with Hardy in freezing, unexpected rain that Barnes took to his bed. In 'An Ancient to Ancients' Hardy does not mingle Barnes's name with those of Etty, Mulready, Maclise, Bulwer, Scott, Dumas and Sand:

> The bower we shrined to Tennyson,
>> Gentlemen,
> Is roof-wrecked; damps there drip upon
> Sagged seats, the creeper-nails are rust,
> The spider is sole denizen;
> Even she who voiced those rhymes is dust,
>> Gentlemen!

In the next to last stanza of that poem he turns the tables on the young:

> Sophocles, Plato, Socrates,
>> Gentlemen,
> Pythagoras, Thucydides,
> Herodotus, and Homer, – yea,
> Clement, Augustin, Origen,
> Burnt brightlier towards their setting-day,
>> Gentlemen.

That I take to be something he learnt from Barnes, who was dead when Hardy wrote it. But the poem of farewell is the one annotated '11 Oct. 1886 . . . Winterborne Came Path' and not published until more than thirty years afterwards. It is moving enough to conclude with, and words like 'yew-boughed' and 'grave-way' derive from Barnes's English. The little poem certainly does follow Barnes in its technique. How curious it is after all if we are right in supposing that Barnes only ever had two disciples who were poets: but those two were Gerard Manley Hopkins and Thomas Hardy.[18]

The Last Signal

(11 Oct. 1886)

A Memory of William Barnes

Silently I footed by an uphill road
That led from my abode to a spot yew-boughed;

Yellowly the sun sloped low down to westward,
    And dark was the east with cloud.

Then, amid the shadow of that livid sad east,
    Where the light was least, and a gate stood wide,
Something flashed the fire of the sun that was facing it,
    Like a brief blaze on that side.

Looking hard and harder I knew what it meant –
    The sudden shine sent from the livid east scene;
It meant the west mirrored by the coffin of my friend there,
    Turning to the road from his green,

To take his last journey forth – he who in his prime
    Trudged so many a time from that gate athwart the land!
Thus a farewell to me he signalled on his grave-way,
    As with a wave of his hand.

Winterborne-Came Path

It is an implacably melancholic poem, but so restrained – so much
is not said – that we must take it as the most personal of tributes.

Notes

Quotations from Barnes's poems are taken from *The Poems of William Barnes*,
ed. Bernard Jones (London: Centaur Press, 1962). Quotations from Hardy's
poems are taken from *The Complete Poems of Thomas Hardy*, ed. James Gibson
(London: Macmillan, 1976).

1. Peter Levi, *Tennyson* (London: Macmillan, 1993).
2. Lane Fox's role as mentor is attested by Barnes's daughter in her
    biography of her father (see note 4 below). However, Alan Chedzoy
    in his *William Barnes: A Life of the Dorset Poet* (Stanbridge: Dovecote
    Press, 1985) p. 23 suggests that Barnes's acquaintanceship with Lane
    Fox began at a later date.
3. Thomas Hardy, 'The Rev. William Barnes, B.D.' [obituary in:] *Athen-
    aeum*, 16 October 1886, pp. 501–2; reprinted in H. Orel (ed.), *Thomas
    Hardy's Personal Writings* (London: Macmillan, 1967) p. 100.
4. Lucy Baxter ('Leader Scott'), *The Life of William Barnes: Poet and Philo-
    logist* (London: Macmillan, 1887) p. 201.
5. Ibid., p. 209.

6. Ibid., p. 84.
7. Ibid., p. 277.
8. Milton, *L'Allegro*.
9. Preface to *Select Poems of William Barnes*, ed. Thomas Hardy (London: H. Frowde [Oxford University Press], 1908) p. ix.
10. 'The Elm in Home-Ground'.
11. 'Hay-Carren'.
12. 'Be'mi'ster'.
13. Gerard Manley Hopkins, 'The Loss of the Eurydice. Foundered March 24 1878'.
14. Original quote by C. H. Sisson is from *Art and Action* (London: Methuen, 1965). Quoted by Robert Nye in his Introduction to *William Barnes: A Selection of his Poems* (Oxford: Carcanet Press, 1972) p. 14.
15. 'The Woodlands'.
16. Baxter, *The Life of William Barnes*, p. 317.
17. Peter Levi, *The English Bible 1534–1859* (London: Constable, 1974). Barnes's translation is entitled 'The Zong o' Solomon' and the quoted extract is from 'Song of Songs II'.
18. This fact was first pointed out by Geoffrey Grigson in an article in *Lilliput* in the 1940s.

6

Hardy and Decadence

GILLIAN BEER

A pervasive theme of Hardy's writing is how things decay, yet how fully and abruptly they are alive. A haunting question is how they survive. Intellectual pressures are emotional pressures too, and for Hardy the implications both of evolutionary theory and of entropy bore in on the life of his fiction and his poems. They are often expressed as a struggle between individuality and energy. Hardy's career as a writer developed alongside the emergence of the Decadent or fin-de-siècle movement in Britain, but he is not often set in a close relation to Decadent writing of the 1880s and 1890s. If we listen to some of the voices by which he was surrounded in the later part of his career we can hear resonances in his poetry and his fiction that we may otherwise miss. We can hear, too, the degree to which new scientific ideas about sound-waves, survival, and the ether of the universe unexpectedly gave Hardy ways out of the impasse of human mortality and decay.

When we think of Hardy and Decadence our thoughts may first turn to *The Return of the Native* with Clym's fine head distorted by the weight of thought, or to Tess, last offspring of a family 'extinct in the male line', or to Jude and Sue willing change but reduced to sports (in the genetic sense) by the death of their children. And in each of these famous examples it is the withering of hope, of the will or capacity to live, that exemplifies decay. Hardy puts into the mouth of the doctor near the end of *Jude* the view that this is how things must inevitably be, that the race will degrade through its own loss of energy. Equilibration or judgment day seems at hand.

But the Decadent movement is not concerned only with exploring sickness. It encompasses also limber play across the threshold between the normative and the monstrous, experimenting with fresh futures; it is preoccupied with new sound worlds; and it is closely involved with New Woman writing. To turn first to that uneasy relationship.

In 1894 George Egerton published a disturbing set of short stories,

Discords, following her recent and immensely influential *Keynotes* (1893), a volume of short stories that turned fiction towards the twentieth century and made their mark in the perceptions and style of D. H. Lawrence. The title 'Keynotes' was adopted as the imprint overtitle for a whole series of works by diverse authors published by the then radical publishing house Bodley Head. One story, 'Virgin Soil', tells of a young woman of 22 returning home after five years of marriage to batter her mother's ears with her deep outrage at having been betrayed into marriage without any warning about sex or men's sexual practices. At the end, exhausted by vituperation and a wan return of sympathy for her mother, she walks to the station, already old in her twenties, surrounded by a premature autumn: .

> The morning is grey and misty, with faint yellow stains in the east, and the west wind blows with a melancholy sough in it – the first whisper of the fall, the fall that turns the world of nature into a patient suffering from phthisis – delicate season of decadence, when the loveliest scenes have a note of decay in their beauty; when a poisoned arrow pierces the marrow of insect and plant, and the leaves have a hectic flush and fall, fall and shrivel and curl in the night's cool; and the chrysanthemums, the 'good-bye summers' of the Irish peasants, have a sickly tinge in their white.[1]

The language displays the stigmata of Decadence: yellow stains foul the dawn and *are* the dawn; the natural world is anthropomorphised as sick, 'a patient suffering from phthisis' – a medical term then so novel that it does not appear in the *Oxford English Dictionary* – and, tubercular, 'the leaves have a hectic flush'; hints of folklore and 'the primitive' edge into the passage: 'poisoned arrow' and, more benignly, Irish peasants. And through all is the melancholy onomatopaeic sough or suff, the sound of the west wind.

   This is the psychic landscape of hope blasted, youth betrayed by oppressive elders, natural joy thwarted by custom, that is both the seed-bed and the site of resistance of the Decadent movement. Moreover, Decadence is here the fall, both part of the natural cycle and of a theological sense of loss, what in the Middle Ages was called 'wanhope', an expression more immediate than despair.

   What makes this passage so powerful within the story is the outrage Egerton conveys – the sense that this *need not be*, that things must change for women. During the 1890s, the period of *Tess of the d'Urbervilles, Jude the Obscure,* and *The Well-Beloved,* Hardy makes particularly strong identifications in his novels with women's plight and women's strength. In this he moves close to writers such as Egerton and Mona Caird, whose spirited and radical *Daughters of Danaus* also appeared in 1894. The emphasis among feminist writers of the time is on resilience as much as torment, on new pathways and endurance; in *Tess* Hardy dignifies those processes, though he shows them overwhelmed at last. But he catches up into his work also other elements from the fin-de-siècle.

In 1893 Arthur Symons wrote what has remained a central description and defence of the Decadent movement in Europe and England, in *Harper's New Monthly Magazine.*[2] Calling it 'the most representative literature of the day – the writing which appeals to, which has done so much to form, the younger generation', he characterises it thus:

> After a fashion it is no doubt a decadence: it has all the qualities that mark the end of great periods, the qualities that we find in the Greek, the Latin, decadence: an intense self-consciousness, a restless curiosity in research, an over-subtilizing refinement upon refinement, a spiritual and moral perversity. If what we call the classic is indeed the supreme art – those qualities of perfect simplicity, perfect sanity, perfect proportion, the supreme qualities – then this representative literature of today, interesting, beautiful, novel as it is, is really a new and beautiful and interesting disease.

Yet, he argues, in representing disease the Decadent movement is truer to life as it is now lived than the classic could possibly be: 'its very artificiality is a way of being true to nature: simplicity, sanity, proportion – the classic qualities – how much do we possess them in our life, our surroundings, that we should look to find them in our literature . . . ?'[3] In Symons's argument the middle way and the norm are falsified, shown as unreal ideals. The vigour, the assertiveness, of Hardy's apparently faint praise of Tess becomes manifest in this context: she is 'an almost standard woman'.

The 'almost' is as crucial to her excellence as the 'standard' – the high type from which all other women deviate. She is both absolute and individual, quirky as well as pure. That combination is itself very typical of late nineteenth-century 'Decadent' writing. We can see it again in the free and magnificent young woman Trilby, in

George du Maurier's novel of that name, who loves men as she chooses and is full of merriment and repose. Alas, like Tess, she is victimised by Svengali and author alike. These pure women do not survive in men's fiction of the nineties, even Decadent fiction; though they may represent potential evolutionary pathways, those ways are blocked. Egerton suggests, even more than Hardy, that 'purity', as interpreted by current society, is a rancorous ideal. Indeed, it is hard quite to measure the pressures of the irony in Hardy's insistence on Tess's purity, the need still to invoke it even if to re-interpret its meaning. Does it set him apart from his younger contemporaries declaredly in the Decadent movement?

During the later nineteenth century the word we now pronounce de'cadence was pronounced deca'dence (decay-dence) with, in the eighteen-nineties a strong undersong of decade (ten-year cycle, fin de siècle). Hardy, I would suggest, added into that chord of meanings and soundings *cadence*. That's a perhaps fanciful way of suggesting how strongly, and in what a diversity of ways, acoustics became part of his thinking and feeling. Pater had declared that all arts aspire to the condition of music, and Egerton prefaces each of her stories with the musical notation of a chord or discord. As we heard in the passage above, Egerton is responsive to the power of natural sound, 'the sough' or suff. Similarly, George Meredith in *One of Our Conquerors* in the early 90s imagines a man haunted by conflicting musical experiences – Donizetti and Wagner – which repeat and grind against each other disturbingly just at the point of consciousness. Music and musical experience are, for writers at the end of the nineteenth century, a means to get beyond the limiting capacity of words and to evoke values other than those of sight. They are part of the Decadent enterprise, often as a mode of salvation: getting out beyond the prescribed expectations of story, through sound, which is peculiarly able to evoke lost or distant memories.

In this discussion I shall suggest that Hardy finds ways of thinking about sound that can become part of his brooding on evolution and entropy and their pressures on the individual life. That is to say also: sound for Hardy becomes a way of thinking about transience and eternity, about decay and continuance, about *being* now. Hardy, as every lover of his work well knows, is sensitive always to sound, which he often merges synaesthetically with touch: the dead heath-bells scoured by the wind to produce a massed buzz and crepitation are, in *The Return of the Native*, heard at once from far off and from within the parched bell of each flower. He registers too the degree to which the viol relies on the body of its player to reach its full resonance – and is infinitely (and often inconveniently) sensitive to the temperature by which it is surrounded.

During the years of Hardy's writing career two major intellectual movements occurred, and for a time seemed to be in contention: evolution and thermodynamics.[4] Evolutionary theory, in Darwinian language, emphasised the movement towards complexity, the subtle relatedness of organism and organism, but also the struggle for life – most vehement between those closely related or needing the same space and nutriment. Darwin inclined to hope that the outcome of such struggle would be not only change but improvement: enhanced beauty, aptitude, strength, and range. Yet he also emphasised the endurance of the simple, the stability of life where the needs of environment and organism well match, and where predations from outside the community can be avoided. For that, he imagined islands or places with closed borders where the inhabitants in their diversity and in the increasing diversification of their descendants can each discover harmoniously an ecological niche without destruction. That is the most 'natural' process, he hopes, of natural selection.

Darwinian evolutionary theory privileged, in theoretical terms, the individual as bearer of the capacity for mutation: 'ordinary succession by generation' and the 'endless forms most beautiful and most wonderful' that 'have been, and are being, evolved' are its subject. That was the optimistic side of evolutionary theory. Hardy taps into the comfort and the menace of forms of survival that discount the individual bearer in his poem 'Heredity':

> I am the family face;
> Flesh perishes, I live on,
> Projecting trait and trace
> Through time to times anon,
> And leaping from place to place
> Over oblivion.

> The years-heired feature that can
> In curve and voice and eye
> Despise the human span
> Of durance – that is I;
> The eternal thing in man,
> That heeds no call to die.

The face lives on; the variety of individual people and their histories is lost.

In the 1870s writers such as Winwood Reade in his widely and passionately read *The Martyrdom of Man* emphasised that individual suffering was not recompensed *for the individual* by being part of a longer evolutionary process. And, alongside that, the introduction of Herbert Spencer's phrase 'the survival of the fittest' into late editions of the *Origin of Species* seemed to license a teleological view of natural selection. In such a plan those who survive are thereby extolled as the justified, the inevitable victors by virtue of superiority rather than simply fortunately apt to the current circumstances in which they live and therefore likely to survive and bear offspring.

Hardy responded vehemently to the contradictory stories that could be extruded from Darwinian thinking and he inclined to position his perceptions alongside those who blench, suffer, are victimised, or (more happily) unknowingly like the ephemerons in *The Return of the Native* pass blithely away.

But alongside this already ruptured and antagonistic set of interpretations came another major scientific movement that first seemed to question the accuracy of evolutionary chronology and then in any case seemed to produce its own inherent contradictions, its own blasting narratives. This was the formulation of the two laws of thermodynamics, then still embraced in the wider formulation 'wave theory'. These ideas also entered public consciousness, particularly in the 1870s with the translation of Helmholtz's essays. Helmholtz's innovative work on entropy, optics, and acoustics was widely disseminated before translation through the publication of John Tyndall's popular expositions, such as *Light* and *Sound*, from the 1860s on. The two laws are, first, that the amount of energy within a closed system remains stable and, second, that disorder is increasing and that energy once consumed is no longer available for work (entropy). Eventually equilibration will be reached and with it the death of the universe. Both evolution and entropy emphasise the irreversible, plummeting or escalating but never turning back.

Now, Hardy, we know, always resisted any attempt to appropriate his work to any system. He emphasised the fugitive, the conditional: writing of W. L. Courtney who had given a sympathetic appraisal of *The Dynasts* he remarked: 'Like so many critics Mr Courtney treats my works of art as if they were a scientific system of philosophy, although I have repeatedly stated . . . that the views in them are *seemings*.'[5]

We do not need to embrace a systematic gridding of Hardy's work to the scientific ideas of his time to become aware of how fully they enter the temper of his creativity, how they distemper and irritate his thought. But why does he so insistently resist system-isation? And why do others need to make this treatment of his work? The menacing paranoia of so many of his plots, where events are ponderously shifted to pound, decimate, or grind down the char-acters' hopes, suggests a terror at work in relation to systems. So rather than simply accepting his denials as ending the question we may do well to consider them symptomatically. Many critics and readers want to stabilise and display accords between his writing and 'scientific systems of philosophy'. Hardy wants to resist settle-ment and hold to seeming: fickle, contingent, temporary, but also absolute. He is claiming the privilege of fiction, its autocracy. Seem-ings are not permanent but they are compelling. 'Impressions', as he described them in the 1892 preface to *Tess*, are the ungainsayable evanishing knowledge of the individual, communicable only so, *as* individual experience. Impressions, moreover, in the new world of entropy, accord well with the organisation of the universe as it ebbs and dissipates.

Like Symons, Hardy is making a claim for a new kind of actual-ity not bound to longer-known laws. Indeed, in terms of loss of faith in life, perhaps the most Decadent document among Hardy's own writing is a letter he sent to Rider Haggard in May 1891. The 'Eric' referred to is Haggard's novel *Eric Brighteyes*, which includes an illustration by Lancelot Speed of 'a huge sword impaled between a woman's naked breasts':

My dear Haggard:
    I called at the Savile a day or two ago, & found Eric awaiting me there. Many thanks for your thoughtful kindness in sending me a copy. My wife, who is with me here, took it as soon as I got home, & has appropriated it ever since. I have, however, read the Introduction, & (I am ashamed to confess) a chapter nearer the end than the beginning – but this was the fault of the artist, not mine, (for I am most conscientious on such matters) in putting such a wild illustration. I shall presently begin & take it straight on.
    Please give my kind regards to Mrs Haggard, & tell her how deeply our sympathy was with you both in your bereavement. Though, to be candid, I think the death of a child is never really to be regretted, when one reflects on what he has escaped.

It is miserably cold here still, & you are well to be away – as I believe you are.

Believe me

Yours sincerely

Thomas Hardy[6]

The appalling combination of a seamy eroticism, the disturbance of narrative trust, and the death of a child so brusquely justified, may well make us quail. But that truncating of life, here so inappropriately addressed to the father of a lost ten-year-old, goes to the heart of Hardy's creative disturbance.

And here I take up again the thread of sound. How to discover some form of eternity without religion? Some form for continuance that will not be mere false optimism? Voice or sound may prove to hold the key. 'Wave theory' emphasises that light, heat, and sound are all interchangeable expressions of a single system of energy which, it was then believed by scientists, pulses through the universe borne in the medium of 'luminiferous aether'. Transformation of energy makes it unavailable for work, but it continues to be, in a space and time not capable of being tapped by us. Some of the implications of these thoughts, derived from John Tyndall's popularising accounts in particular, begin to stir in Hardy's verse. 'The Occultation' imagines a scene never actually entered before air travel: that 'upper air' where day 'continue[s] its lustrous roll'. The technical astronomical term 'occultation', expressing the concealment of one celestial body behind another (usually of stars by the moon), is here applied by Hardy to the sun, and to his own life:

> When the cloud shut down on the morning shine,
>   And darkened the sun,
> I said, 'So ended that joy of mine
>   Years back begun.'
>
> But day continued its lustrous roll
>   In upper air;
> And did my late irradiate soul
>   Live on somewhere?

Time and space are not fixed at one point of observation. Hardy here imagines a continuum of being in which space and time are expressed as all there side by side, not lost as past. This possibility, which acknowledges absence and the irretrievable but asserts deathlessness, gives the pressure to 'A Kiss':

> By a wall the stranger now calls his,
> Was born of old a particular kiss,   `
> Without forethought in its genesis;
> Which in a trice took wing on the air.
> And where that spot is nothing shows:
>   There ivy calmly grows,
>   And no one knows
>   What a birth was there!
>
> That kiss is gone where none can tell –
> Not even those who felt its spell:
> It cannot have died; that know we well.
> Somewhere it pursues its flight,
> One of a long procession of sounds
>   Travelling aethereal rounds
>   Far from earth's bounds
>   In the infinite.

Sound waves never cease; with a frisson of tender comedy, the long ago kiss is added to the procession. 'It cannot have died; that know we well': the authority of schoolbook learning here liberates what has seemed lost.

'In a Museum' wonderfully blends evolutionary and thermodynamic perceptions: Hardy surveys a fossil bird – flight turned to stone – 'mould' indicating both form and decay. As he looks he hears in his head a song sung last evening. Together, last night's song and pre-historic flight cascade through the universe:

I

> Here's the mould of a musical bird long passed from light,
> Which over the earth before man came was winging;
> There's a contralto voice I heard last night,
> That lodges in me still with its sweet singing.

II

> Such a dream is Time that the coo of this ancient bird
> Has perished not, but is blent, or will be blending
> Mid visionless wilds of space with the voice that I heard,
> In the full-fugued song of the universe unending.

Exeter

The bird's species is invisible now, gone before man came. But the song of bird and singer continues; not only – as poets have long declared – because other birds of the same species sing the same song. In Keats another nightingale will sing, but now acoustics and wave-theory allow Hardy's further leap: the song of the bird, though its body is long fossilised, never ends; and neither will that of the woman singing last night. Both continue to pulse as sound-waves through the universe, impulsions in that round which reaches dia-pason in the magnificent last line:

In the full-fugued song of the universe unending.

Unending is here not time only but topography: the universe is with-out bounds, filled with air-waves laden with sounds inaudible to us but physically there, overlapping, 'full-fugued'. 'Wave theory' here implies profound continuance, a medley of transformations that sustain. But, again, individuality must yield, becoming – at most – vibration.

Hardy, so drawn to the obdurate and idiosyncratic in individual-ity, persistently shows that it may not survive in the order of the universe, whether that order is presented as evolutionary or thermo-dynamic, biological or astronomical. Often that recognition is grim. Memory degrades and dies out. Writing matters: in fiction the full flowering of a life may be at least suggested in language that can last. But beyond fiction he seeks solace in the transformations of sound, light, species. The continuance of natural sound, of a recurrent face, can temper loss though not resolve it.

In his late novel *The Well-Beloved: A Sketch of a Temperament*[7] he finds a form closer to comedy to test the resistance of individuality. The work thrives on the comi-tragedy of sexual drive, here without progeny, resisting the toils of evolution. The 'throbbings of noon-tide' are unchanged from youth to age in the human frame: 'One thing it passed him to understand: on what field of observation the poets and philosophers based their assumption that the passion of love was intensest in youth and burnt lower as maturity advanced' (Pt 1, Ch. 9).

In *The Well-Beloved* sex is a form of hope, of revival and light-ness: a 'highly charged electric condition' responding to 'that liquid sparkle of her eye, that lingual music, that turn of the head' (Pt 2, Ch. 1). Here, with an arch self-mockery, the lover is 'inclined to pal-pitate like a sheep in a fair' (ibid.). Teasing innuendo and sinuous sexual allusion ripple the discreet surface of the language. *The Well-Beloved*, as Hillis Miller and others have observed, is sprung on repetition, iteration, and recoil. Here iteration can be self-aggrandising, like the man at the dinner-party' 'a representative of Family, who talked positively and hollowly, as if shouting down a vista of five hundred years from the Feudal past' (Pt 2, Ch. 2). It can renew the quick of life, as with the three generations of Avice – each different and differently alive within the span of a single man's desire: his desire is self-reproducing, not producing new generations as do the women in the book. Pierston finds it hard to recognise difference: 'He could not help seeing in her all that he knew of another, and veiling in her all that did not harmonize with his sense of metempsychosis' (Pt 2, Ch. 6).

Pierston's is, therefore, if severely judged, a sterile desire which greets himself persistently in the likeness of another: a very type of Decadent sexuality. Yet it is also a principle of courage and renewal: of the freshness that lives deep down in things, the way the self stays young. What Pierston questions as a curse he also lives as a blessing: 'When was it to end – this curse of his heart not ageing while his frame moved naturally onward?' (Pt 2, Ch. 12).

And in this book, as opposed to *Tess* and *Jude*, Hardy at last acknowledges the free-loving woman as *not* a tragic figure: enfranchisement indeed. The laundress Avice proves to be, like Pierston, in pursuit of the constant elusive 'one' who manifests so fleetingly in many:

> 'I get tired of my lovers as soon as I get to know them well. What I see in one young man for a while soon leaves him and goes into another yonder, and I follow, and then what I admire fades out of him and springs up somewhere else; and so I follow on, and never fix to one. I have loved *fifteen* a'ready! Yes, fifteen, I am almost ashamed to say,' she repeated, laughing. 'I can't help it, sir, I assure you. Of course it is really, to *me*, the same one all through, only I can't catch him!' (Pt 2, Ch. 8)

Playfully, unportentously, here Hardy draws close to other writers such as George Egerton and Mona Caird who assert women's independent desires. Ruefully, Pierston recognises the implications for men like him of the 'new days' new women: 'To be the seeker was one thing: to be one of the corpses from which the ideal inhabitant had departed was another; and this was what he had become now, in the mockery of new days' (ibid.).

The third Avice, a girl of 'intensely modern sympathies', makes her own choice and leaves Pierston. *The Well-Beloved* (first written in serial form in 1892 and published as a revised whole in 1897) spans a period of gender exploration and limber playfulness among Decadent writers such as Wilde and Carpenter. The book's protagonist never enters the fray of reproduction. He explores ways of *being* without generation, while the women of the book conveniently bear each other. The anxiety about individuality and continuance here keeps within chosen bounds, generating likeness not transformation: a strange comic triumph over the world-ordering systems that dogged his thought.

As we read this work we can hear, chiming in, Walter Pater's perceptions, which in 1873 in the 'Conclusion' to *The Renaissance* so disturbed contemporaries like George Eliot. Like Hardy, Pater teased out new desires and hopes for English Decadence: – a different answer to death:

> a life of constant and eager observation. Every moment some form grows perfect in hand or face; some tone on the hills or the sea is choicer than the rest; some mood of passion or insight or intellectual excitement is irresistibly real and attractive to us, – for that moment only. Not the fruit of experience, but experience itself, is the end. A counted number of pulses only is given to us of a variegated, dramatic life. How may we see in them all that is to be seen in them by the finest senses? How shall we pass most swiftly from point to point, and be present always at the focus where the greatest number of vital forces unite in their purest energy?[8]

Notes

Quotations from Hardy's poems are taken from *The Complete Poems of Thomas Hardy*, ed. James Gibson (London: Macmillan, 1976).

1. George Egerton, *Discords* (London: John Lane, 1894). 'Virgin Soil' reprinted in *Victorian Short Stories: An Anthology*, selected and introduced by Harold Orel (London: Dent, 1987) pp. 163–74.
2. *Harper's New Monthly Magazine*, vol. 87, November 1893, pp. 858–9.
3. Ibid., p. 859.
4. For detailed discussion of these movements elsewhere in my work see

Darwin's Plots (London: Routledge, 1983) and essays on 'The Death of the Sun', 'Wave Theory and the Rise of Modernism' and 'Leaps of the Prepared Imagination: Helmholtz, Tyndall, Hopkins' now collected in *Open Fields: Science in Cultural Encounter* (Oxford: Oxford University Press, 1996).

5.	*The Life and Work of Thomas Hardy, by Thomas Hardy*, ed. Michael Millgate (London: Macmillan, 1984) p. 406.

6.	*The Collected Letters of Thomas Hardy*, ed. Richard Little Purdy and Michael Millgate (Oxford: Clarendon Press, 1978–88) vol. I, p. 235. Letter dated by the editors 'May 1891?'

7.	Quotations from *The Well-Beloved* are taken from the New Wessex Edition (London: Macmillan, 1975–6). Chapter references given in parenthesis in text.

8.	Walter Pater, *Studies in the History of the Renaissance* (1873), later re-titled *The Renaissance: Studies in Art and Poetry* (London: Macmillan, 1910) p. 236.

7

Hardy, George Moore and the 'Doll' of English Fiction

SIMON CURTIS

In 1880, the year before Hardy began to plan his discreetly daring *Two on a Tower*, Maupassant published one of his first, and best-known, short stories, 'Boule de Suif'. Boule de Suif, a patriotic Rouen prostitute, is its heroine, and the tale tells how, when northern France has been overrun and occupied by the Prussians in 1870, she is compelled to sleep with a Prussian officer in order that her travelling companions (a Count, a Councillor, a rich merchant and two nuns: respectable, self-serving and unpatriotic) can continue their flight from danger. It is a cynical story – its satire, though, implicit with humanity – whose main action concerns a prostitute plying her trade, in this case against her will; sex in a hotel bedroom.

Maupassant was a realist, and 'Boule de Suif' first appeared in an anthology of Franco-Prussian war stories by young disciples of the leading realist (or naturalist) of the day, Emile Zola. This 1880 anthology, *Les Soirées de Médan*, was a kind of group manifesto, and marked the neap tide of French realism, whose controlling moon was Zola. Born, like Hardy, in 1840, he had published the first eight of his twenty Rougon-Macquart novels, and was in successful mid-career.

The Pléiade edition of Maupassant's *Contes* reminds us that the subject – the prostitute – was not new.[1] In the 1870s there had been something of a fashion for low-life and prostitute themes in French fiction, the most notorious example being Zola's own story of the courtesan *Nana* (1880). Zola tended to be emphatically frank about sex. But even in 1865, the Goncourts' novel about a servant, *Germinie Lacerteux*, shows how the protagonist, Germinie, in poverty and misfortune, is forced to solicit on the street. The book explores her make-up and sexual psychology interestingly, and not without compassion.

103

Behind her and Zola, of course, lives Flaubert's memorable realist depiction of the life of the provincial adulteress Emma Bovary (1857). Flaubert was a friend and mentor of Maupassant. Behind it, perhaps, we may point to the younger Dumas' *La Dame aux Camélias* (1848), the 'tart with a heart of gold' (source of Verdi's *La Traviata*), and Murger's *Scènes de la vie de bohème* (1847–9) (source of Puccini's *La Bohème*), where starving artists have lovers in their left bank garrets. And behind them live the fictional worlds of Balzac and Stendhal in the 1830s.

Unlike the Victorian novel, sensitive to the expectations of the British matron and her maiden daughter, its distribution largely controlled by the circulating library system (Mudie and Smith), matters such as the direct, realistic analysis of love and marriage, and so sex – and, many would argue, the aspirations of women seen as authentic individuals – were more liberally ordered in France. Balzac's Lucien de Rubempré takes actress Coralie as his mistress in *Illusions perdues* (1837–9); or, preeminent for love psychology and Mozartian sexual intrigue, there is Stendhal's *Le rouge et le noir* (1830). Its heroine, Madame de Rênal, seduced though she is by Julien Sorel, is moreover an 'âme généreuse'; Stendhal is on her side.

Balzac was inspired by Sir Walter Scott, grandfather of the great nineteenth-century narrative novel. But in the general preface to his *Comédie humaine* (1842), he criticises Scott's heroines; they are, to use George Moore's word, 'dolls', their flesh and blood reality undermined by what Balzac saw as Scott's idealising, Protestant conventionality:

> Walter Scott, obliged as he was to conform to the ideas of an essentially hypocritical nation, was false to humanity in his picture of woman, because his models were schismatics. The Protestant woman . . . may be chaste, pure, virtuous; but her unexpansive love will always be as calm and methodical as the fulfilment of a duty. . . . In Protestantism there is no possible future for the woman who has sinned . . . there is but one Woman, while the Catholic writer finds a new woman in each new situation. If Walter Scott had been a Catholic, if he had set himself the task of describing truly the various phases of society which have successively existed in Scotland . . . [he] might have admitted passion with its sins and punishments, and the virtues revealed by repentence. Passion is the sum-total of humanity. Without passion, religion, romance, art, would all be useless.[2]

Balzac helpfully introduces my not unfamiliar theme: how, in the 1880s, Moore and Hardy, for all they were enemies, tried to guide the English novel in a 'French' direction – each of them refers to France – of realism and enlightenment.

For all (let us not forget) that nineteenth-century English fiction produced Elizabeth Bennet, Anne Elliot, Catherine Earnshaw, Becky Sharp, Maggie Tulliver, Dorothea Brooke, Estella, Mrs Proudie and, indeed, Scott's Flora MacIvor, there was a 'doll' problem. This list raises the important question: what do we *mean* by 'doll'?[3] Moore and Hardy at any rate were clear there was a problem to address; put simply, it was the conventional idealising and artistically constricting required stereotype, the 'angel in the house'.

What they opposed is sadly symbolised in the story of one adventurous publisher who in 1889 got sentenced to three months in Holloway prison for being a pornographer (that is, publishing 'obscene libels'). He was prosecuted by the Attorney General for having brought out English translations of seventeen Zola novels in 1884–8.[4]

The publisher was Henry Vizetelly who, author, engraver, wine-connoisseur and journalist in London and then Paris, retired and started Vizetelly & Co. in 1880 at the age of 60. His remarkable firm not only brought out Zola; but also *Madame Bovary*, *Germinie Lacerteux* and some Maupassant; as well as Tolstoy, Dostoevsky and Gogol for the first time in England; as well as texts of Elizabethan and Restoration dramatists (the original 'Mermaid' series, edited by the liberal sexologist Havelock Ellis), with 'UNEXPURGATED' on the covers. One sees, then, how Victorian Grundyism was under pressure in the 1880s. In reaction, the Grundyists saw to it that Vizetelly was sent down, and bankrupted. Among the liberals who signed a letter of protest about this dispiriting miscarriage of justice were both Moore and Hardy. The poet laureate, Tennyson, alas, took the opposite line:

> Set the maiden fancies wallowing in the troughs of Zolaism;
> Forward, forward, ay and backward, downward too into
>   the abysm.[5]

George Moore aided and abetted Vizetelly in his decision to publish Zola in England. His first novel, *A Modern Lover* (1883), had been published by Tinsley who, incidentally, published *Desperate Remedies, Under the Greenwood Tree* and *A Pair of Blue Eyes*, and about whom both Moore and Hardy write amusingly. In *A Modern Lover*, a painter achieves success at the expense of three women he exploits. Early on, too, a girl poses nude for the painter. Little surprise, therefore, that Mudie's monopolistic circulating library more or less vetoed the book's chances of selling by only ordering 50 copies.

Moore, freshly back from ten years in Paris, intended it to be a realistic innovation *à la Zola* (I'm afraid it isn't; Gissing called its milk and water high society melodrama 'unspeakable trash'!). But Moore's combative Irish spirit and French experience meant he wasn't going to take Mudie's disapprobation lying down. He would damn well fight the libraries. His next, ten times better novel, *A Mummer's Wife* (1885), is about a woman married to an asthmatic shopkeeper in the Potteries, who elopes with the manager of a touring theatrical troupe, later turning to drink and dying.[6] It appeared in a new one- (not three-) volume format, and sold at six shillings direct to the public, outflanking the libraries. Thus began Vizetelly's series of 'one-volume' novels, using the selling-point 'realistic' and including Dostoevsky and Maupassant. This bold market initiative helped to undermine the power of Mudie.

Moore also brought out with Vizetelly a witty and effective campaigning pamphlet, 'Literature at Nurse, or Circulating Morals' (1885), in favour of artistic (and sexual) freedom of expression in novels, which was in fact well received in the press. He amplified this in his 1886 preface to Zola's *Piping Hot (Pot-bouille)* and elsewhere.[7] His campaign foreshadows Hardy's own attack on Victorian novel conventions in his 1890 'Candour in English Fiction'.

No matinée idol, with his yellow hair, chinless face and sloping shoulders, the unprepossessing bachelor Moore was nonetheless an irrepressible figure on the literary scene – in a catalogue of literary scenes between 1870 and 1933; he seemed to have a finger in every new artistic pie cooking. By turns funny, perverse, enthusiastic, infuriating, liberal and tendentious, perhaps in the end he cuts a slightly sad figure.

He came from Anglo-Irish Protestant ascendancy stock – Moore Hall in County Mayo – and forsook the family acres at the age of 20 in 1870 to go and be a bohemian in Paris; in short, an absentee landlord. W. B. Yeats wrote:

[Moore] had gone to Paris straight from his father's racing stables
. . . acquired copious inaccurate French, sat among art students . . .
in some café; a man carved out of a turnip, looking out of astonished eyes . . . he read nothing, and was never to attain the discip-
line of style. . . . I doubt if he had read a play of Shakespeare's
even at the end of his life . . . he chose for master Zola as another
might have chosen Karl Marx . . .[8]

Moore himself had described Yeats in Coole Park thus:

[he] was standing lost in meditation before a white congregation
of swans assembled on the lake, looking himself in his old cloak
like a huge umbrella left behind by some picnic-party . . .[9]

He relished the cut and thrust of literary malice and is one of
English literature's most uninhibited gossips. He made a career out
of it. To an era unusually rich in anecdote and colourful personality
– Whistler, Wilde, Beardsley, Shaw, Yeats, Beerbohm – Moore, who
knew most of them, contributed his fair share, dishing it out as well
as taking it. In his 'Lovers at Orelay', in *Memoirs of my Dead Life*
(1906), an account of a weekend in provincial France with a beautiful
lady, he discovers he has left his pyjama suit behind in Paris; story
or tall story, it is readable and comic, and told at his own expense.

The poet Brendan Kennelly writes all the same that Moore 'frequently betrayed his friends through caricature, behaving like some
eloquent Iscariot of the Irish literary scene'.[10] If Moore went for
Hardy, he also went for James, Conrad and Stevenson. Indeed, the
disciple of Zola soon reneged on realism and turned on his erstwhile
French master. There is a disconcerting pattern of enthusiasm and
defection at work in Moore's capricious literary development.

He began as a teenage would-be Shelleyan poet; changed to Paris-
ian art student; became a Baudelairian decadent poet; converted to
Zola and realism, with three novels; then converted to Walter Pater
and aesthetic fiction; next, back to Dublin to take part in the Irish
literary revival at the *fin de siècle*, in uneasy concert with Yeats; a
mythological folk play was next, followed by the Turgenev-inspired
(and fine) stories of *The Untilled Field*, anticipating Joyce's *Dubliners*.
Moore then turned his back on the Irish cause with the rumbus-
tious gossip of *Hail and Farewell*, settling finally in Ebury Street in
London, seeking the 'melodic line' in prose fiction or even 'reverie'
with Biblical and classical themes. He is, in sum, an unnervingly
changeful character to pin down. Postmodernists would have the

whale of a time with him, no doubt, though I hope they may leave him alone.[11]

It was in the mid-1880s – the Zola phase – that Moore, then, attacked the 'doll' of Victorian fiction with Henry Vizetelly. Though Wilkie Collins, Gissing and Charles Reade,[12] among others, criticised the three-volume novel and library system (also deplored by Carlyle and Arnold), Moore has an honorable place as the most outspoken and consistent antagonist of the novel-publishing business. In the preface to *Piping Hot* he says 'It may be a sad fact . . . that literature and young girls are irreconcilable elements, but the sooner we leave off trying to reconcile them the better'.[13] In 'Literature at Nurse', one tactic Moore tellingly employs is to quote three breathily sentimental love episodes from second-rate three-volume novels:

> . . . is the doll showing a little too much bosom, Mr Mudie? . . . The British matron has the public by the ear. . . . I hate you, Mudie . . . because you are the great purveyor of the worthless, the false and the commonplace . . . [you are] a fetter about the ankles of those who would press forward towards the light of truth . . . a religious and sensual passion is as necessary to the realistic novelist as a disease to the physician.[14]

He asks what Pope, Johnson, Fielding and Smollett would say to the present literature of 'bandboxes'?

Five years later, Hardy wrote 'Candour in English Fiction', part of a symposium in the *New Review*. By 1890 he had lost patience with the bowdlerising restraints insisted on by editors and publishers, from Leslie Stephen with *Far from the Madding Crowd* ('I am rather necessarily anxious to be on the safe side . . .') to editor Parson Mcleod with *The Trumpet-Major*, who wanted stories free from anything which a 'healthy *Parson* like myself would not care to read to his bairns at the fireside', and interference in the stories of *A Group of Noble Dames*, as Simon Gatrell has shown.[15] The message of 'Candour in English Fiction' would of course be reverberatingly echoed in the texts of *Tess* and *Jude*; Hardy wished to be able to be candid and sincere in writing about sex.

He approvingly mentions the 'meritorious' (if to him 'crude') attempts by French realists in the direction of 'sincerity'; but his main appeal is to the Greek and Elizabethan dramatists because 'Candour in English Fiction', besides arguing for freedom of speech about sex, is, more constructively than Moore, chiefly concerned about novels which encompass tragedy. The Greeks, writes Hardy, 'reflected life, revealed life, criticised life':

> Life being a physiological fact, its honest portrayal must be largely concerned with, for one thing, the relations of the sexes, and the substitution for such catastrophes as favour the false colouring best expressed by the regulation finish that 'they married and were happy ever after', of catastrophes based upon sexual relations as it is. To this expansion, English Society opposes a well-nigh insuperable bar . . . the magazine in particular and the circulating library in general do not foster the growth of the novel which reflects and reveals life. They directly tend to exterminate it . . . [there is practically a] censorship of prudery. . . . The crash of broken commandments is as necessary an accompaniment to the catastrophe of a tragedy as the noise of drum and cymbals to a triumphal march. But the crash of broken commandments shall not be heard; or, if at all, but gently, like the roaring of Bottom – gently as any sucking dove . . . lest we should fright the ladies out of their wits.[16]

Despite differences of emphasis, 'Candour in English Fiction' shares common ground with Moore's 'Literature at Nurse'.

Two general points are worth adding. First, the defenders of the doll had teeth, so Hardy and Moore were bold. Vizetelly, a 70-year-old man, *was* imprisoned, and ruined. The Bishop of Wakefield, the hymnodist and natural history writer, W. W. How, did burn *Jude*, a novel bitterly and upsettingly attacked. The year before, in another but related sphere of action, Oscar Wilde was sentenced to the maximum, punitive term, two years hard labour, for homosexuality. In the next century, too, Joyce was to undergo the maddening experience of the publishing farrago of his years-long wait to see *Dubliners* appear, because it offended doll susceptibilities.

Secondly, it has to be said that, for all their liberal boldness, Moore and Hardy were in the 1880s swimming with a wider current of literary 'emancipation'. Zola is the joint principal figure, supported by fellow realists, and inheriting the rich tradition of psychological analysis of French literature. He shares the laurel with Ibsen, whose famous middle-period plays, like *A Doll's House* and *The Wild Duck*, were performed originally in the 1880s all over Europe and, in spite of scandal and controversy (*A Doll's House* had first to be given a happy ending in London!), he was securely established as a leading playwright by the 1890s. This can be traced in an appendix to Una Ellis-Fermor's *The Irish Dramatic Movement*.[17]

And yet, these apparently like-minded, quasi-feminist, liberal authors, Moore and Hardy, were personal foes. Let us turn to Moore's characteristic public attacks on Hardy, and Hardy's characteristically reticent response.

When Thomas Hardy OM, the most famous author in the kingdom, was dying, the last verses he penned were epigrams attacking G. K. Chesterton and Moore, each of them notably articulate critics. The 'Epitaph for George Moore' goes:

> *On one who thought no other could write such English as himself*

> 'No mortal man beneath the sky
> Can write such English as can I
> They say it holds no thought my own
> What then, such beauty (perfection) is not known'.

> Heap dustbins on him:
> They'll not meet
> The apex of his self conceit.

This must confirm Hardy's sensitivity to criticism. At the end it was this, perhaps, and not the church bells' outrollings he noticed; was hurt uppermost or innermost? The epigram is, however, untypical. Hardy did not deal in personal satire, of which there is a lively and abundant tradition in our literature – from Nashe to Dryden, Pope, Byron and Burns, or Dunbar with his flytings. Hardy's satires are about life, circumstance, Crass Casualty or the ironic workings of the Immanent Will, not at the expense of literary rivals. There is little personal animus, set in lapidary form, in his work; one could well argue that this is an attractive feature of his personality. As Samuel Hynes wrote in his review of Martin Seymour-Smith's biography of Hardy in *The Times Literary Supplement*, in spite of novels which shocked some readers, Hardy's voice was 'that of the respectable Victorian Man of Letters, a role [he] sought and valued'.[18]

Moore, on the opposite hand, revelled in personal satire, mockery, debunking, comedy, provocation and gossip, and he can be very funny, although I don't think he is enormously funny when he is having his go at Hardy.

There is a first attack on Hardy (after one on James) in his 1888 *Confessions of a Young Man*, the unlikely story of his decadent days in Paris, full of not-entirely-assimilated current French aesthetic commonplaces. He scores a cheap point, more jibe than point, thus:

> . . . I read Mr Hardy despite his name. It prejudiced me against him from the start; a name so trivial as Thomas Hardy cannot, I said, foreshadow a great talent; and 'Far from the Madding Crowd' discovered the fact to me that Mr Hardy was but one of George Eliot's miscarriages.[19]

The novel's development is hare-hearted, too. Moore is affecting cosmopolitan *de haut en bas*. Thirty-six years later, he returns to a more sustained attack in his 1924 *Conversations in Ebury Street*.

In the form of an impressionistic dialogue, and proceeding, typically, more by assertion than reason, Moore first dismisses Hardy's 'tin pot' pessimism, comparing it unfavourably with the pessimism of Ecclesiastes (a work one suspects Hardy knew better than he). Then he castigates Hardy's 'bad prose' by quoting the gurgoyle description in *Far from the Madding Crowd*. He goes on to deplore the melodrama in *Tess* in the seduction, confession and sleep-walking scenes; then, in the unpleasantest passage, which justifies Edward Blishen's adjective 'boorish', he affirms that as soon as Hardy dies he will be forgotten because his popularity depends on mass approval (the 'quackers') but not on the judgement of the discerning. Here one feels that Moore is motivated less by aesthetic principle than by good old-fashioned jealousy. Next, 'Barbara of the House of Grebe' and the descriptions of Egdon in *The Return of the Native* are criticised as unrealistic. It is the business of the Man of Letters, claims Moore, to inquire why the public should have selected for their special adoration Hardy's 'ill-constructed melodramas, feebly written in bad grammar, and why this mistake should have happened in the country of Shakespeare'.[20]

If there is gusto in this assault, there is transparent partiality too. As Moore, I think, never really resolves the tug within his mind

between aestheticism and realism, he criticises Hardy from shakily-
founded aesthetico-realistic ground. It does not, however, surprise
that the attack got home to the sensitive resident of Max Gate.

Middleton Murry came to Hardy's defence in an article in the
Adelphi, and in a letter Hardy thanked him: 'Somebody once called
Moore a putrid literary hermaphrodite, which I thought funny . . .'[21]
(Is there an echo, here, of the 'maphrotight' Christian Cantle?) Then,
we find in Hardy's *Personal Notebooks*:

> The Times in its notices of the monthly reviews agrees with Mr
> Middleton Murry in "The Adelphi" in the latter's smashing criti-
> cism of that ludicrous blackguard George Moore's book called
> "Conversations in Ebury Street," in which I believe I am libelled
> wholesale, though I have not seen the book.[22]

Together with the death-bed epigram, these two angry private
comments about his Anglo-Irish critic are probably the most personally bitter Hardy ever allowed himself to make. He was sorely
provoked.

It is a sad business, not only because Moore in his way was
an ally of Hardy's in his campaign against constricting fictional
conventions in the 1880s, but also because Moore's finest novel,
Esther Waters (1894), has points of interesting affinity with *Tess*.
Esther marked a short-lived, even opportunistic return to Moore's
realistic Zola manner. Each novel treats of working-class, religiously-
inclined heroines, victims each of a seduction, with their subsequent
careers, tragic in Tess's case, in Esther's, ending with a hard-won,
limited, prosaic success: she brings up her son. Malcolm Brown
discusses the affinities in his good critical biography of Moore,[23]
while Peter Casagrande, in *Hardy's Influence on the Modern Novel*,
goes further. The burden of his argument (about the nature of 'influence') is that for all Moore's criticism of Hardy's manner in *Tess*,
Moore secretly admired the book, and set out to emulate it by a
kind of redrafting; '[it] is in one sense a parody of the highest order'.[24]
I am not sure about 'parody'. *Esther* is rather emulation, rivalry, com-
petitiveness, maybe a deliberate critique of *Tess* from the realist
position; a seduced working-class woman would have behaved in
such a way, and not in such another way – in Esther's way, not
Tess's – my way, not yours. To give Moore some due, there is even
an element of the conception of *Tess* seeming too cruel, too wilfully
determined, in a humane view – like Dr Johnson finding *King Lear*
and the putting out of Gloucester's eyes too cruel to bear. *Esther* is

a fine, unmelodramatic, realistic and impersonal book; surprisingly so, considering Moore the personal gossip. It of course lacks the dimension of *Tess*'s poetry, because *Tess* is, or aims at, tragedy. We recall how Hardy was preoccupied with tragedy in the novel in 'Candour in English Fiction'. Moore is (here), in contrast, a humanitarian realist. Peter Casagrande is good on this in his discussion, making the point, for example, about how two contrasting methods, sensibilities, conceptions and genres are at work in the respective seduction scenes. While a guardian angel is rhetorically addressed in *Tess*, in *Esther* the episode is naturalistically told and subdued. In *Tess* and *Esther*, in fact, the tragic and realistic 'modes' confront one another in a fascinating way.

Notes

1. Maupassant, *Contes et Nouvelles*, I (Paris: Bibliothèque de la Pléiade, 1974) p. 1361. The note concerns 'La Maison Tellier', a happier tale whose subject is a brothel.

2. Clara Bell's translation in the original Everyman *At the Sign of the Cat and Racket*, edited by Saintsbury (London: Dent, [no date]). In French, Balzac's *Avant-propos* to the *Comédie Humaine* goes: 'Obligé de se conformer aux idées d'un pays essentiellement hypocrite, Walter Scott a été faux, relativement à l'humanité, dans la peinture de la femme, parce que ses modèles étaient des schismatiques. La femme protestante ... peut être chaste, pure, vertueuse; mais son amour sans expansion sera toujours calme et rangé comme un devoir accompli. ... Dans le protestantisme, il n'y a plus de possible pour la femme après sa faute. ... Aussi n'existe-t-il qu'une seule femme pour l'écrivain protestant, tandis que l'écrivain catholique trouve une femme nouvelle, dans chaque nouvelle situation. Si Walter Scott eût été catholique, s'il se fût donné pour tâche la description vraie des différentes sociétés qui se sont succédé en Écosse, peut-être ... eût-il admis les passions avec leurs fautes et leurs châtiments, avec les vertus que le repentir leur indique. La passion est toute l'humanité. Sans elle, la religion, l'histoire, le roman, l'art seraient inutiles.'

3. Patricia Stubbs in *Women and Fiction: Feminism and the Novel 1880–1920* (London: Methuen, 1981) discusses the place of some of these famous heroines, a subject that could easily fill a whole book.

4. I discussed 'Vizetelly & Co' in the *Bulletin* of the Emile Zola Society, no. 4, Nov. 1992, pp. 7–14.

5. Tennyson, 'Locksley Hall Sixty Years After'.

6. The drink theme owes something to Zola's hugely successful *L'assommoir* (1877).

7. E.g. *Avowals* (1919).

8. W. B. Yeats, *Autobiographies* (London: Macmillan, 1955) pp. 404–5.

9. Moore, *Hail and Farewell* (1911), ed. Richard Cave (Washington, D.C.: Catholic University of America Press, 1976) p. 51.

10. Brendan Kennelly, 'George Moore's Lonely Voices', in *George Moore's Mind and Art*, ed. Graham Owens (Edinburgh: Oliver & Boyd, 1968) p. 165.

11. Moore also rewrote his novels, so there is virtually a 19th and 20th-century version of each – a headache for any potential editor. This does, however, testify to a kind of literary perfectionism, unless one calls it restlessness.

12. Guinevere Griest, in *Mudie's Circulating Library* (Bloomington: Indiana University Press, 1970), discusses the background fully. Charles Reade, novelist and dramatist, adapted Zola's *L'assommoir* for the London stage as *Drink* in 1879.

13. Moore, Preface to *Piping Hot* (London: Vizetelly, 1886).

14. Moore, 'Literature at Nurse' (London: Vizetelly, 1885).

15. Simon Gatrell, *Hardy the Creator* (Oxford: Clarendon Press, 1988) *passim*.

16. Hardy, 'Candour in English Fiction', in *Thomas Hardy's Personal Writings*, ed. Harold Orel (Lawrence: University of Kansas Press, 1966; London: Macmillan, 1967) pp. 125–33.

17. Una Ellis-Fermor, *The Irish Dramatic Movement* (London: Methuen, 1939) Appendix 3.

18. Samuel Hynes, 'The blocked keyhole', *Times Literary Supplement*, 18 March 1994. Review of Martin Seymour-Smith, *Hardy* (London: Bloomsbury, 1994).

19. Moore, *Confessions of a Young Man* (1888) (Travellers' Library. London: Heinemann, 1928) p. 162.

20. Moore, *Conversations in Ebury Street* (1924) (Ebury edition. London: Heinemann, 1936) p. 98.

21. *The Collected Letters of Thomas Hardy*, ed. Richard Little Purdy and Michael Millgate, vol. 6 (Oxford: Clarendon Press, 1987) p. 242. This letter of March 28th 1924 is followed by one of April 9th to Murry where the *Notebooks'* phrase 'ludicrous blackguard' (see below) is repeated. Hardy complains that Moore's 'disciples' (i.e. his friends like Gosse?) don't protest; they remind him of 'performing dogs in a show'. Murry's article, 'Wrap me up in my Aubusson carpet' appeared in the *New Adelphi*, April 1924, and also in New York. See also J. O. Bailey, *The Poetry of Thomas Hardy* (Chapel Hill: University of North Carolina Press, 1970) pp. 647–9; Peter J. Casagrande, *Hardy's Influence on the Modern Novel* (Basingstoke: Macmillan, 1987) pp. 2–3; and Michael Millgate, *Thomas Hardy* (Oxford: Oxford University Press, 1982) p. 553.

22. *The Personal Notebooks of Thomas Hardy*, ed. Richard Taylor (London: Macmillan, 1978) p. 78.

23. Malcolm Brown, *George Moore: a Reconsideration* (Seattle: University of Washington Press, 1955).

24. Casagrande, *Hardy's Influence*, p. 3.

8

'Wives All': Emma and Florence Hardy

MICHAEL MILLGATE

I have for some time been engaged in editing for the Oxford University Press a volume of Emma and Florence Hardy's letters. The work on the texts and annotations is now pretty much finished, and I am writing this paper, as it were, out of that experience, commenting here and there on editorial problems but for the most part talking about the letters themselves, occasionally quoting from them, and using the evidence they provide – or sometimes fail to provide – as the starting-point for forays into wider issues, mostly but not exclusively biographical.

One or two basic points perhaps need to be made right at the start. The first is that I must hope to be forgiven for referring to Emma and Florence in just that discourteous and arguably demeaning first-name fashion: consistently to supply their titles and surnames would, I fear, prove unbearably tedious and indeed confusing. Despite recent precedents, however, I continue to find it impossible to refer to their common – though fortunately not simultaneous – husband as Tom. More importantly, I think it needs to be frankly acknowledged that the volume I am editing would never even have been imagined, let alone undertaken, had it not been for the central thread and focus provided by the figure of Hardy himself. At the same time – and this is a matter to which I shall return – I have sought to represent Emma and Florence as fairly and fully as possible and allow their own distinctive voices to be heard. As Diana Johnson shrewdly pointed out in *The True History of the First Mrs Meredith and Other Lesser Lives*, 'a lesser life does not seem lesser to the person who leads one. His life is very real to him; he is not a minor figure in it.'[1]

Unfortunately, ideal representation of Emma and Florence has been severely inhibited by the nature and scope of the available material. One especially distorting factor has been the extraordinary

discrepancy between the number of Emma's letters that have survived and the number of Florence's. Diligent searches – including
hundreds of letters to libraries world-wide – have succeeded in turning up no more than 120 items written and signed by Emma, only
one of them to a relative and only two to her husband – postcards
at that. Of these I am including rather more than a third – bringing
the total up a little further by adding a few examples of her letters
to newspapers, in the belief that these give an ampler sense of her
most cherished views and opinions than can be obtained from any
of the private correspondence. Florence's letters, on the other hand,
have surfaced in large numbers, and I originally proposed to devote
the entire volume to them – or even to the single series, comprising
some 400 letters in all, to Sir Sydney Cockerell. The subsequent
inclusion of Emma's letters was chiefly determined by the assumption that there would probably never be enough of them to justify
a volume of their own.

The edition as published will necessarily be awkwardly dispro-
portioned, with much more of the space being devoted to Florence
than to Emma, but while Emma's 50 or so letters may seem to be
swamped by the 300 or so of Florence's, they in fact represent a far
higher proportion of those that actually survive. The real problem
so far as Emma is concerned lies in the apparent non-survival of
any letters written prior to 1890. I can only offer the obvious guesses
as to why this might be so: that she wrote few letters; that she wrote
mostly to people who were not in the habit of keeping letters; or
that her letters were not kept even by those who did keep letters,
either for reasons of content and tone that I'll touch upon later or
simply because the recipients were insufficiently impressed by her
status as the daughter of John Gifford or even as the wife of Thomas
Hardy. After all, only a small proportion of Hardy's own surviving
letters date from earlier than 1890, most of them essentially business
letters to his publishers.

The absence of Emma's early letters is truly regrettable, especially
given the scarcity of contemporaneous documentation of the long
courtship of Thomas Hardy and Emma Lavinia Gifford and the first
years of their marriage – given also the inexpressiveness of such
documents as do survive. Eager interrogators of Emma's honeymoon
diary, for example, tend to find themselves answered mostly with
silence, Emma sticking for the most part to food, buildings, furniture,
street-scenes, and the occasional cat. When the chambermaid bursts
into their room unannounced the bride and groom are caught in the

act – of writing. Although I don't doubt that even that naively recorded little episode could be speculatively aggrandised into a kind of fore-scene or dumb-show of the Hardys' entire marriage. More directly relevant is a luckily surviving letter *to* Emma which serves to document her self-conscious romanticism and literary self-dramatisation at the time of her engagement – what she herself once referred to as her 'very sentimental kind of mind'.[2] Writing probably in 1871, Margaret Hawes thanks Emma for 'her sweet photo: and letter full of romantic ideas', and adds: 'They say that a poetical mind keeps one young, & I am sure you do not look more than 18.'[3]

Emma, as is now well known, was in fact thirty-one in November 1871 – though admitting only to twenty-five (rather than thirty) in the April 1871 census – and when Hardy first arrived in St. Juliot in March of 1870 she was living as a dependant of her sister's elderly husband in an extraordinarily isolated location and doubtless despairing of the escape and security that marriage alone could in those days offer. But if Hardy represented for Emma a heaven-sent or even, as she liked to think, pre-destined suitor, she clearly had to adjust to his being some way from the romantic lover of her imagination. Writing again after Emma's engagement, Margaret Hawes refers to the 'fortunate' Mr Hardy and claims to share Emma's expressed aversion for 'handsome *men*' and preference for 'clever, well read ones'.[4]

A few more pre-1890 items are to be found among the little group of letters written to Emma that Florence's executor, Irene Cooper Willis, chose for preservation from among the much larger number she discovered after Florence's death in an ottoman sitting still untouched in Emma's attic retreat at Max Gate. A few business letters of Hardy's written out or copied in Emma's hand also survive from the 1870s and 1880s, together with at least one example of her adding a note to the end of one of Hardy's personal letters: it reads, sensationally, 'Dear Lady Margaret, Many happy returns of the day. Yours always Emma Hardy.'[5] Hardy and Emma presumably exchanged many letters during the four years of their courtship and engagement, but Emma apparently destroyed both sides of the correspondence during the unhappy later stages of the marriage. According to Florence, Emma burned them in the Max Gate garden behind the Druid Stone – where a kettle was sometimes boiled when they took tea outdoors on summer afternoons.

All that now remains of that correspondence – indeed, of Emma's

entire personal correspondence prior to 1890 – are the two fragments, one from 1870, the other from 1874, that Hardy copied down
at the time and then re-copied some fifty years later when searching back through his old notebooks prior to their destruction. 'This
dream of my life [begins the first of the fragments] – no, not dream,
for what is actually going on around me seems a dream rather.'
And from the same letter a second brief passage that reappears,
slightly revised, in chapter 19 of *A Pair of Blue Eyes*:[6] 'I take him (the
reserved man) as I do the Bible; find out what I can, compare one
text with another, & believe the rest in a lump of simple faith.'[7] If
Emma's 'reserved man' seems obviously, and perhaps a little
ominously, to have been Hardy himself, the later fragment, written
just two months before their marriage, strikes a note still more
poignant and premonitory: 'My work, unlike your work of writing,
does not occupy my true mind much. . . . Your novel seems sometimes like a child all your own & none of me.'[8] Little though they tell
us in themselves, these fragments do perhaps indicate that Emma's
literary ambitions and enthusiasms may genuinely have served to
enhance not just her own initial responsiveness to Hardy but his to
her. They don't, however, seem sufficient to endorse Hardy's claim
– made after the destruction of the correspondence – that it had
been comparable to the famous courtship correspondence of Robert
Browning and Elizabeth Barrett Barrett.

The *Collected Letters of Thomas Hardy* includes a fair number
addressed to Emma, the earliest dating from 1885, and while these
tend to deal in domestic details rather than elaborate declarations
of affection – the couple were rarely apart, after all, for more than
a few days at a time – they do provide some evidence that the
marriage, whatever its difficulties, was at least kept up, right to the
end, as a functioning daily domestic operation within which meals
were eaten, conversations engaged in, and guests entertained – if
sometimes in unintended ways. If, as is sometimes suggested, there
was a major rift in the marriage in the early 1890s, or some sort of
crisis or personality change experienced by Emma herself, then it is
all the more regrettable that the lack of earlier letters should have
ruled out the possibility of assessing differences in attitude and tone.
Even so, the available documents do extend over more than twenty
years, projecting a strong sense of Emma herself as she was in her
fifties, sixties, and early seventies, and illuminating, from her point
of view, the later stages of her marriage.

What further skews the record is the fact that by far the largest of

the surviving correspondences is with the American Hardy enthu-
siast Rebekah Owen, who made with her sister Catharine the first
of several 'pilgrimages' to Dorchester in the summers of 1892 and
1893 and later moved permanently to England, taking a large house
in the Lake District. Hardy, by no means as famous as he subsequently became, was at first amused and a little flattered by Miss
Owen's admiring interest in his work and in himself, but as time
passed he wearied of her relentless inquisitiveness and off-loaded
the correspondence and, in effect, the relationship onto the shoulders
first of Emma and later of Florence. With this correspondence, as
perhaps with all correspondences, it's important to keep in mind
the overall character of the relationship when reading and assessing
individual letters. Rebekah Owen is not in herself an important
figure – Richard Purdy used to say that Carl J. Weber had practically
invented her – but, because she wrote so many letters to Max Gate
and kept all the replies, she necessarily looms large in any discussion
of Emma and Florence's correspondence. Unfortunately, in writing
to Rebekah Owen Emma – like Florence after her – was addressing
someone whom she neither understood nor greatly liked and whose
persistent letters were at once a burden to be borne and an intrusion
to be resisted. But since the correspondence did not for the most
part aim at real communication, Emma tended to write with even
more than her usual inconsequentiality, filling her letters with
whatever came most readily to hand – typically household trivia or
references to what she was currently reading or worrying about.
Emma's rapid flitting from topic to topic does at times have a certain
birdlike charm – one is reminded of her own pet term for the Max
Gate sparrows, the 'hoppies' – but again and again her thought
sequences slide through a series of slalom-like shifts of direction
into what by the 1890s had already become a familiar groove of
domestic grievance. Here, for instance, is an extract from her letter
to Rebekah Owen of 19 February 1897:

A friend of ours has sent us some translations of the classics which
he has edited – I have always liked latin prose translations from
a girl. I shall be a subscriber to *Mudie* in the summer – strangely
enough we begin when we are in Town – & not here at all, we
have so many books & periodials [*sic*] to read here. You left behind
you two pages of the "Outlook." Shall I send them? I have just
finished Le Gallienne's "Golden Girl" – which he has *just* published almost the day he married. It is exquisitely poetical at the

beginning – crisply amusing in the middle, though somewhat licentious – & very pathetic at the end – which is quite unexpected. But the *plan* is a judicious blending of Sterne's Senti: journey – & T. H's Pursuit of the W. Beloved. Le Gallienne is quite a *beauty* himself with a kind of Shelly [*sic*] face – & he knows this. I wonder what his bride is like. Anent Mrs Shelley she was a little of the minx kind to fly into his arms as she did whilst Harriet was still out of the depths of water (if not of misery). It strikes me that I ought to have an Author's wives *day* occasionally I wonder if we should get mixed in our words & phrases like your Mrs Lister. One thing I abhor in Authors. It is their blank materialism – (neither do I like Corelli-ism) I get irritated at their pride of intellect – & as I get older I am more interested in ameliorations & schemes for banishing the thickening clouds of evil advancing. I do not care for art for art's sake alone. Yet a friend cannot persuade me to get T. H. to write to Zola to bring out a book on antivivisection. I will not because I know that he wouldn't do it – & I do not want T. H. to be hand in glove with *Zola!* Alas! that *you* are a Jude-*ite* I really ought not to countenance you though you are my New York correspondent. However I will add photographer to my shopping list next summer.[9]

Though Emma's letters to Rebekah Owen are the most persistently peppered – or salted perhaps, from Rebekah's standpoint – with negative comments about her husband, she was in the end no respecter of correspondents. Once latched or launched onto a topic she deeply cared about – religion, animals, Zionism, women's suffrage, the iniquities of her husband and of the male sex generally – she became too passionately engaged to retain any real sensitivity to individuals or to situations. She wrote vehemently to Hardy's friend Edward Clodd about the godlessness of his conventionally Darwinian views on evolution, and when Rebekah Owen converted to Roman Catholicism Emma fired off an outburst of angry remonstrance: 'Ah if you read the Bible with a prayer The Spirit of Truth will reveal it to you & Satan's guile will be gone.'[10] Desmond MacCarthy's mother, seeking Emma's advice as to her son's prospects as an author, was sternly told: 'I fear I am prejudiced against authors – living ones! – they too often wear out other's lives with their dyspeptic moanings if unsuccessful – and if they become eminent they throw their aider over their parapets to enemies below, & revenge themselves for any objections to this treatment by stabbings with their pen!'[11] When the copy of Lady Grove's *The Social Fetich* arrived at Max Gate Emma responded by pointing to what she saw as its grammatical infelicities – doubtless in the knowledge that Hardy had read and commented on the proofs – and then proceeded to offer her own prescriptions for correct English usage:

> After all words were made for man not vice-versa. *Lounge* for "Couch" would be correct for a *one*-end thing – *Sofa* – has two ends – nice old thing – a low-lying-lair! Why do people offer a sugar bowl with a question? – but if any – *like* has a friendly sound. People ought to be well slapped for saying oft*en*. "Chemise" is a pretty word, "Shift" is vulgar & is wanted for "make-shift". People do worry me with their use of prejudice instead of prepossession. About 100 words altogether alone constitute the vocabulary of many even talkers![12]

It's easy to imagine the amused head-shaking, and worse, with which such letters were received. Clodd brushed off Emma's complaints as 'a curious mixture of sentiment and ignorance'.[13] But it must have been different with the truly destructive letter Emma sent in response to an appeal for advice on marriage she had received from the new but by no means youthful bride of Kenneth Grahame, the author of *The Wind in the Willows*. I'll quote just one paragraph:

> Keeping separate a good deal is a wise plan in crises – and being both free – & *expecting little* neither gratitude, nor attentions, love, nor *justice*, nor *anything* you may set your heart on. Love interest – adoration, & all that kind of thing is usually a *failure – complete* – some one comes by & upsets your pail of milk in the end. If he belongs to the public in any way, years of devotion count for nothing. Influence can seldom be retained as years go by, & *hundreds* of wives go through a phase of disillusion, – it is really a pity to have any ideals in the first place.[14]

It's impossible to identify the precise sources of the bitterness Emma here displays, let alone assess the respective degrees of responsibility as between Hardy and herself. There can be little doubt, however, of Emma's profound disaffection – little question, either, of the embarrassment her husband must have been caused by such letters and by Emma's parallel proclivity for openly criticising him on social occasions. And while the particular letters here referred to were of course preserved by their recipients, it's perhaps not difficult to see why Emma's letters might not always have been welcomed, treasured, or preserved.

But Emma does have another voice – as Denys Kay-Robinson was one of the first to insist – a voice that makes itself heard in her public letters and published articles. In my own feline relationships, for example, I'm always mindful of her exhortation, in an article entitled 'The Egyptian Pet', to '[a]lways give a cat free ingress and egress and attend to his voice, remembering that he has no language but a cry'.[15] She wrote to the newspapers about the slaughter of skylarks for food, about the cruelty involved in training animals for performance, about house flies and their status as creatures too, not to be wilfully destroyed. She also wrote, more substantially, about the importance of everyone's becoming what she called a maker of happiness, and especially about women's rights and women's suffrage, of which she became and remained an active supporter – though not to the point of condoning the use of violence, the issue over which she resigned from the London Society for Women's Suffrage in 1912 (the correspondence survives). A long letter of 1908 to the editor of *The Nation* was effectively a claim for the equality of women that saw the achievement of the vote as a mere incident along the way of the future. The final paragraph reads:

> Women have been sacrificed for ages to men. The absurd idea kept up by them, and hitherto humbly accepted by women, that their manhood is a much higher state for a human being than a woman's womanhood, is allied with tyranny and a fearful calcu-lation as to the real capabilities of women, who are abased and crushed by their treatment, and obliged hitherto to cringe to the idea of the superiority of the male, whose praise has seldom been for a good woman except safely on a tombstone.[16]

One of Emma Hardy's most attractive qualities was always her capacity not just for passionate declamation but for passionate action in addressing the issues she really cared about: Hardy himself especially admired the courage with which she would intervene whenever she saw animals suffering mistreatment. In many of her concerns, moreover, she can be said to have had history on her side – if not yet, then in some future that we too can imagine and even hope for. (Though it may be some time before flies become a pro-tected species.) Even those troubling expressions of grievance against her husband need to be seen in relation to the romantic and 'poetic' Emma Lavinia Gifford who still strongly persisted within the public figure of Mrs Thomas Hardy. That letter to Louise MacCarthy also contained a pointed recommendation: 'To those who *marry* authors, & ask my advice, I say, "Do not help – him – so much as to extinguish your own life – but go on with former pursuits".' But Emma herself had *had* no former pursuits of a satisfying kind, and her failure (for whatever reasons) to acquire any new ones during the course of her marriage – motherhood, for instance, or genuine authorial collaboration – threw her increasingly back upon drawing, painting, the writing of verse and prose – in short, upon the still naive and, alas, distinctly limited resources of that very sentimental kind of mind.[17]

Emma Hardy died suddenly in November 1912; some fourteen and a half months later, on 10 February 1914, Florence Emily Dugdale became the second Mrs Hardy. Though the circumstances of Hardy's second marriage were in many respects quite different from those of his first, it's striking that both followed upon a prior acquaintance of several years and that the actual wedding ceremonies were so alike. Hardy had married Emma, not in romantic St Juliot but in a four-year-old church in Maida Vale and in the presence of only three people, Emma's uncle, who officiated, one of her brothers, and the daughter of Hardy's landlady. St Andrew's, Enfield, where Hardy married Florence, dates in part back to the twelfth century, but by 1914 the surrounding area was already densely urban, and the wedding itself was witnessed by only the officiating vicar, the bride's father and youngest sister, and Hardy's brother, Hardy presenting himself on this occasion with at least that degree of family support.

It might occur to a mean-spirited biographer that weddings of this character are significantly cheaper than the standard sort, and it may in any case seem all too typical of Hardy that in arranging the ceremony for 10 February he neatly avoided St Valentine's day. It seems only fair to note, however, that the 14th was a Saturday, when the desired degree of privacy would have been more difficult to obtain. Paramount in all the arrangements was Hardy's determination to avoid reporters and press photographers and the especially dreaded risk of a civic deputation at Dorchester station as he and his bride returned to Max Gate. One of the few surviving examples of Florence's family correspondence shows that those of her sisters who had been excluded from the wedding ceremony were also forbidden to send congratulatory telegrams – for security reasons, so to speak. Florence did, however, send a telegram of her own to one of them early the following morning. It read: 'Business completed all well Florence'.[18]

Emma Lavinia Gifford, aged thirty-three, had married a man only five months older than herself who was still in the early stages of a financially uncertain career; Florence Emily Dugdale, just turned thirty-five, was marrying a man of seventy-three who had become – whatever his fears to the contrary – both immensely famous and securely affluent. As with Emma, Florence's literary interests and enthusiasms were directly contributory to her marriage: it was she who seems first to have approached Hardy, as a hitherto unknown admirer. But whereas Emma had been virtually without occupation prior to her marriage, Florence had for many years been earning her own living. The daughter of a junior school headmaster, she was trained as a teacher and when that career proved both uncongenial and physically beyond her powers she became variously – and perhaps a little desperately – a companion, a typist, a journalist, and a much-employed but sadly underpaid author of children's stories. Her marriage was to provide all too ample occasion for the continuation of her previous secretarial pursuits – interestingly enough, she almost entirely abandoned the typewriter within a year or so of Hardy's death – and the maintenance of a modest level of journalistic activity became one of her few conscious challenges to her husband's displeasure.

Hardy, as Pamela Dalziel has admirably shown,[19] went to a good deal of trouble to foster the writing career of Miss Dugdale, but it is clear from Florence's letters to Lady Hoare and other women friends that he felt altogether differently about publishing wives. Florence, unlike Emma, seems wisely to have avoided verse, but she did appear, typically billed as 'the wife of our greatest novelist', as the author of such Sunday tabloid items as 'A Woman's Happiest Year', 'No Superfluous Women', and 'The Dress Bills of Wives';[20] her unabashedly patriotic contributions during the First World War included ' "Greater Love Hath No Man . . .": The Story of a Village Ne'er Do Well' and 'War's Awakening: How Duty's Call Came to a Bachelor Girl'.[21] Hardy's principal objection to her anonymously published reviews of novels in *The Sphere* was that they took up too much of her time, although he could also quite justifiably have objected, and perhaps did, both to the general worthlessness of the novels Clement Shorter sent her and to the general vapidity of Florence's criticisms. From Florence's point of view, of course, her persistence in such activities can be read, positively enough, as a declaration of partial independence, but Hardy's toleration of them, however grudging it may have been, also seems demanding of a certain respect.

I referred earlier to the sheer quantity of Florence Hardy's surviving letters, and there must indeed be as many of them in existence as there are of her husband's – even when one excepts the many letters that were typed by her and bear her signature but had actually been drafted by Hardy. Examples of Hardy's drafts can be found in the later volumes of *The Collected Letters of Thomas Hardy*; the letters Florence actually sent out usually begin with the tell-tale phrase, 'I write for my husband'. Such items have been excluded from the edition of Emma's and Florence's letters, chiefly for the sake of allowing Florence as much of her own voice as possible. Even so, the vast majority of Florence's known letters date from the period of her marriage – or, to be more specific, from 1914 to the end of 1928, when the turmoil in the immediate wake of Hardy's death was beginning to subside. People tended to keep Florence's letters, clearly, for the same reason as they cultivated her acquaintance and friendship during Hardy's lifetime – for the same reason, indeed, as I am editing a selection of those letters: because Hardy was by the end of the first decade of the twentieth century an immensely famous author and Florence was uniquely placed to speak and write of him with intimacy, because she was so often his direct or indirect spokesperson or interpreter, because she was perceived as the doorkeeper of Max Gate.

Once Hardy was dead and the principal obsequies, testamentary disbursements, and memorialising gestures had been concluded, many of Florence's friends and correspondents tended to drift away: even Sydney Cockerell, to whom Florence had written so regularly for so long, now found it easy to quarrel with her, as he had been careful not to do while Hardy was still alive. But if there are fewer documents available for the period between 1929 and Florence's death in 1937, those years were nonetheless marked by the writing of some of her most interesting and appealing letters, several of them to new friends and acquaintances a good deal younger than herself. And there may be more to come: Florence Hardy items that have recently become available include additional letters to Siegfried Sassoon and a previously unknown correspondence with Wilfred Partington, an active bookman of the period, with whom Florence dined and even went to the cinema on a number of occasions during the early 1930s.

The survival of Florence Hardy's letters in such numbers certainly does not reflect what she would herself have wished. Habits of caution and privacy learned from her husband, reinforced by her own chronically low self-esteem, naturally impelled her towards the destruction of documents rather than their retention. One of her regular New Year occupations was the systematic destruction of all the letters she had received during the twelve months just concluded, and while a few of the letters Hardy had written to her happily escaped this doom, in the last week of her life she specifically asked her sister Margaret Soundy to destroy the letter he had written to her immediately before their marriage – though the empty envelope exists still.[22] Florence's relatives were almost of one mind in destroying whatever personal papers of hers came into their possession, so that only a handful of family letters survive, none of them of early date. Indeed, I have found no letter of any kind earlier than her November 1906 application for a ticket to the British Museum Reading Room in order to do research for *The Dynasts*. Like Emma, therefore, by the time Florence makes her first appearance in the edition she has already come firmly within Hardy's orbit.

Unfortunately for Florence's posthumous reputation, the letters hidden away in Emma's ottoman included a little group written by Miss Dugdale to Mrs Hardy in 1910 and 1911, their survival providing a striking indication of the degree to which – despite all the talk of bonfires – Max Gate was left untouched during the years of Florence's widowhood. What her letters to Emma show is that Florence spent several weeks at Max Gate during the latter half of 1910 and devoted a good deal of time, both there and back home in Enfield, to typing up Emma's stories and religious writings – possibly for some kind of payment – and making efforts to get them published. Although occasionally voicing reservations about what she was being asked to read and type – she suggests, for instance, that the descriptions of clothes in Emma's ageing novella 'The Maid on the Shore', might need to be up-dated – she consistently represents herself as Emma's admiring assistant and ally. She praises 'The Maid on the Shore' itself for its 'vivid & picturesque descriptions of Cornish Scenery'; she urges Emma to write one of her 'delightful poems' about the death of Marky the cat; she says she is 'quite burning with anxiety' to know if one of Emma's religious pieces has been accepted; and she declares that Emma's 'great triumph' will be with 'The Inspirer', evidently a story about a wife who is in some sense responsible for her husband's literary achievements.

Awareness of subsequent events has of course served to throw a somewhat lurid light over everything Florence said and did during this sensitive period, but to suspect her of disingenuousness is easier than to convict her of it. Knowledge of Florence's later agnosticism, for example, might throw doubt on the fervour with which she seconds Emma's struggle against the encroachments of Roman Catholicism, but it's necessary to remember that she was currently conducting an Anglican Bible class in Enfield. We of course know nothing – *nothing* – of any physical relations there may have been between Hardy and Florence at this or any other time, but my own sense, for whatever it may be worth, is that she was attracted to Hardy, ordinarily enough, by a combination of hero-worship, literary aspiration, and yearning to be of use, plus of course a certain element of self-interest. Less than transparent though her dealings with Emma certainly were, I very much doubt whether they were complicated by sexual guilt or by any thought of one day replacing her as the mistress of Max Gate. Very relevant here are the famously indiscreet letters Florence wrote to Edward Clodd during roughly the same period. Given the chance, she would doubtless have destroyed them too, but the letters we despatch customarily remain beyond our control and Clodd's preservation of Florence's correspondence has in practice provided a valuable reality check on what she was more or less simultaneously saying to Emma.

Clodd was Hardy's closest male confidant at this period and one of the very few people who knew how things stood at Max Gate, but it's clear from his diary and from Florence's letters to him that they shared a common detachment, a kind of sympathetic scepticism, towards what she on one occasion called 'the Max Gate menage'. Florence's pre-marital characterisation of Hardy as a great writer but not a great man was one that Clodd adopted for himself, years later, when commenting on Hardy's death, and in November 1910, after telling Clodd of Emma's ever-increasing kindness towards herself, Florence exclaimed: 'I am *intensely* sorry for her, sorry indeed for both.' The letters to Clodd also reflect, however, Florence's gradual cooling towards an Emma who seemed to become steadily 'queerer' even as she was demanding more and more of her young friend's time and attention: in December 1910 Florence narrowly evaded an invitation to accompany Emma on an unseasonable seaside visit to Boulogne, in January 1911 she was interviewing cooks for her in London, and in July 1911 they went on holiday together to Worthing, reputed scene of the familiar snapshot of Florence standing on a beach in a bathing-suit while an overdressed Emma is propped up like a rag doll against a nearby groyne.[23]

One of the responsibilities Florence had to assume in the wake of Emma's death was keeping up the Max Gate correspondence with Rebekah Owen, and she promptly fell into much the same traps as her predecessor had done. Feeling little but suspicion for the woman to whom she was writing, Florence tended to verbalise whatever came most handily to mind, often rambling on until she reached and then transgressed the boundaries of discretion. It was in writing to Rebekah Owen that she revealed the depths of her instinctive dislike of Sydney Cockerell, only to change her mind completely in the next letter and beg that its predecessor be destroyed – as of course it wasn't. Because their length is so often greater than their intrinsic interest would seem to justify, I am including in the edition fewer of Florence's – as of Emma's – letters to Miss Owen than the size of the archive might seem to warrant.

The letters to Gertrude Bugler have presented quite a different kind of editorial problem, in that the importance of the relationship over a period of several years has demanded the occasional inclusion of letters not especially striking in themselves but necessary to the continuity of the story overall. As for Gertrude herself (again I must beg forgiveness for the familiarity), it's clear from the drafts or copies of her own letters that she sometimes kept that she had little real awareness of what was going on, either in fact or in Florence's imagination. Bewildered by Hardy's absorption in the production of the *Tess* play and in Gertrude herself, despairing at the contrast between Gertrude's youthful beauty and what she perhaps too harshly regarded as her own plainness and charmlessness, terrified not just of ridicule and embarrassment but of actually losing her husband and everything that gave meaning to her life, Florence struck out wildly, bringing personally to bear on Gertrude a battery of accusations, threats, sisterly pleadings, and invocations of Hardy's health and reputation that the younger woman was simply powerless to resist. Florence did subsequently feel remorse for her role in denying Gertrude the chance of appearing on the London professional stage, and when *Tess* was revived in the West End after Hardy's death she put herself out to ensure not only that Gertrude was given the heroine's part but that she was properly paid, suitably accommodated, and warned of the dangers of theatrical life. She even tried to guarantee some positive reviews: 'If there is anything I can do for you [she wrote on 11 July 1929] let me know. . . . Three of the leading critics have promised me to do their best for you – & as they are personal friends of many years I can depend upon them.'[24]

Florence appears in a far more consistently happy light in several of her other correspondences – notably, perhaps, that with Charlotte Mew, whose poems she admired and whose personal difficulties she deplored and respected and tried unobtrusively to relieve. She wrote sensibly and well to Siegfried Sassoon and E. M. Forster, although neither perhaps took her entirely seriously, hence entirely kindly: 'I know how you feel about E. M. Forster,' she wrote to Lady Ottoline Morrell in July 1930, 'I have had such-like experiences with so many of T. H.'s friends – so much kindness & sympathy at times, & then silence & long neglect. I often wonder whether selfishness is not at the back of most friendships. I see now why T. H. never poured himself out in friendship to many who flocked around him.'[25] Her many letters to the collector Howard Bliss are repeatedly and sometimes painfully reflective of uncertainties as to her duties as guardian of her husband's literary remains, and it was over just those same issues that her long and complex relationship with Sydney Cockerell finally collapsed into acrimony and eventual silence. Many of her earlier letters to Cockerell, however, display an attractive combination of liveliness and responsibility interspersed from time to time with complaints about Hardy's work-absorption, selective sociability, and occasional stubbornness and tightfistedness. Though such expressions of grievance are reminiscent of Emma's, and doubtless reflective of similar domestic difficulties, Florence's note is generally one of melancholy resignation rather than of strident dissent. I simply don't have space on this occasion to expatiate upon the remarkable scope of Florence's letters to Cockerell, amounting as they do to a running report on life at Max Gate between 1914 and 1928, but I should at least acknowledge that even in their necessarily selective representation they constitute at once the core and principal component of Florence Hardy's portion of the edition.

The record of the years following 1928 is poorer for the absence of letters to Sir James Barrie and T. E. Lawrence, the two men who meant most to her at that time. Letters *to* her from both Barrie and Lawrence certainly survive, and in some quantity, but her own letters to Barrie have apparently been destroyed and her letters to Lawrence seem now to be represented only by a very few typed transcripts of lost originals.[26] There are, however, substantial letters to new correspondents such as Wilfred Partington (mentioned earlier), Sir Arthur Pinero, the dramatist, who is at times almost lovingly addressed, and John Cowper Powys, the novelist – whom she urged not to delete a single line from the lengthening manuscript of *A Glastonbury Romance*. She was in touch with all the Dorset-dwelling Powyses, and in answer to a question of Llewelyn Powys's she once replied: 'Am I happy? No – not quite. I think my nature only allows me to be happy at rare intervals – for a short time – but *when* I am happy I *am* happy – filled to the brim, with an ecstacy that the generally cheerful person can never know.'[27] I'm obliged, as an editor, to observe that the effect of that pronouncement is slightly marred by Florence's misspelling of the word 'ecstasy' itself – as if she *didn't* in fact know quite what it was. Even so her declaration will come as a relief to those who might reasonably have concluded, on the basis of available evidence, that she was always the depressive, socially insecure personality brilliantly evoked in Sylvia Townsend Warner's *Diaries* as resembling 'a very sad subdued seal, looking out of her face and then diving under again'.[28]

A notable feature of Florence's last years was her responsible and energetic discharge of the duties she had accepted locally as a Justice of the Peace, as a member of the Dorchester Hospital Management Committee, and as chairman of the Mill Street Housing Society – aspects of her life to which Robert Gittings and Jo Manton were the first to draw proper attention. Since she scarcely ever makes reference to such activities in her personal correspondence, I have sought to give them minimal representation in the shape of one of her letters to *The Times* about housing problems in general and the progress of the Mill Street scheme in particular. Also included in the edition are a few of the helpfully informative letters she wrote near the end of her life to people whom she judged to be seriously interested in her husband's work. Most of them, as it happened, were Americans, and she wrote with special warmth to two young transatlantic visitors – Richard Purdy and Frederick B. Adams – whose scholarly interests had happily brought them to Max Gate at a time when house, garden, and Hardy's study all remained very much as they had been in Hardy's lifetime.

Max Gate, indeed, and the never-resolved question of its eventual fate, becomes a recurring theme of the letters written after Hardy's death. At that date the Scots pines Hardy had planted remained standing thick and dark around the house and its garden, and while Florence could still be moved by the summer beauty of the place she more often speaks as if in terror of its winter gloom and isolation – which of course meant, since the death of Hardy and of the dog Wessex, its aching loneliness. In October 1930 she wrote to John Cowper Powys: 'It is late at night – or what I call late – in this silent house – a clock ticking near me – in the room where we have so often sat together with T. H. & it is rather like a grave. Do you know his poem "The House of Silence", which begins "This is a quiet place"? It described Max Gate then, & even more aptly describes it now – when I am the phantom left alone.'[29] Tempted at times to move away altogether, she found that she could not in practice abandon a place so profoundly associated with Hardy and his work – indeed, with her own marriage and everything that had given purpose and value to her life. Nor was Hardy the only ghost that haunted appealingly there: 'Today is the 22nd anniversary of the death of E. L. H.,' she wrote to Howard Bliss on 27 November 1934, '& she has been in my mind all day – & I have been up in the sad little attic where she died – still full of her presence.'[30]

Although Florence seems never quite to have forgiven Emma for becoming so profoundly and so publicly the object of Hardy's retrospective devotion – especially in the 'Poems of 1912–13' – she does on several occasions allude to her predecessor in sympathetic terms. When, for example, Hardy proposed to destroy the numerous leaves of The Woodlanders manuscript that were written out in Emma's hand, Florence successfully protested that to do so would be unfair to the memory of the woman who had carefully copied out so many pages with no thought but to be helpful. As time passed, and especially during the many backward glances of her widowhood, Florence increasingly recognised how much there was in common, not so much between Emma and herself as between their experiences of marriage to Thomas Hardy – to a great writer whose primary loyalties necessarily lay elsewhere. Her own letters, so much more numerous than Emma's, are to a remarkable degree a record of a literary marriage, showing with particular fullness and poignancy both the rewards and the costs of finding oneself – to quote the heading of one of Florence's obituaries – the helpmate of genius.

Both Emma and Florence made deliberate choices to marry Hardy – Florence with what ought to have been the more widely opened eyes – and they must both have felt, and with good reason, that they had fulfilled their part of the implicit creative bargain as well as of the explicit marital compact. A great deal is known about Florence's secretarial and other labours, and although it appears from Emma's letters that by the 1890s Hardy had effectively excluded her from his study and from any active participation in work in progress, she had certainly made earnest attempts in the earlier phases of their marriage to assist her husband in his professional pursuits — chiefly by writing out some of his business letters, recopying heavily corrected pages of manuscript, and keeping notes of the characters and place-names used in the various novels and stories.

It was Emma, indeed, who most memorably articulated the need of both women for some form of independent expression, registering even in that early fragment her unease at Hardy's book being so exclusively his own and protesting more directly to Rebekah Owen in February 1899: 'T. H. has always so much to say by voice, & pen, that letter-writing is my only resource for having all the say to myself, & not hearing his eloquence dumbly.'[31] Emma's and Florence's literary efforts inevitably seem trivial, sometimes embarrassingly so, when set alongside their husband's, and yet it is easy to see, especially since each had first related to him on a quasi-literary basis, why they found it necessary to resist hearing his eloquence dumbly, why they sought voices of their own. Florence's journalism seems in this respect a kind of distant echo of Emma's letters to the newspapers, her acceptance of public duties a form of fulfilment of Emma's involvement in the suffrage cause.

I have tried, within the limits of the space and documents available, to give as much substance as possible to the edition's value as a portrait of Florence's marriage and, to a lesser extent, of Emma's. My working title has always been *Voices from Max Gate*, and while that may sound a little too funereal, in its obvious allusion to 'Voices from Things Growing in a Churchyard', it does seem to put the emphasis in the right place. But if Emma's and Florence's voices serve to counterbalance Hardy's, that doesn't in itself establish any inherently truthful equilibrium: politicians equally attacked from both sides of an issue like to take this as proof of their essential correctness when it may in fact be evidence only of comprehensive error. Phyllis Rose's study of five Victorian marriages is entitled *Parallel Lives*, in endorsement of the proposition that every marriage is in truth two marriages, one for each spouse, hence demanding of two separate narratives, and it's important to keep in mind that while Emma and Florence both wrote and spoke quite freely about their marriages, Hardy himself kept silent, except in private conversations with Clodd and perhaps with one or two other close friends. Some of his novels, poems, and public statements did of course reflect – to Emma's anger and distress – his scepticism about marriage as an institution, but there exists almost no direct evidence of what he felt about his personal experiences of the married state.

There may in any case be little point in blaming Hardy overmuch for his dominance over both his wives, for the selfishness of which Emma accused him, for his exploitation of Florence's secretarial skills, or for those long hours of inviolable isolation in his study that so often left Florence, as she once said, with only the dog Wessex for company and conversation. Given – as it surely must be given – that Hardy was a great artist, marvellously creative even into extreme old age, then his errors and faults and marital offences seem to rank well down by comparison with those of other admired artists whose sometimes outrageous misbehaviour is customarily viewed as essential to their lives as artists and even as a kind of guarantee of genius. Part of the difficulty, perhaps, is that Hardy's crimes were never sufficiently of passion, his very emotions, even when generated by the women who became his wives, seeming not to feed back into those relationships but rather into his work, and especially into his later poetry. It's also, perhaps, that so much has been heard – generally from prejudiced sources and in response to highly directive questioning – about those trivial meannesses and obstinacies of Hardy's old age that are arguably more characteristic of old age in general than of Hardy in particular.

One can't really ask that biography be non-judgemental – it would surely be a pallid affair if it were – and since biography can never know or understand all, it's never quite in a position to pardon all. But neither, surely, should it deliberately take sides, identify villains, scapegoats, and objects of mockery, or deny to anyone their meed of imaginative sympathy. Although the 'wives all' of my title was intended ironically and even a little humorously, it of course comes from the scene in The Woodlanders in which Fitzpiers's mistresses, the upmarket Felice Charmond and the downmarket Suke Damson, come rushing to his house upon news of his accident and are taken into his empty bedroom by his already disenchanted spouse: 'Wives all,' says Grace derisively, 'let's enter together.'[32] Wonderfully, however, Grace is moved – to tears and, indeed, to graciousness – by a sudden tenderness towards her rivals, recognising them as victims equally with herself of the same underlying situation. It is an episode important to take into account when judging Grace within the novel: she is not, I suspect, among the best loved of Hardy's heroines. It is also an episode whose implicit message might appropriately be applied to the much-moralised subject of Hardy's own marriages.

Notes

This paper draws on the introduction to *The Letters of Emma and Florence Hardy*, ed. Michael Millgate (Oxford: Clarendon Press, 1996).

1. Diana Johnson, *The True History of the First Mrs Meredith and Other Lesser Lives* (New York: Knopf, 1972) p. xiii.
2. Emma Hardy, *Some Recollections*, ed. Evelyn Hardy and Robert Gittings (London: Oxford University Press, 1961) p. 4.
3. Dorset County Museum.
4. Dorset County Museum. In Emma Hardy's unpublished novella, 'The Maid on the Shore', the transparently named hero, Alfred During (Hardy himself had already used up such surnames as Strong, Mayne, and Oak), is somewhat deprecatingly viewed by the heroine as possessing an 'insignificant face and figure and quiet thoughtful manner [that] had an interest for her more matured mind that no merely dashing handsome man . . . could have for her again'. (Quoted in Millgate, *Thomas Hardy: A Biography* [Oxford: Oxford University Press, 1982] p. 124.)
5. *The Collected Letters of Thomas Hardy*, ed. Richard Little Purdy and Michael Millgate, 7 vols (Oxford: Clarendon Press, 1978–88) vol. I, p. 161.
6. Wessex edition (London: Macmillan, 1912) Ch. 19, pp. 208–9.
7. *The Personal Notebooks of Thomas Hardy*, ed. Richard H. Taylor (London: Macmillan Press, 1978) p. 6.
8. *Personal Notebooks*, p. 17.
9. Colby College Library. All quotations in this paper from Emma Hardy's and Florence Hardy's letters are made with the permission of the Miss E. A. Dugdale Will Trust.
10. Letter of 16 June 1908, Colby College.
11. Letter of 3 November 1902, Mrs Michael MacCarthy.
12. Letter of 9 December 1907, Beinecke Library.
13. Clodd diary, Alan Clodd.
14. Letter of 20 August 1899, Bodleian Library.
15. *The Animals' Friend*, March 1898, pp. 108–9.
16. *The Nation* (London), 9 May 1908, p. 189.
17. Emma Hardy personally believed that her mind had 'served [her] very well through the proof of life's occurrences' (*Some Recollections*, p. 4).

18. Telegraph form, 11 February 1914, Daphne Wood.
19. Thomas Hardy, *The Excluded and Collaborative Stories*, ed. Pamela Dalziel (Oxford: Clarendon Press, 1992) pp. 333–46.
20. In, respectively, *Weekly Dispatch*, 27 August 1922, p. 8; 17 September 1922, p. 8; and 8 April 1923, p. 2.
21. In *Sunday Pictorial*, 13 June 1915, p. 7, and 22 August 1915, p. 7.
22. Information from R. L. Purdy, who knew Margaret Soundy well; the envelope is in the Beinecke Library.
23. See, for example, Robert Gittings, *The Older Hardy* (London: Heinemann, 1978) plate 11.
24. Letter in Bugler collection.
25. Letter of Sunday [mid-July 1930], University of Texas.
26. See Ronald D. Knight, *T. E. Lawrence and the Max Gate Circle* (Weymouth, 1988) pp. 102–3, 106–7, 135–6.
27. Letter of Thursday [Spring 1935?], Frederick B. Adams.
28. Quoted in *Times Literary Supplement*, 3 June 1994, p. 8.
29. Letter of 26 October 1930, University of Texas.
30. Princeton University.
31. Letter of 14 February 1899, Colby College.
32. Wessex edition (London: Macmillan, 1912) Ch. 35, p. 313.

9

Bodily Transactions: Toni Morrison and Thomas Hardy in Literary Discourse

ROSEMARIE MORGAN

The most rudimentary of all literary transactions begins with the body – the body expressive, symbolic, figurative and vocalic. As an extension of the human body, as also of the common English tongue, 'voice' embodies, for both the modern Afro-American Toni Morrison, and the Victorian Wessex regionalist Thomas Hardy, the cultural diversity it simultaneously differentiates and mediates. But it is by infusing the voice of the poet not only into the prose narrative but also into the idioms of the unlettered, that Morrison and Hardy sustain the essential salt-of-the-earth commonness of the English tongue, the vigour and richness of the voice vernacular. Both are self-avowed champions of dialect.

Regional and racial dialects are, in themselves, diverse. The deeply musical speech of Afro-Americans, for example – what Toni Morrison calls 'speaking black' – constantly re-invents its own rhythmic expressiveness, its own vivid linguistic colour. Equally, being more conversive than discursive, and less politically regulated than standard forms, dialect actively flourishes its glorious dominion over inglorious grammatical tropes. In this sense, I would say that where standard English regulates, dialectal form transparently articulates, the social formation.

In the 1870s, Thomas Hardy begins, in the writing of *Far from the Madding Crowd*, by paying close attention to dialectal speech in each and every one of his characters, from Gabriel Oak right down to Boldwood's factotum. He explores, experiments with, revises and ultimately forges such a fine balance between standard forms and dialect that variation itself pre-empts slippage into the 'clod-hopping' or too (implausibly) 'cultivated' voice in equal measure. But it was a complicated business. For Hardy's editor, the fervidly class-conscious Leslie Stephen, there was still too much of the 'educated-sounding' labourer; for Hardy's reviewer it was rather the reverse, that the 'quaintness' of the dialect implied authorial condescension to the 'masses' (Stephen's word – not Hardy's). For Hardy himself it was vital that his workfolk retained their natural-born expressiveness together with their irreverent good humour and, most important of all, that they should not come across as that country-bumpkin stereotype so fondly patronised by Victorians as 'Hodge'. On these points Hardy laboured lovingly and long, enriching his countrymen's talk (as Martin Seymour-Smith puts it) so as 'to articulate their souls'.[1]

But twenty years on, in the 1890s, matters had become far more complicated. Hardy has by now attracted notice to his radical views. From what we might call his regionalist stance – which seeks to preserve the autonomy of a race by championing its dialectal forms – Hardy is now openly iconoclastic. In the earlier novels, for example, he has his rustics scorn all forms of colonisation by 'standard' urban, middle-class codes and practices, particularly those voiced in local pulpits which evidently inspire the unlettered members of the congregation to misuse, misquote, and to otherwise make profane as much of the Bible as possible. But by the 1890s, lighthearted scorn has intensified to show a sharper edge of consciously-politicised resistance to the socialisation and acculturation of the 'masses'. He now confronts, with *Tess*, the issue of replacing dialect with standard English and, with *Jude*, of introducing standardised forms of domestic organisation: the bureaucratic regularisation of marital relationships. In turn, class acculturation (or assimilation) intersects with the standardisation of language, and this some considerable time before George Orwell's Newspeak.

The implications of this acculturation for Tess, for whom the public world utters itself in standard school English and the private in local dialect, are those of appropriation. For, as Hardy presents the case, the public world of standard speech is indivisible from the public world of standard patriarchal values: Alec's values; Angel's values. Values that enable the former, in taking forcible possession of her body, to charge her with acts of incitement, or in his words, 'temptation', and then to smugly override her protestations as merely provocative words, the kind of words every woman says and does not mean; likewise, values that enable the latter first to idealise then to commodify her person – brutally devaluing it at the last on the (double-standard) basis that he has not got what he had bargained for.

Following this continuum, Hardy then has Sue Bridehead experience a more impersonal, a more socially alienating appropriation of her person. This, by means of the imposition of such a crude standardisation of language (in matrimonials), coupled with such a crude enforcement of patriarchal values (also in matrimonials), that all self-responsibility, all personal autonomy and all sense of identity are gradually eroded and finally destroyed.

Thus a primary transaction, between the body and language, as between language and the social formation, exposes deep conflicts of class and sex in Hardy. What had begun (in Wessex) as solid resistance to colonisation by standard, middle-class language and values, ends in total defeat for those who resist. The deadly war between spirit and flesh remains in mortal combat with the Word.

For Toni Morrison's characters, a century later in the 1970s, for whom the social controls of the dominant culture operate not only through sexism and classism but also through racism, these kinds of issues continue to remain painfully unresolved. In her first novel, *The Bluest Eye*, published in 1970 but set back in the 1940s,[2] Morrison structures her narrative with variant versions of a standard, school reading-primer – the Dick and Jane reader so prevalent in schools at the time. Symbolic of the lifestyles explored in this tale, which is set (as Hardy's tales are also set) in the author's birthplace and initiation-period of youth, the first version of the simulated Dick and Jane reader is rendered in Standard English, orderly, correct, uniform:

> Here is the house. It is green and white. It has a red door. It is very pretty. Here is the family. Mother, Father, Dick, and Jane. . . . They are very happy. See Jane. . . . She wants to play. . . . See Mother. Mother is very nice. . . . Mother laughs. . . . See Father. He is big and strong . . . (p. 7)

This first version corresponds in form and content to the Fisher family: white, middle-class, suburban and secure, with homemaking mother, career-making father and standard pets, all (by reading-primer standards) clean, comfortable, and content – a world alien to the black community at the centre of the novel.

The second version of the primer replicates the first but assumes a different format on the page – less intelligible, with missing capitals and inconsistent punctuation, but still comprehensible. This corresponds to the lives of Claudia and Frieda, the two black McTeer children of devoted parents endlessly struggling with poverty and racism. The third version maintains the same word-order but packs it into a chaos of vowels and consonants. This corresponds to the dysfunctional black Breedlove family in which the young Pecola embarks on the hazardous voyage to womanhood and does not survive the journey.

If, then, for Hardy, the themes of initiation into adulthood depict youthful trials and painful confrontations with the tensions of sex and class, for Morrison it is sex and race. And it is in *The Bluest Eye* that these confrontations are seen at their most destructive. Pecola Breedlove, measuring her self, her identity, her hopes and dreams, her entire universe, by the language and values of a standard Dick-and-Jane world to which she will never belong but with which she constantly identifies, cannot escape the tyranny of white, middle-class ideologies she feels she should value. In her struggle through innocence to experience she enters – as does Hardy's Tess – a man-made world in which power and privilege sustains itself by exploiting the vulnerable, the defenceless and the innocent; but unlike Tess's self-immolating act, Pecola's holds out no redemptive grace. Thus, as she loses her reason and mentally collapses into the Dick-and-Jane world she has unconsciously internalised, so (correlatively) the standard language of the school primer disintegrates before the reader's eyes.

Pecola's self-hatred and denial of her own existence finally engender a mental collapse of the kind Sue Bridehead suffers at the end of *Jude*. Reverting to the world she had imbibed as a child, Pecola, in her derangement, now takes on the 'blue eyes of a little white girl', and the wings to fly away – away from the blackness into the light:

> She spent her days, her tendril, sap-green days, walking up and down, up and down, her head jerking to the beat of a drummer so distant only she could hear. Elbows bent, hands on shoulders, she flailed her arms like a bird in an eternal, grotesquely futile effort to fly. Beating the air, a winged but grounded bird, intent on the blue void it could not reach – could not even see – but which filled the valleys of her mind. (p. 158)

As with Sue Bridehead's crazed descent into the world of the biblical word, mentally reverting to the relative security of orthodoxy, of embracing a familiar world and having it embrace her in turn, of

finding a certain protection in derangement, so too with Pecola
Breedlove.

As with the later Hardy, Morrison likewise presents acculturation
as an insidious form of social control that annihilates both individual and cultural identity. Equally, language is seen, by both, as
the agency of control, agency of the fall: 'the letter killeth'.

Some seventeen years on, in 1987, when Morrison comes to
Beloved,[3] in which the woman's sacrificial act serves as a most tragic
and most terrible response to unbearable oppression, the written
word in standard school English does more than shape the unconscious mind of the child learning to read: it also shapes the mind
of the child learning to write. The scene is a plantation estate in Ohio,
shortly after the Civil War. Here, Sethe (who despite her escape
from slavery works as servant to the Garner family) tells how she
was heading for the kitchen one day when she heard the voices
from Schoolteacher's class coming from the side porch, and how
she is suddenly caught by the sound of her own name. 'I couldn't
help listening to what I heard that day', she says.

> [Schoolteacher] was talking to his pupils and I heard him say,
> 'Which one are you doing?' And one of the boys said, 'Sethe.'
> That's when I stopped because I heard my name, and then I took
> a few steps to where I could see what they was doing. School-
> teacher was standing over one of them with one hand behind his
> back. He licked a forefinger a couple of times and turned a few
> pages. Slow. I was about to turn around . . . when I heard him
> say, 'No, no. That's not the way. I told you to put her human
> characteristics on the left; her animal ones on the right. And don't
> forget to line them up.'

Numb with shock, Sethe momentarily loses all sense of time and
place: 'I just kept lifting my feet and pushing back. When I bumped
against a tree my scalp was prickly' (p. 193).

Sethe's pain and mortification at the hands of Schoolteacher is at
all times associated with The Word. In the very beginning it had
been his godlike power over the word, and his abuse of this power,
that had first put the 'tree' on Sethe's back – as she describes it to
Paul D. 'What tree on your back?' asks Paul D. 'What tree on your
back? Is something growing on your back? I don't see nothing growing on your back' (p. 15). But as he takes her in his arms and rubs
his cheek on her back he learns, we are told, of

her sorrow, the roots of it; its wide trunk and intricate branches. Raising his fingers to the hooks of her dress, he knew without seeing them or hearing any sigh that the tears were coming fast. And when the top of her dress was around her hips and he saw the sculpture her back had become, like the decorative work of an ironsmith too passionate for display, he could think but not say, 'Aw, Lord, girl.' And he would tolerate no peace until he had touched every ridge and leaf of it with his mouth, none of which Sethe could feel because her back skin had been dead for years. (pp. 18–19)

The tree growing on Sethe's back has been there for eighteen years, ever since she was very young, very pregnant and at the same time nursing a baby daughter; ever since Schoolteacher's boys came in and held her down and forcibly took her milk; ever since School-teacher heard of it and had her beaten for telling on them – beaten so hard it opened up her back and when it closed, there was a tree.

So Sethe has a tree on her back and Schoolteacher, dictator of words, had it beaten into her living flesh for speaking out. And just as Hardy, in *Tess*, devises a parody of the creation myth, of the garden of Eden, in order to disable the mythic implications of the fall and the false stain they might cast upon Tess's purity, so with Morrison in *Beloved*. Although in Sethe's case Morrison collapses the New Testament/New World into the Old with the crucifixion motif. Backed up against a tree already scored upon her body, and with thorny prickles on her scalp and words of betrayal in her ears, Sethe is clearly aligned here with the crucified figure on Calvary.

And among the animal characteristics ascribed to Sethe in School-teacher's class there are, no doubt, words like 'dumb', 'stupid', 'weak' and 'unclean'. Yet, in actuality, she is remarkably wise, under-standing, compassionate, and possesses unusually strong mental powers – a keen philosophical grasp of the unknowable, invisible world (or what Hardy would have understood as 'essences', Essen-tialism). Thus, in being driven back against the tree she experiences Schoolteacher's denial of her person as a renewed scourge upon her body, for, to her way of thinking, all words partake of some kind of material reality: as the spirit is made flesh so words also manifest being. Attuned to a kind of Platonism (or, in modern terms, 'morphic resonance'), she feels that things more shadowy and insub-stantial than material objects remain in the world for all to see, hear and know, that images, words, memories, do not just disappear into the mind. They stay. 'Some things just stay,' she tells her daughter, Denver.

> I used to think it was my rememory. You know. Some things you forget. Other things you never do. But it's not. Places, places are still there. If a house burns down, it's gone, but the place – the picture of it – stays, and not just in my rememory, but out there, in the world . . . the picture of what I did, or knew, or saw is still out there. (pp. 35, 36)

So the horror for Sethe is that what she overheard 'is still out there' and will always remain.

Hardy's Tess would have understood that.[4] Some things 'just stay' for Tess also. As, for example, when Angel startles her in the garden after her ecstasy and she begins to feel, in her sudden sense of naked exposure, that the trees have inquisitive eyes. Her sensations, like Sethe's images and rememories, seem almost palpable, tangible, visible for all the world to know and see.

In one small measure then, in the passage from Hardy to Morrison over time and space, we have a single but lofty tread. In articulating the shadowy forms of half-understood words, of indelibly imprinted images, of sensations transmuted into essential modes, of self-expressive dialectal formations, both writers share the same world. Both give immediacy, bodily presence and authenticity to those who are otherwise marginalised, disenfranchised or, by virtue of the internal politics of the novel, absented in one way or another from public discourse.

And, no doubt, the Hardy who expressed the view (in his Preface to *Jude*) that there may be more in a book than the author consciously puts there, would find complete affinity with a Morrison who consciously seeks, she says, to provide a 'subtext that either sabotages the surface text's expressed intentions or escapes them through a language that mystifies what it cannot bring itself to articulate but still attempts to register'.[5]

At a completely different level of literary discourse, there is also a less-than-rudimentary command of irony.

Even in his most grave and serious mood Hardy's sense of humour gets the better of him, as also with Morrison. Both, for example, take a mischievous delight in bestowing droll names on their characters. For Hardy, this becomes a satirical satisfaction when endowing Leslie Stephen's fictional counterpart in *The Hand of Ethelberta* with the name of 'Neigh': neigh like a disgruntled, petulant horse, 'nay' – sounding like the niggling nay-sayer Stephen proved to be when faced with Hardy's delightfully open candour.

Morrison's 'baptisms' are no less impudent. This is how it is for the good Doctor Foster's son-in-law in *Song of Solomon*:[6]

> He had cooperated as a young father with the blind selection of names from the Bible for every child other than the first male. And abided by whatever the finger pointed to, for he knew every configuration of the naming of his sister. How his father, confused and melancholy over his wife's death in childbirth, had thumbed through the Bible, and since he could not read a word, chose a group of letters that seemed to him strong and handsome; saw in them a large figure that looked like a tree hanging in some princely but protective way over a row of smaller trees. How he had copied the group of letters out on a piece of brown paper; copied, as illiterate people do, every curlicue, arch, and bend in the letters, and presented it to the midwife.
>
> 'That's the baby's name.'
>
> 'You want this for the baby's name?'
>
> 'I want that for the baby's name. Say it.'
>
> 'You can't name the baby this.'
>
> 'Say it.'
>
> 'It's a man's name.'
>
> 'Say it.'
>
> 'Pilate.'
>
> 'What?'
>
> 'Pilate. You wrote down Pilate.'
>
> 'Like a riverboat pilot?'
>
> 'No. Not like a riverboat pilot. Like a Christ-killing Pilate. You can't get much worse than that for a name. And a baby girl at that.'   (p. 19)

But Pilate she is and Pilate she remains. One of the most splendidly pagan and triumphal of Toni Morrison's unconventional women, Pilate's naming makes a clear statement about the semiotic arbitrariness of language and the ambiguity of the pedagogic text, as also about the vicissitudes of its interpreters. Thus 'Pilate' signifies 'Christ-killer' by one reading, but by another ('by whatever the finger pointed to'), it signifies the reverse: the sacred 'tree' of redemption. The biblical 'sign', in this particular instance, points (by means of

Morrison's own pointing finger) to the 'tree' that this particular Pilate will incarnate. As she grows to maturity so she actually becomes 'strong and handsome', 'princely' and 'protective' and more: as the keeper of knowledge, secrets, mysteries, omens and oracles, she embodies the very Tree of Life itself.

Hardy devotees may instantly perceive that Pilate is not the first in the literary canon to be named in this mischievous way. As Henery explains to Bathsheba in *Far from the Madding Crowd*, Cainy Ball's mother, 'not being a Scripture-read woman, made a mistake at his christening', and named her infant son Cain thinking it was Abel who did the killing.[7]

Such guileless transactions clearly charm and delight Hardy and Morrison, both of whom pay fond and irreverent homage to the richness of the biblical text – frequently with recourse to the voice vernacular, to the open-eyed, *tabula rasa* of the unlettered mind. And perhaps it is inevitable, given the ideological tradition in American literature, that themes of the Fall, of being cast East of Eden, surface again and again in Toni Morrison's work, but with a difference. By merging myths and ancient folkloric beliefs of Africanist origin with those of the Hebraic, she places a unique slant on the myths and belief-systems of Christianity. In *Sula*,[8] for example, the prophetic if deranged Shadrack, who has been 'blasted and permanently astonished by the events of 1917' (p. 13), and who exemplifies the divided self torn between consciousness and unreason, functions as something of a hybrid consciousness shaped partly by race memories from an irretrievable, long-lost Africanist past, and partly by a more recent Messianic culture from which he has inherited the faceless, nameless, identity-less status of slave some fifty years after abolition. In this dualistic sense, as a divided self and a hybrid consciousness, Shadrack symbolises (and to some extent, catalyses) the conceptual duality of innocence and experience, of good and evil, within the community, within the consciousness of a people for whom knowledge of the difference sets the stage for the fall. But it is Shadrack's National Suicide Day that specifically embraces myths of Africanist origin. These hark back to a non-Christian, non-Edenic tradition and recall a long-held, long-valued belief-system so antithetical to zealous Christian missionaries in Africa that they made every attempt to have it outlawed as barbaric and savage in practice. The practice was suicide. Tribal custom among, for example, the Yoruba, held that the chosen few who followed their revered mentors and leaders to the grave would gather the highest spiritual grace in the afterlife. The privilege of suicide was, thus, sought after and highly prized.

And so it is that the shellshocked Shadrack,

> began a struggle that was to last for twelve days, a struggle to order and focus experience. It had to do with making a place for fear as a way of controlling it, for he could not anticipate it. It was not death or dying that frightened him but the unexpectedness of both. In sorting it all out, he hit on the notion that if one day a year were devoted to it, everybody could get it out of the way and the rest of the year would be safe and free. In this manner he instituted National Suicide Day.   (p. 14)

It is not long before Shadrack's National Suicide Day becomes part of local custom and belief. As in Hardy's Wessex, where shared beliefs or communal superstitions also help to make a place for fear as a way of controlling it, so in Morrison's township of Medallion, Ohio. Just as Hardy's rustics find consolation in exchanging premonition stories of black cats or the new moon seen through glass or deathheads shaped in candlegrease, so in Medallion, the story goes that

> Somebody's grandmother said her hens always started laying double yolks right after Suicide Day.
> Then Reverend Deal took it up, saying the same folks who had sense enough to avoid Shadrack's call were the ones who insisted on drinking themselves to death or womanizing themselves to death. 'May's well go on with Shad and save the Lamb the trouble of redemption' says he.   (p. 16)

In this respect, as much in irony as in iconoclasm, Morrison and Hardy again come together – linked by their mutual love of custom and folklore, and of the manner in which belief-systems evolve from ancient mythologies, pagan superstitions and magical revelations.

Moving on to yet another transactional level of discourse with the body, Hardy and Morrison also make similar approaches to sexuality – in particular, female sexuality and erotic relationships between women, which both celebrate with candour and delight. Subverting sexual codes and practices, both choose to challenge the status quo, although Hardy seems to present the more radical front by virtue of the stronger opposition he faced in his Victorian audience.

Of course, it is true of iconoclasm (in the broader view) to say that the bootlegger was created by repression, that the Speak-Easy was created by prohibition, and that Thomas Hardy had Leslie Stephen. But it is not alone his rebellious spirit, his love of the forbidden and his literary anarchism that make him the revolutionary. It is rather the sudden indeterminacy (so aptly human and contradictory) with which he configures his topic, just as it is the dramatic use of inconsistency (so appropriate to human psychology) with which he configures sexual relationships – these give him the radical edge. And, most important of all, in the context of female sexuality, Hardy has a truly supreme genius for making palpable and real the *incompletion* of intimacy – particularly in woman-and-woman erotic relationships.[9]

On the other hand, for Morrison, the lovely, flowing intimacy between women is sensual and very, very physical: women console each other, caress each other, fix each other's unwanted pregnancies, deliver each other's babies and keep silence on each other's homicides. There is fierce loyalty, unbreakable solidarity, shared powers of healing, cathartic storms of violence, unspoken acts of devotion, and deep affinities of mind and body.

Such is the intimate love and wordless affinity between Nel and Sula (in the novel of that name) that with the death of the one there is no end to the grieving of the other. For Nel, there is now only the stark realisation that the person she has been missing for all these years is not the man she had wed and lost, but Sula. With a final heartrending cry, a cry, we are told, that has no bottom and no top, but just 'circles and circles of sorrow' (p. 174), Nel howls her pain to the earth and sky in the pure and terrible knowledge that she will never know the love she never realised she could have known.

And at the other end of the Morrison spectrum there is sheer physical sex, sheer lovely euphoric sex. Sula's household is a good example, where her mother, Hannah Peace, will not live without the attentions of a man. Hannah luxuriates in her sexuality, in the pure and simple joy of it for its own sweet sake.

Her flirting was sweet, low and guileless. Without ever a pat of the hair, a rush to change clothes or a quick application of paint, with no gesture whatsoever, she rippled with sex . . . barefoot in summer, in the winter her feet in a man's leather slippers with the backs flattened under her heels, she made men aware of her behind, her slim ankles, the dewsmooth skin and the incredible

length of neck. Then the smile-eyes, the turn of the head – all so
welcoming, light and playful. . . . If the man entered and Hannah
was carrying a coal scuttle up from the basement, she handled it
in such a way that it became a gesture of love. He made no move
to help her with it simply because he wanted to see how her
thighs looked when she bent to put it down, knowing that she
wanted him to see them too.

But since in that crowded house there were no places for private and spontaneous lovemaking, Hannah would take the man
down into the cellar in the summer where it was cool . . . or in the
winter they would step into the pantry and stand up against the
shelves she had filled with canned goods, or lie on the flour sack
just under the rows of tiny green peppers. . . . What [Hannah]
wanted . . . and what she succeeded in having more often than
not, was some touching every day.   (pp. 42–4)

Given a shift in time, space and ethnicity, I think the Hannah Peaces
of Morrison's world could find their way into Hardy's without much
trouble – not into the media-controlled world of his novels, but
rather into the more sequestered domain of his poems – say, the
world of 'Voices from Things Growing in a Churchyard', where the
free-loving Eve Greensleeves enjoys, in perpetuity, being 'kissed by
men from many a clime'.[10]

Subject to the Grundyan controls of the day, such Eves do not, of
course, appear in Hardy's novels. Unlike Morrison's matriarchal
world in which birth, death and life are authorised as the women
– bearers of the race – see fit to authorise them, in the Victorian
patriarchal world there is no comparable female authority: every
aspect of a woman's life, physical, intellectual, spiritual, sexual comes
under the control of men.

Covert, subtle, and surreptitious then, Hardy has to be in returning to his women their birthright of bodily authority, of self-
responsibility, in endowing his Bathshebas and Tess's with a voluptuous delight in their own sexuality. No openly luxurious Hannah
Peaces in Parson Swancourt's pantry![11] Moreover, as far as homo-
erotica is concerned, Hardy's was an age in which sexual ideology
sanctioned only a limited sexual desire in healthy women – limited
to matrimonial activity and then further limited to arousal by the
male solely. This would seem to leave women free to indulge, discreetly, in every manner of intimate activity were it not for the heroic
force of ideology – a force equally powerful, if differently structured,

today, which urges a woman to be dietary-bound, depilitarised, deodorised, siliconised and lipo-suctioned down to the last ounce of her customised flesh. Female sexuality still remains a thing to be beaten into shape.

Ideology no doubt led many a Victorian woman – certainly if Havelock Ellis is to be believed – to suffer her flushed, hot, wet, body as unclean (to use Mrs Oliphant's word), as gross (to use Sue Bridehead's), or as just plain unladylike (as Sarah Stickney Ellis might say). And no doubt there were others, less oppressed by ideology, who did not experience their bodies in this way at all, as Hardy evidently knows quite well. But what he also appears to know quite well is that, given their social conditioning, women might never even recognise the latent existence of a homoerotic passion. This might never emerge at all from under so strong a heterosexist ideology. This aspect of the libidinous affections might well remain permanently unknowable, permanently unfulfilled. It is so in Hardy's fiction. And it remains a latent, undeveloped, marginalised aspect of woman's experience not, I think, because he would willingly marginalise it but because he would more willingly represent it truthfully – as women would, in actuality, have experienced it: barely recognisable even to themselves, unrealisable even to themselves.

In so far as this aspect of female sexuality still impinges, today, on women's experience, I shall conclude with Hardy's visionary treatment of it, which has paved the way for countless other representations, including the Nels and Sulas of Morrison's world.

Hardy's first published novel, *Desperate Remedies* (a good title here), is probably the first to spring to mind, in the homoerotic context. For although not a single Victorian critic appears to have detected it, many moderns have, thanks largely to the incursion of feminism into Hardy scholarship to adjust the kind of reading that C. J. P. Beatty, for example, makes in his 1970s introduction[12] to the novel. Beatty claims that Miss Aldclyffe's passion for Cytherea is merely frustrated maternal longing.

This is not the case. From the very first encounter between the older Cytherea Aldclyffe, and the younger, Cytherea Graye – the former described by Hardy as having a 'masculine cast' of countenance (Ch. 4.2) – the emphasis is upon their powerful physical attraction to each other and the electric passion that flashes between them. In Miss Aldclyffe's bedroom, they talk heatedly while gazing admiringly on each other's bodies – the one letting her eyes linger on 'the fair white surface, and the inimitable combination of curves' of her mistress's breasts (Ch. 5.3), the other intensely aware of '[feeling] the back of Cytherea's little hand tremble against her neck' (Ch. 5.2). And if the older woman rages passionately at the younger, this looks to me very much like the volatile surge of thwarted sexual arousal. Hardy virtually says as much – or says as much to those who are familiar with his figures of speech: 'The maiden's mere touch', he writes, 'seemed to discharge the pent-up regret of the lady as if she had been a jar of electricity' (Ch. 5.3). We know that phrase pretty well. It occurs again in *The Woodlanders* where Fitzpiers responds to Winterborne's jealous probes by talking in pseudo-scientific terms about getting electrically 'charged with emotive fluid like a Leyden jar'; Winterborne's flat response is, 'Well, it is what we call being in love down in these parts.'[13]

Being in love is what it is, too, for our lady of Knapwater House, who takes on the younger maid, in the very first place, purely and simply on the basis of physical attraction. This includes her 'sweet method of turning which steals the bosom away and leaves the eyes behind' (Ch. 4.2). Even more is left behind, as it happens. Cytherea also leaves such an alluring impression upon our 'motherly' lady that she cannot help but nourish erotic fantasies about such a 'creature who could glide round my luxurious indolent body in that manner, and look at me in that way'. How she longs for the touch of such light fingers upon her head and neck! (ibid.).

And touch they do. But first, alone in bed and in the dark, Cytherea has her own fantasies – visions of the youthful Miss Aldclyffe in her first 'awakening of the passion'; visions that keep the young maiden sleepless, hot and restless, visions that keep her alert to the smallest sound outside her room. And then it happens. Miss Aldclyffe enters and, 'It was now mistress and maid no longer; [but] woman and woman.' Climbing into Cytherea's bed and flinging her arms around the young girl's body, Miss Aldclyffe presses her close and begs for kisses with the cry, 'Why can't you kiss me as I can kiss you?' (Ch. 6.1).

And if Hardy now speaks, at this point, of Miss Aldclyffe's planting 'a warm motherly' kiss on the lips of the shy young girl, I do not think it is simply to mute the erotic impact of the scene. Nor do I think it is designed simply to divert the reader's attention away to merely commonplace maternal affections. It is rather in the interests of plausibility. The experienced woman is hardly going to take the inexperienced one by force. As Hardy apparently knows full well (and as young girls in their school dormitories also know equally well), the more experienced, or older woman, frequently makes her sexual advances to the less experienced girl with a good deal of so-called 'motherly' affection – whispering affinities of blood, of maternal feelings, of sisterly love. Nor would Hardy have Cytherea become so excited and embarrassed (his words), if Miss Aldclyffe's kisses were simply motherly. Nor would Miss Aldclyffe rise to such vehement jealousy, upon hearing that Cytherea has already been kissed by a man, if her feelings were just maternal. And if we have heard, elsewhere in Hardy, of pent-up electrical forces, we have also heard elsewhere the words, 'Why can't you kiss me as I can kiss you?' Not verbatim – but close enough, these are Alec's words to Tess. In both instances the words of passion used by Hardy in this scene recur in an erotic context elsewhere in his novels.

Miss Aldclyffe appears to be remarkably sexually experienced for a woman of her time and clime. She has known enough young girls whose hearts have been 'had' (as she puts it) to have become cynical about the socially-prescriptive notion of female chastity. And she knows enough about men, also, to have developed a taste – like Eustacia after her – for sexual ardour over sexual fidelity – erotic fervour over moral virtue.

The relationship between the two Cythereas improves considerably as time goes on. So much so that the servants begin to talk about 'some secret bond of connection exist[ing] between Miss Aldclyffe and her companion. But they were woman and woman, not woman and man, the facts were ethereal and refined, and so they could not be worked up into a taking story' (Ch. 8.1).

Here we encounter one of Hardy's favourite narrative devices – the intervening voice of a bystander narrator. This is not, surely, the choric voice of servants saying there can be no 'taking story'? *They* would scarcely concern themselves with epistemologies and *they* would, in fact, be the first to 'work up a taking story' from whatever gossip-fragments they might find – ethereal or otherwise. The 'taking story' that cannot be worked up is, as it turns out, a 'carnal plot', as Hardy has it in the first edition. So what his interloper implies here is that there can be nothing in a woman-and-woman relationship that promises properly to stir the public imagination. Since there is no such thing as a carnal relationship between women – as this exists in the social imagination – there is nothing here to narrate. This 'bystander' view thus coheres with Victorian orthodoxies but not with Hardy's narrator who, being temporarily displaced by the interloper, has *not* at any point suggested that the facts do not exist.

Seemingly hamstrung, at this juncture (with no story that will 'take'), and already one-third of the way through the book, Hardy now promptly consigns Cytherea to the newly introduced steward, Mr Manston (in a matter of pages), almost as if a 'taking story' has to be found somewhere and that it has to be found heterosexually. This much, at least, can bring in the gossip, the kind of story readers can openly talk about in respectable, middle-class drawing rooms.

Possibly aware that this manner of setting female friendships apart from the erotic sets a limit on the life of the passions itself, Hardy now draws attention to this disjuncture by limiting his own narratorial voice to a passionless monotone:

> The month of October passed, and November began its course. . . . New whispers arose and became very distinct (though they did not reach Miss Aldclyffe's ears) to the effect that the steward was deeply in love with Cytherea Graye. Indeed, the fact became so obvious that there was nothing left to say about it except that their marriage would be an excellent one for both; – for her in point of comfort – and for him in point of love. (Ch. 9.1)

A very wooden account, I would say, but cleverly ambiguous just the same. If, in one voice, we are delivered a somewhat sour view of marriage as excellent if it provides comfort (and nothing much else) for our refined but impoverished Cytherea, in quite another we are offered a subtly complicit point of view. For, with the advent of so lifeless a 'story' as this heterosexual marriage portends, and for readers who have already judged the affection between the women to be too deep and too irreplaceable to be supplanted by a conventional marriage, there is at least the satisfaction that (in this instance) both author and reader secretly share the same world, that both – in opposition to the status-quo – share the perception that if the woman-loving Cytherea, like Paula Power after her, goes the way of the Laodicean, it is not at all because she is wanting in passion but rather because the world within and beyond the novel is wanting in understanding and wisdom.

One of the most truncated of these woman-and-woman non-'taking stories' occurs in *The Woodlanders*. As with the Cythereas, the first encounter between Grace and Felice Charmond is highly emotionally charged, and here again it is with a slight turn of the head and a backward glance that the gazing intimacy of their first connection fixes the moment of mutual attraction – as figured in the looking-glass sequence:

> their faces in immediate juxtaposition, bringing into prominence their resemblances and their contrasts. Both looked attractive as glassed back by the faithful reflector.   (Ch. 8)

Faithful to what? To their attraction to each other? Presumably – for as Grace leaves and mounts the adjoining hillside, she turns, looks back and sees that Felice is standing at her door gazing steadily – as if 'glassed back' to her still.

The difference between this mirror scene, which brings the two women together in a single frame, and the later parallel scene in which Grace enters yet another house for the very first time (this time the house of her male lover, Fitzpiers), is that in the latter she catches a glimpse in the glass of his half-conscious gaze only. He too catches only a half-conscious glimpse of her – as if, he feels, someone is visiting him in a dream (Ch. 18). There is no exchange of intimate gazes, only the shock of something unreal. There is no sudden and startling affinity, only a dreadful sense, on both their parts, that their eyes have deceived them. Prophetic stuff.

Now, Hardy is very good with mirrors: mirrors as objectifying devices imaging the self as other (Bathsheba's looking-glass scene, for example); mirrors as thieving devices stealing a look, a glance, from the unsuspecting (as with Eustacia and Clym); and mirrors as reflecting endangerment, returning a wounding image to the vulnerable self (as with the shorn Marty South who dreads catching herself in her glass for fear of 'break[ing] her heart' [Ch. 3]). So, with this kind of focus in which the reflecting glass shapes an alternative dimension, or a kind of Platonic outer reality where the inner is but a hazy shadow, a blurred consciousness, a dimly perceived understanding – in which the lips that move in Bathsheba's mirror, for example, shape a vivid image of sexual voluptuousness which is, as yet, only nascent in reality – with this kind of close focus Hardy offers his reader an alternative dimension which, in the case of Grace Melbury and Felice Charmond, allows us to know something of their intense sexual attraction to each other.

We note, for example, that following Grace's meeting with Fitzpiers, it is not of him but of Felice that she dreams; it is of Felice she thinks longingly, and it is Felice's presence that she deeply misses

(Ch. 19). But no sooner has the narrative veered in this direction than it abruptly switches (as in *Desperate Remedies*), to a flatly stereotypical scene in which heterosexuality takes over and rules the day: suddenly, and with no cause whatsoever, Grace's hitherto perfectly stationary horse breaks out of control, and instantly Fitzpiers is there to the rescue, and thus in a bright flash of melodrama we immediately have the makings of a nice little 'taking story'. And from thereon, at almost every point of their courtship, Grace and Fitzpiers are offered some kind of conventionally melodramatic scene in which she supplies the shrieks and screams and he the strong, manly arm.

Even so, at the very point when Fitzpiers is at his rare and imperfect best – affectionately musing on their future home and thinking Grace might like to live in a place like Hintock House – her response is still neither deeply tender nor fully engaged. On the contrary, she is, even now, preoccupied with sad thoughts about Felice's continued absence, 'for she could not forget that she had somehow lost the valuable friendship of the lady of this bower' (Ch. 23). This heartsore reversion to Felice is, however, shortly to be arrested, and just at the very moment, at their passionate night-meeting, when it seems possible the two women might now, at last, come together and declare themselves. Grace has, by now, suffered stultifying months of a miserable marriage, during which she has contemplated her husband's meetings with Felice Charmond with a weary sense of their inevitability and a deep sense of loss – not of the man, but of the woman.

But the woodland night-scene of their meeting turns out to be remarkable only for its irresolution. To be sure, Hardy does come close to the kind of voluptuous intimacy that so enraptured the two Cythereas in *Desperate Remedies*, but not quite close enough. First, he prefaces the scene with Melbury's visit to Hintock House to plead for his daughter's happiness, to openly declare his daughter's love:

> She loved you once ma'am; you began by loving her. Then you dropped her without a reason, and it hurt her warm heart more than I can tell ye ... (Ch. 32)

Secondly, Felice breaks down in the knowledge that 'the allusion to Grace's former love' touched her 'more than all Melbury's other arguments'. Thirdly, she dismisses Melbury, bursts into tears and tries to recover herself by taking a walk in the woods.

This is where she meets Grace. And this is where the narrative action promises so much more than it can fulfil. The women talk, they express themselves with candour and simplicity, with defensiveness and anger, with reproaches and insults, and with such intense excitement that when they break up they each find themselves wandering mindlessly into the woods and getting hopelessly lost. Hours later, they find each other again. Tired, cold and weary they fall instinctively into each other's arms. Clinging tightly, they share intimate confidences, tender confessions, gentle consolations, and hold each other so close that 'the younger woman could feel her neighbour's breathings grow deeper and more spasmodic, as though uncontrollable feelings were germinating' (Ch. 33).

But nothing more happens. They go their separate ways, meet on one last occasion in the 'Wives all' scene, and never meet again. Felice dies on the Continent where she is shot by her jealous lover; Grace rejoins Fitzpiers to spend the remainder of her days in what her father describes as a marriage of 'forlorn hope' (Ch. 48).

The nature of the mix, in these relationships, is invariably complementary: the charismatic, sexually-passionate, rather dangerous older-woman-with-a-past, and the more dutiful, prim-and-proper young miss. This mix (one might say 'conflict') of sensuality and repression occurs again in *The Mayor of Casterbridge*, where the dynamics of the relationship between Elizabeth-Jane and Lucetta follow the customary Hardyan line of arrested development. Thus the prim-and-proper young maid, fascinated by a glimpse of the sensuous older woman, pursues her devotedly with what Hardy calls 'almost . . . a lover's feeling',[14] but just at the point when the two women discover a deep affinity of thought and feeling their intimacy comes to an abrupt halt. As in *The Woodlanders* and *Desperate Remedies*, all carnal passions are eventually channelled into heterosexuality.

A less truncated form of woman-and-woman love does, however, occur in what Barbara Hardy calls Hardy's 'feminist' novel. This is in *A Laodicean*,[15] and here the two women-lovers, Paula Power and Charlotte de Stancy, live so openly in such devoted intimacy that theirs does, indeed, very nearly become a 'taking story'. Although old Sir William de Stancy is oblivious to the fact, and speaks of his daughter's 'intimacy' with Paula Power as sheer opportunism (now that Paula has become the owner of Stancy Castle), to the sexually-interested Somerset it is quite evident that the two women are engaged in what he calls an 'eccentric or irregular' relationship (Bk 1, Ch. 5). They had, he thinks, found sweet communion a necessity of life, and by pure and instinctive good sense had broken down a barrier which men thrice their age and repute would probably have felt it imperative to maintain. (Bk 1, Ch. 4)

And although Hardy, at this point, sees the need to legitimise the whole issue by assimilating the homosexual implications to Greek mythology, he does permit Somerset a further (pointedly patronising/aptly defensive) observation that this kind of relationship is both desirable and progressive:

an engaging instance of that human progress on which he had expended many charming dreams [when such matters had seemed] of . . . importance to him. (ibid.)

But, more typically, Hardy extends the voice of honest candour not to the bourgeois Somerset but to the local innkeeper, for whom the two women 'be more like lovers than maid and maid' (Bk 1, Ch. 5).

Less typically, Hardy does not now suppress but instead gives vivid dramatisation to this intimacy between the women. Separated physically for more than a few hours, they keep closely in touch by telegraph – the tenderness of the messages rousing the infatuated Charlotte to hot-red blushes (Bk 1, Ch. 6). Separated emotionally by Somerset's flirtatious attentions to Paula, they come together instinctively and instantly as the one crosses the room to caress the other reassuringly (Bk 1, Ch. 10). Then, separated from Charlotte and finding herself alone and uncomfortable with Somerset, Paula immediately contrives to bring Charlotte in on the scene; and when left entirely alone in her empty castle, it is not the man but the woman she longingly misses and lovingly awaits (Bk 3, Ch. 2). Later, it is to Charlotte that Paula makes a lover's gift of diamonds and pearls (Bk 3, Ch. 6). And it is Charlotte's physical discomfort (at the Hunt Ball) that preoccupies Paula, and it is Charlotte whom Paula insists on taking home while the discomfitted Somerset is left in misery to nurse his ruined hopes alone (Bk 3, Ch. 6). And to all of this Hardy adds a delightfully ambiguous touch as Paula's maidservant recounts how, in the gymnasium, her mistress 'wears such a pretty boy's costume . . . that you think she is a lovely young youth and not a girl at all' (Bk 2, Ch. 6).

Male desire, however, shapes all of this differently. The irked Somerset repeatedly takes Paula's cool responses to him to be coquettish behaviour, her indifference to be a 'passive way of assenting' (Bk 1, Ch. 15), her undemonstrative attitude to be just another indication of the 'pleasing agonies' of love (Bk 1, Ch. 15), her weary resistance to his emotional pressure to be mere playfulness. Irritated by these false assumptions and coercive misreadings, Paula is driven, at one point, to expostulate that men are 'a dreadfully encroaching sex' (Bk 3, Ch. 3). Hardy, though, makes it clear that such encroachments are necessary. A man (under such circumstances) must needs plot diverse inroads into a homoemotional relationship so strong that without remorseless tactics of scheming and bombardment there can and will be no entryway for the male. Evidently this strong woman-bond is felt, by Somerset, to be a very real threat – particularly to what he assumes to be man's right-of-access to woman.

Hardy reinforces this motif of incipient male domination and encroachment upon the female by devising a mirror plot within his narrative. That is, he not only creates an entire theme of encroachment – male upon competing male, architectural style upon architectural style, medievalism upon eclecticism or upon hellenism, or vice-versa – but he also devises an ending to this novel which shapes an appropriate 'defeat' of the male stronghold – the symbolic male stronghold of patriarchy and the property which bears the name, Stancy Castle.

In fact the closure of this novel performs in all ways Hardyan and subversive. There is ambiguity, indeterminacy and more. For what we have, to all intents and purposes, is a conventional Victorian ending (getting married and living happily ever after), undercut by an altogether unconventional ending in which the theme of encroachment and the crisis of closure in the women's relationship combine to tell a rather different story. It tells, very subtly, of the narrative's purposeful dismantling of the Victorian myth that women search for emotional and sexual fulfilment only through men.

It happens thus. First there is Somerset's proposal of marriage, to which Paula responds with resignation, not joy. If we were to give this 'Laodicean' response a name in the canon of Hardy closures, we might name it the politics of reluctance. The reluctance, for example, of Fancy Day, in *Under the Greenwood Tree*, to give herself body and soul to her future husband Dick Dewy. The reluctance of Bathsheba, in *Far from the Madding Crowd*, to give herself to Gabriel Oak in anything other than a companionate bond. And the more radical reluctance of Sue Bridehead in her relationship with Jude: Sue's renunciation of the dominant culture's institutionalisation of

heterosexual marriage (with Jude) – which, after all, purportedly promises love and fulfilment and not the self-loathing and tortuous sex she experiences with Phillotson – openly raises the question (with Hardy) as to what it is all these reluctant brides are unconsciously rejecting. Institutionalised marriage, no doubt. Monogamy, possibly. Confinement to an exclusively heterosexual relationship – probably. Perhaps it is enough, for our purposes here, that Hardy is prepared to raise the question.

Returning to the closure of *A Laodicean*, we find that Paula had hoped, she says, to have lived with Charlotte for the rest of her days. Charlotte opts, however, for conventual life. So Paula offers Somerset her reluctant acceptance. Thus, the imaginative continuum of all such subdued moments in Hardy's fiction, from Fancy Day's withholding to Sue's recalcitrance, comes full circle with Paula's descent into matrimony. As her inexpressible regret – mutely conveyed by a repressed sigh – draws breath from feelings of utter resignation and the ghastly finality of her loss of Charlotte, so an even more fiery breath erupts in the world outside: a conflagration engulfs the castle. The house of De Stancy is in flames. The male stronghold collapses on the outside while, on the inside, the woman's heart goes out, in a sigh, to the lost beloved who now makes her last and final call:

> . . . my own very best friend, and more than sister, don't think that I mean to leave my love and friendship for you behind me. No, Paula, you will *always* be with me. . . . My heart is very full, dear – too full to write more. God bless you, and . . . Good-bye!   (Bk 6, Ch. 5)

Notes

1.   Martin Seymour-Smith, *Hardy* (London: Bloomsbury, 1994) p. 193.
2.   Toni Morrison, *The Bluest Eye* (New York: Washington Square Press, 1972). Page references for quotations given in parenthesis in text.
3.   Toni Morrison, *Beloved* (London: Chatto & Windus, 1988). Page references for quotations given in parenthesis in text.
4.   See also Hardy's poem 'Beyond the Last Lamp', in which 'morphic resonance' completes the idea of a mood-imprint upon the landscape with,

There they seem brooding on their pain,
And will, while such a lane remain.

The Complete Poems of Thomas Hardy, ed. James Gibson (London: Macmillan, 1976) poem no. 257. Hereafter abbreviated to *Complete Poems*.

5.   Toni Morrison, *Playing in the Dark: Whiteness and the Literary Imagination* (Cambridge, Mass.: Harvard University Press, 1992) p. 66.
6.   Toni Morrison, *Song of Solomon* (New York: Alfred A. Knopf, 1977). Page references for quotations given in parenthesis in text.
7.   Thomas Hardy, *Far from the Madding Crowd*, New Wessex Edition (London: Macmillan, 1974–5) Ch. 10.
8.   Toni Morrison, *Sula* (New York: Alfred A. Knopf, 1973). Page references for quotations given in parenthesis in text.
9.   I am reluctant to use the word 'lesbianism'. In one sense it is too limiting, and in another, too generalising. It also carries, nowadays, too much political and ideological baggage to be useful in this context.
10. *Complete Poems*, no. 580.
11. Although Hardy did once, in his early married life, apparently find his own pantry filled up – so to speak – with more than canned goods and rows of tiny green peppers, when his maid was found to be pregnant.
12. See Beatty's 'Introduction' to Hardy's *Desperate Remedies* in the New Wessex Edition (London: Macmillan, 1975–6). Chapter references for quotations from the novel identified in parenthesis in text.
13. Thomas Hardy, *The Woodlanders*, New Wessex Edition (London: Macmillan, 1974–5) Ch. 16. Chapter references for subsequent quotations identified in parenthesis in text.
14. Thomas Hardy, *The Mayor of Casterbridge*, New Wessex Edition (London: Macmillan, 1974–5) Ch. 21.
15. See Barbara Hardy's 'Introduction' to *A Laodicean*, New Wessex Edition (London: Macmillan, 1975–6) p. 13. Chapter references for quotations from the novel identified in parenthesis in text.

10

The Far and the Near: On Reading Thomas Hardy Today

PETER ROTHERMEL

When I was asked to make a contribution to this book, I was somewhat dazed. What could I say that hadn't been said before, probably better than I could say it? Thus I decided not to add another elaborate thesis to the ones already existing, but to re-read a good number of Hardy's major novels and take note how they impressed me today. In addition, I asked some of my students to support me in my plan.

I propose this to be an occasion of sharing with you, this and that point, this and that passage, so you will not be surprised to find my contribution moving more in the direction of a Homage to Hardy than in that of an academic paper. I do apologise for not being what is called an authority on Hardy, but I hope that you may not be displeased to realise that a friend and admirer of Thomas Hardy from the Continent has made observations not unlike your own.

The categories of the Far and the Near, I should make clear, are preliminary, and refer to the contents of the texts, not to Hardy's rhetoric or point of view, interesting though these may be. You remember the beautiful scene in *Tess of the d'Urbervilles* when Tess, stirred by the emotion of beginning love for Angel Clare, feels as if she had left herself and all material objects behind:

> It was a typical summer evening in June, the atmosphere being in such delicate equilibrium and so transmissive that inanimate objects seemed endowed with two or three senses, if not five. There was no distinction between the near and the far, and an auditor felt close to everything within the horizon.   (Ch. 19)

We, too, may find that the distinction between the near and the far, though initially helpful, may dissolve into a greater whole. Yet a key-word occurring in this passage is 'seemed'. Hardy, as we know, saw life as a 'series of seemings', which explains – partially at least – his frequent use of 'seem' and related verb phrases. Thus we may be both justified and forgiven when, in talking about Hardy's characters, we resort to words like 'seem' and 'appear' quite frequently. Not from an attitude of evasiveness but in awareness of the fact that truth and the appearances of truth are something immensely personal and idiosyncratic, delicate and complex.

When I was a young student – many decades ago – my English professor suggested in one of her lectures a reading of Hardy's *The Return of the Native*. I followed her suggestion and was impressed by Hardy's use of language, his presentation of characters and his immensely rich vocabulary – at that time I still had to fight my way through dictionaries – and I was vaguely intrigued yet not really enthralled by the slow movement at the beginning, the famous chapter on Egdon Heath. It seemed, by and large, all rather far away. That went, for my as yet untutored mind, for plot and conflict as well – for that strange story of passion, jealousy, frustration and pointless death, as it struck me then – a year after the end of the war. I failed to comprehend Mrs Yeobright's fury and mortification at seeing her niece return from her wedding appointment unwed, all the more as she professed no great liking for the prospective groom. My readiness for Hardy was not yet awakened.

It was many years later that I, for professional reasons, came to embark on the adventure of really getting lost in Thomas Hardy. I read novels I hadn't read before, shame to say. In doing so I detected an uncertain feeling – later shared by my students – of puzzlement bordering on irritation in response to the nature and reason of the conflicts which brought protagonists to ruin and despair. Tess being seduced by the libertine Alec d'Urberville offered no problem. It was in keeping with the well-known eighteenth-century topos: Lovelace in Samuel Richardson's *Clarissa* could be seen as a forerunner of Alec. Seductions of dependants or near-dependants occur everywhere still, and have formed the topic of fiction for centuries. More difficult to follow and thus further away from our own time and understanding was Angel's reaction to Tess's story. His career appeared to be of greater importance to him than her love. And – although another topos of eighteenth-century novels – Tess's unquestioning, utterly demure compliance, her self-effacing submissiveness to Angel's order of separation, appeared hard to stomach, seemed far away. And Angel Clare was far away, who had such strange notions of himself and his life that he felt he 'had utterly wrecked his career by this marriage' and thought himself 'a dupe and a failure', who had to make for Brazil, because there 'the conventions would not be so operative which made life with her seem impracticable to him here' (*Tess*, Ch. 39). What message could such a weak character have for us today? Well, granted, his behaviour had its function for the sake of the plot. No weak Angel, no reappearance of Alec. But Tess's submissiveness? Even if the plot asks for it, it causes – caused – annoyance, irritation, pain. Why should a stable, even-tempered, self-reliant young woman prostrate herself so much as to say that she feels 'utterly worthless'? Why should she be willing to let herself be frightened and subdued by the 'picture of possible offspring who would scorn her' if they heard of her alleged misdeed (Ch. 36)? Or are we *meant* by Hardy to become furious at such unresisting acquiescence in a preposterous demand? At the whole attitude of mind represented by it? Perhaps a not impossible conclusion. Hardy himself felt the need of some explanatory, almost restrictive comment: 'she might have seen that what had bowed her head so profoundly – the thought of the world's concern at her situation – was founded on an illusion'. And further: 'Most of [her] misery had been generated by her conventional aspect' (Ch. 14). It is noteworthy that most of Hardy's plots centre in the minds of his protagonists, not in outer events. In fact, in a 'series of seemings', the world being 'only a psychological phenomenon' (Ch. 13).

Far from a modern reader's point of view appears, on first reading, the plot of *Jude the Obscure*. It isn't so much Jude's own development. His susceptibility to women's charm and influence explains his predicament to any contemporary reader, though he or she may have some difficulty in swallowing his long-sustained innocence. It is Sue Bridehead who causes bewilderment, her radical change – somersault rather – from being a modern, clever, progressive, emancipated woman to one whose sore mind reflects nothing but stale conservatism, abject self-denial, remorse and the very medievalism that she, previously, despised so much. It is only the soreness of her mind that offers some kind of explanation. Our resort to psychoanalysis leads us inevitably to a masochistic mind. 'Our life', Sue wails before Jude, 'has been a vain attempt at self-delight. But self-abnegation is the higher road. We should mortify the flesh – the terrible flesh – the curse of Adam!' (Pt 6, Ch. 3). Is it that Sue has never come to terms with her own and Jude's sexuality? And further: 'We ought to be continually sacrificing ourselves on the altar of duty! . . . I well deserved the scourging I have got! [here she refers to the death of her children by the hand of Father Time] . . . I wish my every fearless word and thought could be rooted out of my history. Self-renunciation – that's everything! I cannot humiliate myself too much!' (Pt 6, Ch. 3). Such pathos connected with such views seems very far from us. Unless – again – Hardy intended even his contemporary readers to be annoyed and so to rebel against such perverted notions. Only: even such rebellion seems far away; those particular prison doors of narrow minds have been standing open for quite a time.

Sue's self-abasement goes even further than that of Tess. Only once after her reversion does she seem to have a clear moment when she says: 'Perhaps the world is not illuminated enough for such experiments as ours! Who were we, to think we could act as pioneers!' (Pt 6, Ch. 3). And yet, Hardy adorns Sue with many lovable qualities, qualities which struggle to bring the whole person closer to us and only partly succeed. There is this lovely story that her aunt tells of the young Sue:

> Why, one day when she was walking into the pond with her shoes and stockings off, and her petticoats pulled above her knees, afore I could cry out for shame, she said: 'Move on, aunty! This is no sight for modest eyes!'   (Pt 2, Ch. 6)

A story that in its subject seems far, is in its humanity, however, very near. It makes us even see the impish smile in Sue's eyes.

I have arrived – taking a few shortcuts – at what may be described as the turnpike of my paper. Let us then leave the Far and turn to the Near. And I'll begin this section with an apparent paradox: what is far and yet near? The past is far, and yet the look into the past is near. Hardy liked to look at and into the past – if 'liked' is not too weak an expression. And in this we moderns feel very near to Hardy. We, perhaps more than preceding generations, have learned to value certain contents and manifestations of the past which now seem to be hopelessly disappearing and destroyed. I cannot quite side with C. H. Sisson, who speaks of Hardy's 'morbid, retrospective temperament'[1] unless he is thinking of Hardy's concern with Victorian morality. May Hardy speak for himself: 'I have instituted inquiries to correct tricks of memory, . . . in order to preserve for my own satisfaction a fairly true record of a vanishing life.'[2] Hardy knew and loved the value and significance of things as they had been: the old churches, cottages, and roads, the trees and springs and wells, the old ways of toil and soil, of pasture and pleasure, of shepherd and sheep. All the manifold and individual ways that were the outgrowth of custom and of nature; an unquestioning and unquestioned obedience to her laws – contrary to the modern, arrogant, self-complaisant ways of the vulgar rich, with their ugly pseudo manor houses, their modern harvesting machines, their streamlined furrows, drawn in indifferent ignorance to the destroyed harmony that lay beneath; the more and more accelerated dissolution of a social structure and life which had, at least, afforded community, stability, and security if not wealth, and was now gradually withdrawing like a beaten army under the impact of modernism, of an insipid, brainless materialism.

Hardy's love of the past did not include love of backwardness, of dogmatism and bigotry. That, to his mind, was opposed to life. Yet he may have felt, as Matthew Arnold did, the spread of insecurity following in the wake of a growing scepticism that threatened the very centre of traditional belief. Its herald was the publication of a widely discussed book *Das Leben Jesu (Jesus Christ's Life)* by David Friedrich Strauss in 1836. It drew away the ground under the feet of many who had nothing else to tread on. Nothing but a doubtful trust in science and in what was called progress; in the inventiveness and persistence of the human mind. Not, in Hardy's eyes, a salutary, sustaining conception or hope. However, he, who may have believed like others that morals could be preserved without dogmatic religion, had little to offer instead. His alleged pessimism may spring from this awareness. Like Arnold he may have felt himself to be living between two worlds, 'one dead, the other powerless to be born'. One day, when Angel Clare asks Tess to give him an idea of what she thinks of life and of the future (not in those words, of course), she, responding, strikes a mood that seems almost Hardy's own: 'You seem to see numbers of to-morrows just all in a line, the first of them the biggest and clearest, the others getting smaller and smaller as they stand farther away; but they all seem very fierce and cruel and as if they said, "I'm coming! Beware of me! Beware of me!"'. (And who doesn't here think of Macbeth's famous soliloquy?) Hardy's comment to those words is: 'She was expressing in her own native phrases – assisted a little by her Sixth Standard training – feelings which might almost have been called those of the age – the ache of modernism' (*Tess*, Ch. 19).

Into this dilemma, between the two worlds, between dogmatism and scepticism, retrospection and progressiveness, reverence of (sometimes hollow) tradition and emancipatory desire, Hardy puts some of his best-known central characters. They may, in the last consequence, die of it like Tess and Jude; or they may find a modest corner in the perpetual flux of things that affords them a survival in serenity, like Bathsheba, like Elizabeth-Jane.

Hardy had no illusions about the possibility of preserving what was lovable about the past. Individual and contagious strife for higher living standards, for more amenities, for progress would see to that. In 1883 he writes in his essay 'The Dorsetshire Labourer': 'Progress and picturesqueness do not harmonise. They [the labouring class] are losing their individuality, but they are widening the range of their ideas, and gaining in freedom. It is too much to expect them to remain stagnant and old-fashioned for the pleasure of romantic spectators.'[3]

Quite a few of my students were struck by the 'nearness', the modernity of some of Sue Bridehead's remarks *before* her reversion. As when she expresses her wish to dissolve her first marriage to Phillotson: 'I am certain one ought to be allowed to undo what one has done so ignorantly! I daresay it happens to lots of women; only they submit, and I kick. . . . When people of a later age look back upon the barbarous customs and superstitions of the times that we have the unhappiness to live in, what *will* they say!' (*Jude*, Pt 4, Ch. 2).

We know that many of Sue's progressive notions were hers only second-hand, taken over from her undergraduate boy friend. That may be part of the reason why they could later on so easily and totally be replaced by the backlash of an imagined compulsion to obey irrational dogmatism. The second-hand derivation becomes fairly clear in her young, almost funny and affected seriousness: 'I have no respect for Christminster whatever, except, in a qualified degree, on its intellectual side', and: 'Intellect at Christminster is new wine in old bottles' (Pt 3, Ch. 4). Such young wisdoms may surprisingly bring back to us the slogans of the students' protest movement in the late 1960s.

One suspects, when weighing Sue's earlier, i.e. 'modern', views against her later, reactionary ones, that both were in fact substitutes in lack of the real thing her heart longed for. It is not fair, as has been done, to derive her blatant discrepancies from her being repelled as well as attracted by sexuality. I don't overlook the part that jealousy played in her reversion nor the fact that she regarded the death of her children as God's punishment for her 'sins'. And yet, all such efforts at explanation seem poor rationalisations in view of her vehement, irrational thirst for self-effacement.

Into Phillotson's mouth, who, again, wavers between truly humane conceptions and conventional, accepted, and therefore useful morality, Hardy laid words of a distinctively modern flavour. Against the exhortations of his friend Gillingham not to let Sue go he retorts: 'I know I can't logically, or religiously, defend my concession to such a wish of hers; or harmonize it with the doctrines I was brought up in. . . . I simply am going to act by instinct, and let principles take care of themselves' (Pt 4, Ch. 4). How near to our own understanding and contemplation of such things, and what a contrast to Angel Clare's decision not to stay with his newly wedded wife 'on principle'!

Viewed and recognised from a different angle, even Gillingham's admonishing protestations to Phillotson strike us as 'near'. They come from a source as old as human society which will last as long as the desire for distinction lasts: 'But if people did as you want to do, there'd be a general domestic disintegration. The family would no longer be the social unit' (ibid.). To this well-known threat of Armageddon Phillotson gives this astonishing, really revolutionary and clearly 'feminist' reply: 'I don't see why the woman and the children should not be the unit without the man.' What could be nearer? Whereupon we hear all the good old grandmothers and grandfathers cry out with Gillingham: 'By the Lord Harry! – Matriarchy! . . . It will upset all received opinion hereabout. Good God – what will Shaston say!' I think we would not be mistaken if we, watching Hardy write these lines, thought we could discover a smile around his generally straight lips.

The Far and the Near, categories which do not seem to hold a great deal of water, perhaps. They may be tentatively useful in letting us estimate the width of Hardy's span, comprising the conflicts and tensions of his time and sublimating them in the creation of his characters. And there is this: what may and did strike us as far – all those manifestations of prejudices, of narrow-mindedness, of intolerance and bigotry – are they really so far from us? Their contents may be; their essence is not. They are present, around us, wherever we look, alas.

I would now like to ask you to let your minds dwell on the central question: what, do you think, remains beyond the Far and the

Near, what strikes you as permanent and, at the same time, decidedly Hardyesque? There is, to begin with, Hardy's extraordinary and very personal gift of observation, which is linked to his admirable genius for characterisation. The permanent products of his gift of observation can only be explained by his sensitivity; a sensitivity that is not confined to the sense of sight but includes all senses, a sixth sense as well: that of intuition, his ability to put himself into the minds and souls of others. Permanent evidence of the fruit of such perceptiveness can be found on almost every page. There are, furthermore, the many well-remembered instances of his art of revealing the close interrelationship of man and nature, their intrinsic interdependence.

What strikes home, too, because it reflects a permanent trait of the human condition, is Hardy's presentation of his main characters as lonely people; people who crave for love and companionship and cannot find it.

Permanent, at least to me, are also the many examples of Hardy's humour, always humane, though it may be spiced with irony. Then his presentations of rural life, always functional, always accurate and illuminating. Last not least – and this may be personal – I regard as permanent Hardy's general contemplations and wisdoms which he puts into the mouths of his characters.

When, in order to be more explicit, I will be briefly pointing to some facets of Hardy's art, I do so in full realisation of the fact that they form integral parts of his work as a whole.

Speaking of Hardy's sensitive observation in connection with characterisation, take, as one of many possible examples, the scene where Bathsheba (in *Far from the Madding Crowd*) sits waiting in her open waggon, unwrapping a package:

> . . . her eyes crept back to the package, her thoughts seeming to run upon what was inside it. At length she drew the article into her lap, and untied the paper covering; a small swing looking-glass was disclosed, in which she proceeded to survey herself attentively. She parted her lips and smiled.
>
> It was a fine morning, and the sun lighted up to a scarlet glow the crimson jacket she wore, and painted a soft lustre upon her bright face and dark hair. The myrtles, geraniums, and cactuses packed around her were fresh and green, and at such a leafless season they invested the whole concern of horses, waggon, furniture, and girl with a peculiar vernal charm. What possessed her

to indulge in such a performance in the sight of the sparrows, blackbirds, and unperceived farmer who were alone its spectators, – whether the smile began as a factitious one, to test her capacity in that art, – nobody knows; it ended certainly in a real smile. She blushed at herself, and seeing her reflection blush, blushed the more.   (Ch. 1)

What a great piece of 'showing', pointing to the trait in Bathsheba's character which, by a hair's breadth, could have been her undoing.

As an example of Hardy's art of showing the mood of characters by describing landscape, setting thereby the tone to a whole novel, I quote the passage from the beginning of *The Mayor of Casterbridge*, where the lonely Henchard and his no less lonely wife are:

approaching the large village of Weydon-Priors, in Upper Wessex, on foot . . . hedges, trees, and other vegetation . . . had entered the blackened-green stage of colour that the doomed leaves pass through on their way to dingy, and yellow, and red. . . . For a long time there was [no sound] beyond the voice of a weak bird singing a trite old evening song that might doubtless have been heard on the hill at the same hour, and with the self-same trills, quavers, and breves, at any sunset of that season for centuries untold.   (Ch. 1)

Isn't there an echo of Keats's 'Ode to a Nightingale'?: 'Perhaps the self-same song that found a path / Through the sad heart of Ruth'.

The close interrelationship between character and fate (or destiny) is very noticeable in Hardy's work and sets him near great writers in other languages. Friedrich von Hardenberg – known as Novalis – held that 'Charakter ist Schicksal' – character is destiny or, as Hardy translates the phrase in *The Mayor of Casterbridge* (Ch. 17): 'Character is Fate.' When reflecting the tragic fate of Tess we cannot do so without taking note of Hardy's comment that it was her 'reckless acquiescence in chance too apparent in the whole d'Urberville family' which paves her way into Alec's trap (Ch. 37). And 'but for the slight incautiousness of character inherited from her race' she would have been 'an almost standard woman' (Ch. 14). As regards Angel Clare's character, it is his 'fury of fastidiousness' which makes him act as a coward in the face of Tess's revelations (Ch. 37).

The supposition that 'character is destiny' can bring about an attitude of fatalism, with destructive results. Tess, in an attack of despair, reflects: 'What's the use of learning that I am one of a long row only – finding out that there is set down in some old book somebody just like me, and to know that I shall only act her part' (Ch. 19). Was this Hardy's own belief? Destiny understood as genetic destiny?

An outstanding feature of Hardy's characters, lifting them beyond temporal truth, is their longing for something far, something outside themselves, felt like an open wound. In *The Return of the Native* Eustacia is craving for the great bustling world, for Paris; if not Paris, at least for London, away from Egdon Heath; in *Jude the Obscure* it is Jude's 'magnificent Christminster dream' that decides his movements; in *Far from the Madding Crowd* it is Boldwood's irrepressible desire to get possession of Bathsheba which decides his fate; in *The Mayor of Casterbridge* it is Michael Henchard's untameable desire to hold on to Elizabeth-Jane which prepares the way to his doom. And Tess? There is her love for Angel Clare and her conscious longing for his return to her. But there is something else. The core of her longing seems to be directed at something beyond tangible or even ideal objects. She gives voice to it when she speaks of the possibility that our souls may 'go outside our bodies when we are alive': '[you must] lie on the grass at night and look straight up at some big bright star; and, by fixing your mind upon it, you will soon find that you are hundreds and hundreds o' miles away from your body, which you don't seem to want at all' (Ch. 18). Is this a foreshadowing of her life's end? A similar experience occurs to her when listening to Angel playing his harp: 'Tess was conscious of neither time nor space. The exaltation which she had described as being producible at will by gazing at a star, came now without any determination of hers; she undulated upon the thin notes of the second-hand harp, and their harmonies passed like breezes through her, bringing tears into her eyes.' The sheer beauty of this piece of writing puts a million lines of so-called erotic literature to shame. It goes on: 'The floating pollen seemed to be his notes made visible, and the dampness of the garden the weeping of the garden's sensibility. Though near nightfall, the rank-smelling weed-flowers glowed as if they would not close for intentness, and the waves of colour mixed with the waves of sound' (Ch. 19).

As the impossibility of fulfilment makes Hardy's characters lonely, so the excess of desire leads them into catastrophe. Eustacia in *The Return of the Native* was 'framed to snatch a year's, a week's, even an hour's passion from anywhere while it could be won', and 'Her loneliness deepened her desire' (Bk 1, Ch. 7). Michael Henchard is driven to his end by his failure to rest content with what he *can* have, and by his excessive possessiveness regarding Elizabeth-Jane. Jude is consumed by his longing for Christminster and all it stands for and is only thwarted in reaching his goal by his susceptibility to women and his ignorance about them. Sue Bridehead's fading away like a flower cut is the result of an excessive sense of sin and consequent atonement; Bathsheba runs into a near-catastrophe owing to her excessive vanity, which cannot suffer Boldwood's apparent indifference towards her person; her Valentine to him with 'Marry Me!' is the source of so much misery.

Tragedy developing from excessive emotions, from unrestrained passions, is a basic element underlying practically all great dramatic art – Shakespeare's no less than that of the Greek playwrights – Euripedes, Sophocles, Aeschylus. Their protagonists have often an elevated stature or function – politically, socially – which makes their eventual fall all the more moving and impressive; their height of fall – 'Fallhöhe' – provokes awe and sympathy among the audience. The result is, according to Aristotle, a 'catharsis', a purification of the passions and of the mind. Hardy's main protagonists are given that 'height of fall'; others, like Alec d'Urberville, Angel Clare, Wildeve (*The Return of the Native*), Sergeant Troy (*Far from the Madding Crowd*), Donald Farfrae (*The Mayor of Casterbridge*), even Eustacia, lack it. They have no or only an insignificant past, or they disown it and thus have no depth. Their lives are shallow. Yet even though the theme itself is not Hardy's, the execution of it certainly is. A very personal, unique execution.

It is noteworthy that Hardy, in the case of his tragic protagonists, seems to feel the need to give the reader some cognitive help in order to better understand their fall, particularly in view of obvious discrepancies in their actions. In Sue Bridehead's case Hardy asks: 'Was Sue simply so perverse that she wilfully gave herself and him [i.e. Jude] pain for the odd and mournful luxury of practising long-suffering in her own person?' And he essays an answer himself: 'Possibly she would go on inflicting such pains again and again . . . in all her colossal inconsistency' (Pt 3, Ch. 7).

In the case of Tess, Hardy lets us know: 'The firmness of her devotion to him [i.e. Angel Clare] was almost pitiful. . . . She might just now have been Apostolic Charity herself returned to a self-seeking modern world' (Ch. 36). (To a modern reader it begs the question, however, whether it would not have been much more charitable towards Angel – and thus to herself as well – if she had given him a good piece of her mind and not waited for a year!)

In the case of Michael Henchard – who makes the reader waver between admiration and repulsion – Hardy comments: 'Henchard was constructed upon too large a scale' (*Mayor of Casterbridge*, Ch. 26). And, after he has departed on Newson's return: 'Externally there was nothing to hinder his making another start on the upward slope, and by his new lights achieving higher things than his soul in its half-formed state had been able to accomplish. But the ingenious machinery contrived by the Gods for reducing human possibilities of amelioration to a minimum . . . stood in the way of all that' (Ch. 44). Henchard 'did not sufficiently value himself' to try and explain his actions to Elizabeth-Jane (ibid.).

Certainly, there are inconsistencies. But far from trying to explain them away, Hardy seems to affirm them. That's how I understand his sentence in his autobiography: 'it is not improbabilities of incident but improbabilities of character that matter'.[4] Does 'matter' here mean that they are wrong because inexplicable, or that they are important and valid? I think the latter. Man, Hardy seems to say, is not a logical entity, not a rational one. He is, when truly alive, full of contradictions, always good for surprises to others and to himself.

A writer's approach to the creation of character can hardly be separated from his own understanding of man and the world. In a good number of Hardy's major novels an overbalance of dark tones, of sombre hues seems to prevail, and these are closely linked to the fate of the protagonist. This has been interpreted as being symptomatic of Hardy's own mind, at least at the time of writing. Some of Hardy's own comments may support this assumption. When writing about Eustacia in *The Return of the Native*, Hardy says: 'we see [her] . . . arriving at that stage of enlightenment which feels that nothing is worth while' (Bk 1, Ch. 7); and in the same novel we read about Clym Yeobright: 'He had reached the stage in a young man's life when the grimness of the general human situation first becomes clear; and the realization of this causes ambition to halt awhile. In France it is not uncustomary to commit suicide at this stage; in England we do much better, or much worse, as the case may be' (Bk 3, Ch. 3). Tess, when asked whether she thinks we live on a splendid or on a blighted star, answers: '[on] a blighted one' (Ch. 4). And Elizabeth-Jane seems to give voice to the author when she reflects about Farfrae: 'He seemed to feel exactly as she felt about life and its surroundings – that they were a tragical rather than a comical thing; that though one could be gay on occasion, moments of gaiety were interludes, and no part of the actual drama' (*Mayor of Casterbridge*, Ch. 8). Elizabeth-Jane had been taught – here Hardy adds 'rightly or wrongly' – 'that the doubtful honour of a brief transit through a sorry world hardly called for effusiveness, even when the path was suddenly irradiated'; her youth had seemed to teach her: 'that happiness was but the occasional episode in a general drama of pain' (Ch. 45).

And yet. Thomas Hardy, it is true, was at times gloomy, depressed, unhappy, for reasons – if particular reasons there must be – which have to remain mere conjectures, as he took great pains to leave no relevant personal papers behind. Perhaps it had something to do with the reception of his novels by the critics, perhaps with his marriage. Perhaps just with Hardy being a thoughtful man. It is not necessary to know. The truth that 'the serpent hisses where the sweet birds sing' (*Tess*, Ch. 12) can hardly be refuted.

Yet there is something else as well. In the scene where Tess buries her child in unconsecrated ground she, for lack of any other container, puts her farewell bunch of wild flowers into a jar with the label 'Keelwell's Marmalade' (Ch. 14). Though this snapshot of life may seem to contain some rather macabre humour, Hardy's sense of humour is nevertheless sound and well-developed. It comes to the fore in the descriptions and conversations of secondary characters, of labourers, farmers, artisans. Examples abound. It may contain a grain of ironic salt: Bathsheba spoke 'in a tone which showed her to be that novelty among women – one who finished a thought before beginning the sentence which was to convey it' (*Far from the Madding Crowd*, Ch. 3). There is the famous beginning of that novel, setting its tone: 'When Farmer Oak smiled, the corners of his mouth spread till they were within an unimportant distance of his ears, his eyes were reduced to chinks, and diverging wrinkles appeared round them, extending upon his countenance like the rays in a rudimentary sketch of the rising sun' (Ch. 1). Think of the bull story in *Tess*, when William Dewy is chased by an aggressive bull, which he can only pacify by continuing to play on his fiddle: 'a sort of smile stole over the bull's face' (Ch. 17). Gabriel Oak and his sheep dog come to mind with the unforgettable comparison: 'His dog waited for his meals in a way so like that in which Oak waited for the girl's presence that the farmer was quite

struck with the resemblance' (*Far from the Madding Crowd*, Ch. 4).
Or remember the story of that same sheep dog, which ruined Oak
when it chased practically his whole flock of sheep over the cliff
in misinterpretation of its duties, whereupon its life was terminated
as the dog was considered 'too good a workman to live'. This is
followed by Hardy's comment which expresses, to my mind, so
very English an observation: the dog's fate was 'another instance of
the untoward fate which so often attends dogs and other
philosophers who follow out a train of reasoning to its logical
conclusion, and attempt perfectly consistent conduct in a world
made up so largely of compromise' (Ch. 5). Delightful!

For all his sombreness, his awareness of the state of the human
condition, Hardy never drags his readers down or leaves them with
a sense of the absolute vanity of human endeavour. Although, for
example, Michael Henchard's behaviour, his egotism and that grain
of ruthlessness in his character cause not a little irritation and displeasure to the reader, he is nevertheless a giant, an uncut and
uncouth rock, an echo from times immemorial. His personality and
his fate are not merely depressing. We can sympathise with him
because he overcomes his fate by finally accepting it, by accepting
the lessons it taught him. He is ready to do so because he has
eventually succeeded in dumping the remains of his own egotistical
and possessive self into the mire of his own creation. He bowed his
head to and obeyed the noble challenge that the German dramatist
and poet Friedrich von Schiller carved into the words:

> Nehmt die Gottheit auf in euren Willen
> Und sie steigt von ihrem Weltenthron.

(This comes from his ode 'Das Ideal und das Leben', and a free
paraphrase would be: 'Make the will of the Gods your own and
they will come down from their high horses.')

The feeling of awe, of compassion that is often raised in readers
by being made engaged witnesses of the fall of one of Hardy's
great characters is evidence of his art to make us identify with them;
an art that Hardy shares with the greatest writers. His gift of sensitive imagination, of making himself, as it were, at home in the minds
of his characters, of hoping, despairing, suffering, rejoicing with
them, is the root of this art. And he made us the gift of letting us
participate in it.

I should also like to draw your attention to some of Hardy's characters who appear to have grown directly out of the soil of the country he loved. They do not make a great show of themselves, prefer to remain more in the background. From Hardy's major novels I pick four: Diggory Venn and Clym Yeobright from *The Return of the Native*, Gabriel Oak from *Far from the Madding Crowd* and Elizabeth-Jane from *The Mayor of Casterbridge*.

Venn and Oak have essential qualities in common. They are patient, they are able to suspend their egos, they help others where they can without being obtrusive, and are ready to jump into the breach with all they are worth without expecting a reward. They are free from that fatal quality of selfishness which leads others into their doom and is, in Hardy's words, 'frequently the chief constituent of the passion and sometimes the only one'. Passion, in the context used, stands here for sexual urge and infatuation. Both Venn and Oak are deeply immersed in nature, in the course of the seasons, in farming and in farmers' needs. Like Egdon Heath, they are slighted and enduring. They have been slighted by the one they love, repeatedly. And they endure. Their make is of a mythological quality, yet they are bursting with humanity. And they possess the saving grace of modesty. Like Clym Yeobright, who finds contentment in being a furze-cutter, they do not want to reach beyond themselves: 'The more I see of life', says Clym, 'the more do I perceive that there is nothing particularly great in its greatest walks, and therefore nothing particularly small in mine of furze-cutting' (*Return of the Native*, Bk 4, Ch. 3).

Later, and half blind, Clym Yeobright, like Thomas Hardy himself not a dogmatic Christian, finds inner satisfaction in sharing with others the lessons that life and piety have taught him: 'He left alone creeds and systems of philosophy, finding enough and more than enough to occupy his tongue in the opinions and actions common to all good men' (Bk 6, Ch. 4). Doesn't that sound an echo of Hardy's own belief?

Last, but perhaps most important, the message which Hardy conveys through Elizabeth-Jane. Through what she found to be most valuable in the end, which breathes not resignation, but serene contentment. She, too, is ready to share, unobtrusively, her secret with others:

the finer movements of her nature found scope in discovering to the narrow-lived ones around her the secret (as she once had learnt it) of making limited opportunities endurable; which she deemed to consist in the cunning enlargement, by a species of microscopic treatment, of those minute forms of satisfaction that offer themselves to everybody not in positive pain; which, thus handled, have much of the same inspiriting effect upon life as wider interests cursorily embraced.   (*The Mayor of Casterbridge*, Ch. 45)

Sometimes Hardy needs to be bitten into; he is never smooth, never easy, but the reward of perseverance is high. By his perceptive and perceptible love of people, by his sympathetic, unreserved participation in their joys as well as in their sufferings, Hardy makes us forget whatever may have struck us, initially and perfunctorily, as 'far'.

Personally I admit that I found and find, in addition to what I have discussed, great pleasure in some of Hardy's contemplations and observations which, to my mind, may well deserve the name of wisdoms. I pick up one that refers to Michael Henchard but has certainly a wider application: 'There are men whose hearts insist upon a dogged fidelity to some image or cause thrown by chance into their keeping, long after their judgment has pronounced it no rarity – even the reverse' (*Mayor of Casterbridge*, Ch. 42). And this one, from the many that would deserve to be quoted: 'Of love it may be said, the less earthly the less demonstrative. In its absolutely indestructible form it reaches a profundity in which all exhibition of itself is painful' (*Return of the Native*, Bk 3, Ch. 3). Though this was written in reference to Mrs Yeobright, I've been wondering whether Hardy did not have his own mother in mind, as well.

Hardy can give us a wealth of thought and enjoyment, a wealth of secondary experience – a not always adequate term, as to some of us the so-called secondary experience may well be more pertinent, more piercing, moving and enlightening than the so-called first. I don't think that we, as book addicts, make a great deal of difference here anyway. Hardy can make us forget that his characters are creations of the mind. Although their language and a portion of their attitudes are no longer ours, they are wonderfully alive and continue being alive when the book is on the shelf. They have become friends and we are sorry to have them leave us.

When one has seen through some idiosyncrasies, such as his fondness for footnotes and for references, his display of erudition, his occasional predilection for complex, not to say complicated, sentences (proof of his painstaking effort to find the 'mot juste', the exactly suitable formulation and expression); when one has recognised the relativity of the furnishings of his characters with attitudes and opinions which to us appear out-dated; then we are free to see that Hardy is not a writer of the past about the past but of all times, and so of ours. As to his so-called regionality, Hardy found the best retort himself: 'domestic emotions have throbbed in Wessex nooks with as much intensity as in the palaces of Europe'. His 'delineations of humanity' breathe truth; they are universal.[5]

Strange as it may seem today, for reasons of narrow-mindedness Hardy was – in his own time and even afterwards – not always as much appreciated as he is in ours. He was deeply hurt by the criticism directed against him and some of his novels – especially against *Tess of the d'Urbervilles* and *Jude the Obscure*, which made him discontinue writing novels altogether.

He knew that the bigotry and prudery of his time would continue to curtail his literary freedom. But he was grateful to those who stood by him, who understood and appreciated him, and he wanted to thank them. In his Preface to the Fifth Edition of *Tess of the d'Urbervilles* he gave vent to this particular desire in terms which, to my mind, afford us a glimpse into the heart of a great writer, who had tasted, together with the joy, also the bitterness of life, like many of us:

> My regret is that, in a world where one so often hungers in vain for friendship, where even not to be wilfully misunderstood is felt as a kindness, I shall never meet in person these appreciative readers, male and female, and shake them by the hand.

Perhaps we are not unjustified in supposing that we might have been amongst those whose hand he would have shaken.

Notes

Quotations from Hardy's novels are taken from the New Wessex Edition (London: Macmillan, 1974–6). Chapter references are given in parenthesis following quotations.

1. C. H. Sisson, 'Introduction' to Penguin English Library edition of *Jude the Obscure* (Harmondsworth: Penguin Books, 1978) p. 26.
2. 'General Preface to the Novels and Poems', in Macmillan's Wessex Edition (London: Macmillan, 1912).

3. 'The Dorsetshire Labourer', *Longman's Magazine*, vol. 2, 1883. Reprinted in Harold Orel (ed.), *Thomas Hardy's Personal Writings* (Lawrence: University of Kansas Press, 1966; London: Macmillan, 1967) p. 181.
4. *The Life and Work of Thomas Hardy, by Thomas Hardy*, ed. Michael Millgate (London: Macmillan, 1984) p. 183. Hardy is specifically referring to *The Mayor of Casterbridge*.
5. 'General Preface to the Novels and Poems', in Macmillan's Wessex Edition (London: Macmillan, 1912).

11

Hardy, *The Hand of Ethelberta,* and Some Persisting English Discomforts

EDWARD BLISHEN

After I had accepted the invitation to write this paper, I kept forgetting why it had been said that it might make sense for me to do so. I found myself thinking instead of the reason why it didn't make sense: that is, that I am not a Hardy scholar. And it doesn't help that the best words I can think of for such scholarship as I have – that it always resolves itself into a confused heap of impressions – were the words used by Hardy to describe his fiction. I am simply, like many others, someone who has read Hardy most of his life: and of whose outlook, and way of seeing things, and way of attempting to say things, Hardy is a part. But when I say that, I suddenly remember the argument that was offered for my writing: which was that an unremitting, relentless reader, who has thought much and over many years about what he has read, might have something to offer as that sort of person: as someone who owes part of what he is to Hardy: a reader under the influence.

I have been struck, when I have mentioned that I was writing this paper, by the number of friends and acquaintances who have said, in the quick way you do, responding to a name, that they recoil from Hardy a little, from the sense of him as a gloomy man living in a gloomy house among wives made gloomy: his knotted secrecy is something they shrink from. And I am surprised by how actually hurt I am by such responses, partly because I cannot think of any writer to whom I am more grateful, but partly because the gloom is such a rich gloom, because the secret man was so marvellously and deviously and intricately open, and in such important ways demonstrated the indispensable difficulty of being truly open: the paradox that to be secret is common but that to be secret *and* open is not. As Martin Seymour-Smith splendidly put it in his eccentric recent biography: 'for all his natural reticence, he could not live without candour'.[1] And I am hurt because by any judgement he wrote some of the best novels and some of the most beautiful poems in the language, and I am also particularly hurt by these responses because I cannot think of any writer who was from the beginning more hobbled, presented with more handicaps. You may remember a note of his, written when he was 30: 'It is, in a worldly sense, a matter for regret that a child who has to win a living should be born of a noble nature. Social greatness requires littleness to inflate & float it, & a high soul may bring a man to the work-house.'[2] He had a high soul when the social verdict was that he shouldn't have had one, and when his own verdict, expressed in that note, was that it might have made better sense for him to have been without one.

Well: in short, Hardy is to me a hero. His life and work were about as hardwon as could be. He is wonderfully impossible to get to the bottom of. There were some things he said in that hard-fought-for language of his that, if they had been all he had ever said, would have made him memorable: 'An object or mark raised or made by man on a scene is worth ten times any such formed by unconscious Nature. Hence clouds, mists, and mountains are unimportant beside the wear on a threshold, or the print of a hand.' It might be some old Greek fragment. 'The most prosaic man becomes a poem when you stand by his grave at his funeral & think of him.'[3] As to that last, I have always been haunted by the thought that no human being is unremarkable, and that most come and go with no attempt made to paint even the simplest portrait of what they were: and I know no writer who is more exercised by pity than Hardy is for this general doom of anonymity and inattention, or who is more likely to incline us by his own feeling for this fate to make something of our memories of those we have known: simply to make something of memory.

Anyway, I hope that a confused impressionist might have something to offer, and in fact my saying 'yes' to the invitation did rest on something besides the strange dangerous delight of the idea of being licensed to write about Hardy. I knew at once there was something I had longed to say, longed to sort out in my own mind, longed to make if I could some sort of pattern of: and that it arose partly out of the circumstances in which I first encountered Hardy, over a period of four or five years, something like sixty years ago: I having fallen under the spell of his *face* round about 1932. I hope that this account of how an English child came to read Hardy nearly a century after Hardy's birth, the mishaps and especially the intensities of his reading, might be of value as a very tiny part of the everlasting labour of attempting to say what Hardy is, and of taking grateful measure of him.

I was at a grammar school: I was a first generation grammar school boy. I had never loved anything more than reading and attempting to write. I first met Hardy by way of *Under the Greenwood Tree*, which was a classroom text during a period when we were miserably mistaught English and Latin by a man called Judson, whom we called Judy. He had no intention, I am sure, of misteaching us, and I look back at him with great sympathy, as a man who should out of common kindness have been prevented from becoming a teacher. In an ideal state such acts of prevention would be built into the system. He was disqualified by being very deaf, and by really wishing to perfect a pamphlet which at last came out during his retirement, a pamphlet on the Lesser Clergy of Bradford during a period in the seventeenth century: and he was disqualified by being simply an honest boring man, with one of the driest minds I have ever encountered. The dryness of his mind had fed back into his whole being: he was utterly dry. He was Hardy's 'most prosaic man'. Had he taught us Boredom we would all have passed brilliantly. You could always slightly brighten a Latin lesson by asking him to give an account of the *pilum*, the Roman throwing spear. For some reason, perhaps for the very reason why we invited him to do it, he never tired of describing the *pilum*, and drawing it on the board. It was his one excitement, as it became ours. When it came to English we spent most of our time in the boiler-room of language, among the parts of speech, bolting and unbolting them, stoking and shovelling: assembling a sentence only instantly, almost guiltily, to break it up again.

And there was *Under the Greenwood Tree*. This he made us read round the class – that perfect method of making any book whatever intolerable. To the fact that we were dismal untrained readers was added the further misery (as it was to me) that my classmates enjoyed turning over two pages instead of one, four if it could be managed instead of two: Judy seemed to be without any normal sense of having lost his place in a narrative: and he clearly regarded a novel, anyway, as an essay in foolish invention justified only by

footnotes. I think he may have been following the pages of notes at
the end, and never the text, so that the great gaps in the tale were
not quite evident to him. There was a portrait of Hardy at the
beginning of the book, that melancholy, rapt, remarkable, small,
secret face, surely one of the most mysterious faces any writer ever
had: and I seemed to know from it two things about him – that he
would have winced of course from this treatment of his text, and
that at the same time he would have been amused. The man who
on the basis of his intense noticing of people invented Robert Penny
and Thomas Leaf would have seen the comedy in there being a
Judy, who, poor man, could never come to terms with that to others
obvious effect of his great deafness – that he could not make out
what was bawled at him – and in there being a W. E. Jones: he
was the ringleader of those classmates of mine whose attitude
towards the text was that of literary terrorists; reading a critic or two
since, I have thought of them. And of course he would have seen
the comedy in this other boy, already drawn so deeply into his
world, and so anxious to have *Under the Greenwood Tree* taken
seriously. Among my friends I remember being infamous for liking
the descriptive passages in fiction: I loved being held up by a
landscape or a seascape or a building or a sunrise; in this novel of
Hardy's you were not even held up by such things: they seemed
to me curiously a means of increasing the pace of the narrative. You
could not peel apart the people and the world they lived in. It was
my first experience of that sort of intense, rapt integrity in a piece
of fiction. I had of course the involuntary incompetence of a thirteen-
year-old reader. I identified with Dick Dewy, I adored and had my
heartstrings torn by Fancy Day, I took it that it was only too probable that so desirable a young woman would be tempted to betray
me – oh, Dick Dewy – in favour of a parson or a farmer: my own
world was full of persons one could expect a young woman to
prefer to oneself: I lived at the lower-middle-class semi-detached
bottom of a road the rest of which was full of large middle-class
residences: I knew what it was to be one of the world's Dick Dewys,
doubtfully able to hold his own among gentlemen. Our headmaster
addressed us all as gentlemen: he was hoping by doing so to push
a few of us further up the road, to a larger house: or to a greater
expectation that Fancy Day might turn to us despite our semi-
detachedness. Well, I was *inside* the novel, as a child eager I guess
for erotic torment, and, inevitably – a scholarship boy, at the wrong
end of most of life's roads – as a child with a sense of formidable

social unease. I thought I would never again read anything that enchanted and hurt me so much as when they went nutting. And somehow I thought of Dick as someone whose torment might not be at an end at the end of the book. I fed my own distrust into him.

In due course I read *The Trumpet-Major*, taking it from the library shelves; in the résumé of the year 1934 in the ponderous diary I kept at the time, I put it in the first place among the books read in the last half-year. It triumphed over *The Poor Gentleman* by Ian Hay and *Mr Perrin and Mr Traill* by Hugh Walpole. I explained my liking it far more than these others. 'The *Trumpet-Major* owes its place', I wrote, 'to that peculiarly homely feeling that Hardy always imparts.' I think that was an attempt to describe this sense Hardy's writings gave me that I was gathered into the story. Then I wrote: 'I like to forget his particular creed and read lightly.'

Well, what did I know about his 'particular creed'? I had read, I guess, about his pessimism. How odd it is to look back on oneself as a child, and to attempt to shake out what was truly felt from what the child was able to say. I know, at that moment – I was fourteen, within the next year my handwriting would dwindle in size from day to day, all manner of secrecy and complexity would beset it – I know at that moment I was on the eve of being assailed by the idea, the idea that there were ideas, by the idea of there being philosophies – and I remember how similar to the gulf that stretched, for instance, between the headmaster's insistence that we were gentlemen and our blunt knowledge that we were not, and between a blandness there was at the top of our road that came from being at the top of the road, and an abrasive discomfort there was at the bottom of our road, that came from being at the bottom of the road – how of that order of desperately important distinctions was the distinction between having a comfortable and having an uncomfortable head: between being – soon a few of us were earnestly using the terms – more or less optimistic, and being more or less pessimistic. And very quickly it was clear that this was no matter of gentle, tolerated preference where one might without any notion of disgrace be one or the other.

About this time I had the ill-luck to be included in a sort of general studies class run by the headmaster. I think we were supposed to be studying the Great Civilisations: but what we chiefly studied, or were battered by, were the headmaster's opinions on almost everything, a general context of great civilisations being taken to justify perfectly his, I have to say, noisy soliloquies. He warned us off the Russians: 'Always, gentlemen, examining their own rather unlovely insides'. He warned us against Shelley: 'Tuppenny ha'penny blackguard, bolshevising his way across the face of the earth'. (These are verbatim quotes: I was already a committed spy.) And he warned us again and again against Hardy. There was another similar offender, A. E. Housman, but his crimes seemed pale beside those laid at Hardy's door. Hardy was that immensely easy thing to be: a pessimist. Being a pessimist was rooted in a despicable refusal to put one's shoulder to the wheel. You moved away, a shirker, covering your absence of guts (our headmaster's word), with words and concepts drawn from foreign brands of philosophy. If I had not already been deeply committed to Hardy, I would have been bound to become – as I thought of it – a confederate of his in simple reaction to the headmaster's assault on him. Thomas Hardy, in this grammar school in the 1930s, was an outlawed person, and to be found to read and admire him was worse even than that other great misdemeanour, of being caught playing association rather than rugby football: 'The wrong-shaped ball', said the headmaster on one infamous occasion. I remember once, when I had written a determinedly miserable essay for him, he said: 'Blishen – too much Hardy, too much Hardy, too much Hardy!' (He made almost everything he said even worse by saying it three times.) If you were drawn to Hardy, it was a sort of declaration that you were choosing to stand aside, to throw up your hands, to mock honest faith, to take no part in the great struggle to become a gentleman. You were electing, our headmaster implied, to be without a backbone. I felt with an incoherent fury then, I feel with a coherent fury now, how unacceptable that was as an implied statement about the man with the small secret face: who may, as a recent biographer has suggested, have found gloom congenial, but who looked unflinchingly at the worst of things and made marvels out of doing so.

An interesting fact of our cultural history, I believe: that it was possible then, and remains possible now, to present Hardy (and in this case, in a grammar school, much of its time given to literature) not as a great writer, but as some sort of subversive.

Now, what happened next might seem rather odd. The novel of Hardy's that I went on to read was *The Hand of Ethelberta*. I am fairly clear why this was the book I chose from the row of Hardys in our local library. Growing up in an unbookish home, I was greatly dependent on libraries: and on such collections of books as I came across in the houses of relatives, most of whom, though themselves unbookish, seemed to have somewhere a shelf or a box of books, wonderfully miscellaneous and generally inexplicable: I still have my barely literate grandmother's copy of *England As It Is, Political, Social and Industrial, in the Middle of the Nineteenth Century*, by William Johnston, Esq., Barrister-at-Law, published by John Murray when Hardy was eleven years old, and originally part of the library of A. M. Forbes at Ahmedabad. And there were secondhand bookshops that had penny and tuppenny shelves. For a time at ten, eleven, twelve, I was grateful to draw upon a tiny library that was part of a Sunday School I belonged to, and that was confined to a cupboard unlocked for favourites by the Sunday School superintendent, who stood at the borrower's elbow until the flustered choice had been made, and then locked the cupboard again. For some time I thought it was the fate of books to be locked up. Our town library had not notably caught up with the twentieth century: and the effect of all this was that I read an immense number of run-of-the-mill Victorian novels. *The Hand of Ethelberta* must have seemed to me the almost archetypal title of the kind of book I was most at home with. I can easily imagine myself choosing it. It would be full of bombazine and bustles, and there might be a man decorously dressed but having laid aside his jacket who was burying a body, not improbably that of his wife, in a cellar.[4]

And I remember the astonishment of reading *The Hand of Ethelberta*. I did not know of course that it was among the books Virginia Woolf had in mind when she said it was 'seldom, and always with unhappy results, that Hardy [left] the yeoman or farmer to describe the class above theirs in the social scale'.[5] The essence of what at fourteen I made of *The Hand of Ethelberta* I can fairly claim to recall with some accuracy. I was bothered, of course, that Ethelberta, with whom I fell in love within two pages, was the least straightforward heroine, indeed, the only perverse heroine, I had as yet encountered: I wanted her to be sensible and, since she patently loved Christopher Julian, to succumb to what I thought to be the logic of such a situation: perhaps, indeed, after inflicting interesting miseries upon them both – and all those secondhand and library books had convinced me that amorous misery was an indispensable step towards amorous bliss – she should consent to marry him. I made nothing much of her sister Picotee, who you remember does marry Julian, never having imagined that in these matters there might be a reserve, A. N. Other, who would do, instead of the heroine, what I thought heroines inflexibly did. I wrung my young hands over Ethelberta's decision to marry the, as I thought, wholly abominable Lord Mountclere. I was inside this book with the typical title that turned out not to be a typical book at all, but a book that turned my typical expectations upside down. I was at once dismayed and, I must say, rather *proudly* aware that I had moved . . . I had taken a rather large step, forward: I had become, in some curious fashion, adult: being adult lying exactly in the fact that expectations were overturned. In some way I grew up, made *that* step, saw that life was much more complicated and perverse than I had believed; in a couple of days I felt life grow ten times as dense as it had been, in reading this often despised novel of Thomas Hardy's.

But it's not exactly *that*, important experience though it was to me, that most moved me when I read, for the first time, *The Hand of Ethelberta*. What actually struck me, imprecisely, of course, in a blurred way, in a way I could not make too much of then, was that the novel was about being the lower-middle-class semi-detached creature who was being urged to take the first steps towards feigning to be a middle-class detached creature living at the top, and not at the bottom, of a road. I jump a little here and say, as I hope to say more gracefully in a moment, that of course I recognise that in writing *The Hand of Ethelberta* Hardy was not doing what he did best: but I have to say I know few texts that confront that sort of social cruelty, and absurdity, more interestingly, more knottedly, in some odd sense, more brazenly – with a more awkward and painful boldness, than *The Hand of Ethelberta*. Hardy never did anything easily. I am angry sometimes when there is talk of his use of language being clumsy, not the handling of a born master of it, when as it seems to me the problems Hardy had with language – problems that he usually set himself – were all directed towards making easy statement impossible. There *was* the problem that, like Tess, he had two disparate tongues: that he was deeply at ease in one – oh that moment in *The Hand of Ethelberta* when Ethelberta's sister Cornelia says of her new bonnet, deplored by Ethelberta as untownlike: 'If there's one thing I do glory in it is a nice flare-up about my head o' Sundays'[6] – and that he had to *climb* into the other language: but it seems to me the most foolish failure of understanding to hold that, after a certain point in his development as a writer, Hardy was daunted by the business of using words. He said of the reception of *Wessex Poems* that there was the usual 'ascription to ignorance of what was really choice after full knowledge'.[7] He knew what he was doing. Point anywhere in Hardy to an easy sentence such as an orthodox fluent writer might produce out of his orthodox fluency! I am angry also at times when *The Hand of Ethelberta* is easily disparaged. Of course it is not *Far from the Madding Crowd*, of course it is not *Tess of the d'Urbervilles*; it is not *The Mayor of Casterbridge*. But it is also not any commonplace novel you can think of, concerned with what it is concerned with: questions of candour and concealment, of kinds of fiction, of the attempt to be happy or fruitful in the midst of social arrangements designed to produce unhappiness or sterility.

You will understand, I know, that in speaking of my responses to *The Hand of Ethelberta*, I am not making any ridiculous claims for the child I was, for his percipience or anything of the sort: but I do find it remarkable that this unlikely and not in the least straight-forward novel should have gone home so directly to a callow reader who recognised in it, understanding without understanding, the essence of his own situation, of a persisting English situation: of the tormented difficulty of being rooted in one social world and being required to grow up into another.

I did not go back to *The Hand of Ethelberta* until about ten years ago, when I read it rather hastily in a rare gap between obligatory kinds of reading, and found myself impatient with it. 'Well,' I thought, 'here is Hardy trying to do what it is not in his gift to do.' I was of Michael Millgate's mind: that it seems 'to have been written without any intense creative engagement, and it certainly lacks that dense texture of personal experience which toughens all of Hardy's major fiction'.[8] It was a novel untoughened. I have notes I made at the time of this second reading. I thought you could tell the absence of conviction by the failure of images: Ethelberta is described as 'a plump-armed creature, with a white round neck as firm as a fort' – which made me think of a Martello tower (Ch. 4). That would-be lover of Ethelberta's, Ladywell, by name and char-acterisation, is plucked straight out of Restoration comedy, and not reclothed for this later epoch: and when Christopher Julian says of Ladywell that he is 'that perfumed piece of a man . . . with the high eyebrows arched like a girl's' (Ch. 4), I had no faith in the possibility of his having used those words, which I thought came from literature, not life. I felt the novel took on a solidity, later, a kind of confidence even, an alteration of quality difficult to explain. I loved the account of the abortive journey of Ethelberta's brother Sol and the brother of Lord Mountclere – both intent for different reasons on preventing Ethelberta's marriage to Mountclere, and described splendidly by Hardy as sitting 'in a rigid reticence that was almost a third personality' (Ch. 44) – that abortive journey into Swanage Bay: because Hardy is marvellous always about the sea: 'They retreated further up the beach [these were spectators of the struggles of the steamer Sol and Mountclere's brother were aboard, the *Spruce*], when the hissing fleece of froth slid again down the shingle, dragging the pebbles under it with a rattle as of a beast gnawing bones.' And when the *Spruce* has given up the struggle: 'The bay became nothing but a voice, the foam an occasional touch upon the face, the *Spruce* an imagination, the pier a memory' (Ch. 43). But I put the book down (hastily, as I had taken it up), disappointed. Was this the novel that I had this odd sense of having grown up on, fifty years earlier?

I don't suppose this is the place to discuss the subjective nature of almost every reading of almost every book: and the sense one has of the especially subjective character of one's reading of particular books. I think *The Hand of Ethelberta* is an eminent example of a book it is very difficult to be certain about. For the purpose of this paper, because I wanted in it to look again at, and come to conclusions about, that early reading, that invasion of an English child's life by a profound Englishman, I have read it again and re-read it: and each reading strengthens my admiration of it. Well, of course it isn't those other books: and of course it hasn't that 'intense creative engagement' that lay behind *The Woodlanders*, say, so that you know that every nerve of the writer, every atom of himself, is involved: he is creating an amazement: everything in the novel grows from everything else in the novel. The bloom is marvellous: you know the soil was right, the weather was right, the husbandry was right. But I think it has intense creative engagement of another sort. Remember what Hardy said about it, or allowed to be said about it, in the *Life*: 'It was, in fact, thirty years too soon for a Comedy of Society of that kind.' It had nothing whatever in common with anything he had written before, and gave him the satisfaction of proving, 'amid the general disappointment at the lack of sheep and shepherds, that he did not mean to imitate anybody'.[9] He did not mean to write for ever about sheep. It's a bit as if, at some relevant moment, Shakespeare had declared gruffly that you needn't look to him for an everlasting sequence of kings. Hardy was cross. He was cross, I believe, partly because he was thought to be attempting to ride in George Eliot's slipstream – oh, the fury of being thought to do that! – and partly because he knew that he had other things in him besides those that drew him to the writing of marvels. Think of all that incidental activity of Hardy's: those notebooks, those aphorisms! He had, alongside supreme gifts for tragedy and comedy, the gifts and habits of a deeply-thinking man, an awkwardly deeply-thinking man, a relentless observer of all the worlds he moved in. In the *Life* he arranges for it to be said that 'he took no interest in manners, but in the substance of life only'.[10] This perfectly describes what we ideally think about him: but I suggest it is not absolutely true. He spent much time, very much of his life, in a world the substance of which you had to approach through an examination of manners: and though I believe there is a sense in which Hardy made the suitable gestures which manners required, without ever being wholly involved (because he was, after all, one of the world's great deep celebrators of the substance of life), nevertheless I think there was this part of Hardy that, out of sheer natural talent, knew it could make something of the world of manners (as the best strangenesses in *The Hand of Ethelberta* would do), with the world of substance: and that, in short, *The Hand of Ethelberta* is – not a mistaken step in the career of a great writer, no stumble, but an expression to be valued for its own sake of this other Hardy coiled inside the marvellous Hardy. I dare to think that he might have been glad that this was said.

And I would like to add something else that springs from my sense of being, in an immensely minor way, of course, someone who has been in something like his position, knowing in my bones what it is like to enter . . . the cultivated world from the uncultivated world. 'But alas . . . The wretched homeliness of Gwendoline's mind', Ethelberta thinks, having talked to a beloved sister (Ch. 23); talking to a beloved mother, she says: ' "O mother, don't!" '– 'tenderly, but with her teeth on edge' (Ch. 15). Hardy at home must have had his teeth on edge again and again. Remember also the discomforts between Stephen Smith and his parents in *A Pair of Blue Eyes*. He was the 'clever lad'. It 'read like some clever lad's dream', said John Morley of *The Poor Man and the Lady*:[11] and I imagine easily how that term 'clever lad' must have hurt Hardy. I remember, as many must, being a 'clever lad' in an unsophisticated setting: my parents half-proud and half-appalled. My uncles, and I had an operatic chorus of uncles, coarse mocking men whom when I was small I loved deeply, who made of my being alleged to have brains a family joke, of which I was uncomfortably gratified to be the target: I was a cause of one of their jokes, a great thing to be:

they spoke of having brains as a disability, a reason why one could not expect to be much liked or trusted, a constitutional weakness: one ought to wrap up, step carefully, avoid manly exertion. They were townees, of course, Londoners: and in *The Hand of Ethelberta* Hardy comments on what he calls 'the usual law by which the emotion that takes the form of humour in country workmen becomes transmuted to irony among the same order in town' (Ch. 26). (Notice, by the way, how much is packed into that: 'the *emotion* that takes the form of humour' – clumsily roundabout, some would say, but how in fact it invites us to look behind the idea that humour might be some self-igniting instant quality in us instead of the form taken by an emotion.) My London uncles – glazier, stallholder, van driver and others – were enormously ironical about any in their midst who had some touch of the clerk about them.

And there was another angle of irony involved for Hardy, the 'clever lad', I am sure: I believe there is a reflection of that in the scene where Ethelberta finds herself among the members of Lord Mountclere's archaeological group. It's a scene in which Ethelberta is actually set free, for a moment, from the anxieties of her situation: an oddly charming scene: as a celebrated person, and a woman, she who is appallingly tethered seems, for that hour, to be quite untethered. She is enlisted in a sort of numinous group of women who, says Hardy, had a charter to move abroad unchaperoned: 'the famous, the ministering, and the improper'. And in the idle benignity of the occasion these ladies and gentlemen look upon her tenderly: and by way of what Hardy calls 'a pleasant whim', their spirits are felt to be brisk enough 'to swerve from strict attention to the select and sequent gifts of heaven, blood and acres, to consider for an idle moment the subversive Mephistophelian endowment, brains' (Ch. 31). The cruel weight of the usual disapproval of cleverness is in that phrase: the disapproval, it is clear, might come from any point of the social compass. That face of Hardy's: such an unconcealably clever face, too. Clever is a word designed to cause discomfort. For the English it has always been close to such words as cunning, crafty, untrustworthy.

Oh, all these forms of hurt! There are moments in the novel when Hardy, I think, bares his teeth; there are ferocities: as when he writes of Mountclere and Ethelberta – 'the viscount busying himself round and round her person like the head scraper at a pig-killing' (Ch. 31). Well, ferocities! I often think of that story Emma told Hardy five months after they met, and he recorded in a notebook:

E's story of Miss R., the aristocratic old lady in Cornwall whom she knows. When she, Miss R., had fallen down in the street she was approached by some workmen to pick her up. 'How dare you think of touching me!' she exclaimed from the surface of the road. 'I am the Honourable Miss —' And she would not be helped to rise.[12]

Behind that small secret face – the memory of humiliations, actual or always possible, and the responding ferocities! 'The viscount', or 'the man', he calls Mountclere: in Rouen, 'the fascinated man, screaming inwardly with the excitement, glee, and agony of his position' (Ch. 34). It isn't that he does not know enough about viscounts to write temperately of them: it is that he does not want to write temperately about them.

And always, that sense of having fallen irrevocably out of the nest. Ethelberta thinks: 'It was that old sense of disloyalty to her class and kin by feeling as she felt now which caused the pain, and there was no escaping it. Gwendoline would have gone to the ends of the earth for her: she could not confide a thought to Gwendoline!' (Ch. 23). She felt 'a gloom as of banishment' (Ch. 13). At one moment she reflects: 'I wish I could get a living by some simple humble occupation, and drop the name of Petherwin, and be Berta Chickerel again, and live in a green cottage as we used to do when I was small' (Ch. 28). I suspect it was following some sudden need to have it said by *someone* that Hardy put into the mouth of Christopher Julian, who had no special reason to say it, the statement that: 'The only feeling which has any dignity or permanence or worth is family affection between close blood-relations' (Ch. 21). What agonies by way of swings of feeling this poet and storyteller must have suffered! Perhaps one of the reasons for the ultimate unsatisfactoriness of *The Hand of Ethelberta* as a novel, its failure to become a self-discovering whole, but a reason for (as I think) its great value as something else . . . a document? (a document that offers far more fun than documents usually do), is that things pressing to be said out of Hardy's own predicament as he moves through his thirties get said in it in a sometimes desperately haphazard way. This is a novel I believe with items from some of those carefully destroyed notebooks embedded in it. 'A story-teller seems such an impossible castle-in-the-air sort of a trade for getting a living by' (Ch. 23). Who can doubt that that is Hardy, waking in the night in 1875, horrified as one easily may be in the night. How, he asks himself, as Ethelberta asked herself, can he solve his agonising social problems, which are the problems of his life, by way of such an evanescence, such a transparently vulnerable and unreliable trade, as that of storyteller? Especially when the intentions of this storyteller have little that is banal about them: especially when the storyteller is moved in his storytelling to make what way he can against 'the inert crystallized opinion – hard as a rock – which the vast body of men have vested interests in supporting'.[13] And again, a cry in the night (I think): 'that complete divorce between thinking and saying which is the hallmark of high civilization' (Ch. 27).

That is said . . . is cried out, rather . . . of the practice of a society couple of Ethelberta's acquaintance: they have no habit of pressing what they feel or think to the point of utterance; rather, whatever they actually think or feel is, for its being actual, forbidden expression. I believe, I must say, after my latest readings of the novel, that *The Hand of Ethelberta* says more about Hardy in London than any other document: certainly, far more, in terms of the truth of it, than the *Life* ever does. I have never been quite able to imagine convincedly his London existence. He was much there, we know, and all those accounts of dining here and dining there in the *Life* are not included for the irony of it. My own guess is that the clever lad from the country was always a little dazzled to be among 'the cool men and celebrated club yawners', as he calls them in *The Hand of Ethelberta* (Ch. 9) – and I think one must notice that these terms do cover the cultured fellows, the Ladywells and the Neighs, as well as the aristocratic emptyheads. I suspect that when he allowed them to be listed in the *Life* he satisfied one strand of himself: I perfectly see that, great tragedian though he was, the clever lad who made rather more than good never lost his satisfaction at being accepted in those circles; but there was this other greater man in him, and I would guess that some element of self-disgust at his own pleasure in being a fully accepted part of the London world might have helped to create that private gloom, and might have contributed to the secrecy of that face. There is talk of him, that always astonishes me, in terms of Hardy being, or not being, a snob. Those who think it's snobbery that is involved should read *The Hand of Ethelberta*. It's a game that is involved, a heroic game: the storyteller with his essential concern for the substance of life, a man able to take his place in the great succession of artists throughout history, had to win a simple game of acceptance or rejection. It interests me that he tried out, as I think, in his imagining of Ethelberta's fate, a particular cool solution of the game. When Ethelberta enters Enckworth Court, Lord Mountclere's home, for the first time, she declares that the mysteriously sustained staircase that rises out of the entrance hall is in itself worth marrying the man for. But then it becomes clear that she counts his library, the command and use of his library, as the superior gain. And sitting in that, making use of that, she is said to have begun an epic poem: this being about the time, the time of the writing of this novel, that Hardy made the first known reference to the possibility that one day he might produce such a poem. I will fight a duel with anybody who sees nothing of Hardy in Ethelberta. If it is asked why he did not do what was natural to him, and explore her destiny in tragic terms, I believe the answer is that he was interested in her as a valiant gameswoman, the creation of a gallant gamesman.

Yes, Hardy in London! There are exchanges, in this novel, of simply smart remarks – sound bites they would now be called – and I do not think Hardy was ever, in his London years, aloof from these. I think he could turn a cynical phrase like any of those in *The Hand of Ethelberta*: 'The one almost cynical comedy'– you remember D. H. Lawrence's comment.[14] In fact, I don't think *The Hand of Ethelberta* is, in the end, cynical: but I think it grapples with the fact of the everyday cynicism Hardy encountered. There is a moment when a countryman discovers that Christopher Julian cannot tell an oak from an elm. I have an Austrian friend who when she stumbles across such, as she thinks, incapacitating ignorance, says the offender doesn't know where God lives; this anonymous countryman thinks Julian doesn't know where God lives: and behind Hardy's cultivation of drawing-room manners, clubroom manners, must have lain a very strong charge of such scorn. It would give great edge to his mimicry of fashionable cynicism or shallowness, or display of that complete divorce between thinking and saying that was the hallmark of high civilisation.

There's so much more that I want to say about *The Hand of Ethelberta*, but I must exercise economy. I want to say for example how oddly Shavian parts of the novel are. There were only sixteen years between the man from Dorset and the man from Dublin who helped to carry him into Westminster Abbey. They were, of course, wildly different literary persons, but I think there was a curiously strong shadow of Shaw in Hardy. There are exchanges out of a sort of ur-Shaw comedy in *The Hand of Ethelberta*. This is Chickerel addressing his daughter: 'getting on *a little* has this good in it, you

still keep in your old class where your feelings are, and are thought-
fully treated by this class: while by getting on *too much* you are
sneered at by your new acquaintance, who don't know the skill of
your rise, and you are parted from and forgot by the old ones who
do. Whatever happens, don't be too quick to feel. You will surely get
some hard blows when you are found out, for if the great can find
no excuse for hitting with a mind, they'll do it and say 'twas in fun'
(Ch. 7). Mr Chickerel, challenged by his employer when the news
is out that he is Ethelberta's, now Lady Mountclere's, father: ' "Do
you mean to say that the lady who sat here at dinner at the same
time that Lord Mountclere was present, is your daughter?" asked
Doncastle. "Yes, sir," said Chickerel respectfully. "How did she come
to be your daughter?" "I – Well, she is my daughter, sir" ' (Ch. 42).
Read it as a Shavian exchange, and the idea that here is Hardy quite
out of his element weakens. Mrs Doncastle, pierced to the quick by
the knowledge that she helped the butler's daughter (then Mrs
Petherwin) to marry the viscount, cries out that Chickerel should
have owned up to the relationship. She meets with no sympathy
from her husband, who has a touch of Jane Austen's Mr Bennet
about him but much more of some ruthlessly rational character
out of Shaw: 'You didn't tell Mrs Petherwin that your grandfather
narrowly escaped hanging for shooting his rival in a duel.' In defeat
Mrs Doncastle turns Shavian herself: 'The times have taken a strange
turn when the angry parent of the comedy, who goes post-haste
to prevent the undutiful daughter's rash marriage, is a gentleman
from below stairs, and the unworthy lover a peer of the realm!'
(Ch. 42). There came that moment, more than thirty years on, of
course, when Hardy was to point out that the scenes in which the
butler is present at the dinner at which his child shines, scenes
pointed to as improbable and subversive, had been successfully
echoed in Shaw's play *You Never Can Tell*.[15]

Then there are the moments that remind us that, as David Lodge
has demonstrated in a splendid essay,[16] Hardy is at his most marvellous when he looks at the scene from a physically amazing angle.
After the archaeological gathering at Corvsgate Castle, Ethelberta
looks across to the edge of things and sees a line of trees being
felled to let in sky and sea, this at Mountclere's order following a
more or less idle comment of hers. Ethelberta stands at the top of
the flèche of the cathedral in Rouen, with the panting peer at her
side. These last two scenes are sometimes cited as typical grotesque
flaws in the novel, and I can only say: I don't see that. All Ethelberta's

lovers being at Rouen at once, and in Rouen because Hardy was there the year before writing it, is also mocked: and I agree it is not *The Mayor of Casterbridge*, where similar unlikelihoods are knit into a tale so consequent that no one makes much of a point of them: but I do not believe for a moment that Hardy was amateurishly miscalculating or so creatively cold that every move was clumsy: this was part of the artificiality of the artificial comedy he was writing. The 'Comedy in Chapters': what to say of his reply to Leslie Stephen, arguing against the use of this subtitle for the serial form of the novel: 'I should certainly deplore being thought to have set up in the large joke line – the genteelest of genteel comedy being as far as ever I should think it safe to go at any time.'?[17] Hardy making his way through the minefield of Victorian magazine fiction, and being memorably ironical. Imagine a Sophocles, caught up in the English class system, feeling bound to disclaim any intention of causing guffaws, but not disowning a certain tendency to smile politely. And a Sophocles who had quite a bit of Aristophanes tucked up inside him.

May I end with the boy I was. From *The Hand of Ethelberta* I moved on to the rest of Hardy. *Tess* was thrown into my lap by an Irish master of ours as he made his way towards the platform for assembly; he was required to teach us mathematics, at which he was an ass, though he quickly switched to physical education, at which he was not, but he influenced a great many of us in the matter of our reading, which the headmaster did not mean him to do. He knew how to flatter us with books, to make little conspiracies of reading, and much that he commended to us went against the grain of what the headmaster favoured. 'Keep it quiet!', he would whisper, when throwing a book into your lap: it could be any recent, or any remote, novel: at times it was D. H. Lawrence: it was several decades too late to keep *Tess* quiet but I knew what he meant. Through him I came to Hardy the poet. I could not afford to buy the *Collected Poems*, which cost a sum that still represents to me, when it comes to books, the unattainable: twenty-one shillings, or that gentlemanly amount, a guinea. I have still the copies I made of fifty or sixty of the poems, taken from our Irish master's copy. I noted much later that Hardy believed his complete poetical works should be available 'at a reasonable price so as to be within the reach of poorer readers'.[18] It was a long time before I realised that there might be a line of succession, not much spoken of, from *The Poor Man and the Lady* (what one would give to read that!) through *The*

Hand of Ethelberta to *Jude the Obscure.* I have a sense of why it is that the author of the major novels is the Hardy I came for a long time to think of as the only Hardy. I have carried with me for most of my life a reference of his that, I think, covers both the Hardys – or the many Hardys: to 'that fieldmouse fear of the coulter of destiny despite fair promise, which is common among the thoughtful who have suffered early from poverty and oppression'.[19]

Having been taught Latin by Judy, I made at my first reading nothing of the epigraph to *The Hand of Ethelberta: Vitae post-scenia celant.* 'People conceal the back-scenes of life', 'People hide what goes on backstage'. My ancient Latin dictionary, without a title-page, bought long ago on a threepenny shelf, and offering a synopsis of the Horatian metres, extracted from Dr Casey's *Latin Prosody Made Easy* – perhaps a dictionary Hardy was familiar with – proposes *Post-scenia vitae* as the self-sufficient quotation, and attributes it, not to Lucretius, but to a certain Vitruvius. It offers the translation: 'Actions hidden from the sight of the world'. The small secret face of the man who *revealed* so much in his poetry and his fiction and his jottings, and who *hid* so much. . . . No need to struggle with Latin when it comes to another quotation I cling to, from Hardy himself, in the preface to his *Select Poems of William Barnes*: 'The history of criticism is mainly the history of error.'

Notes

1. Martin Seymour-Smith, *Hardy* (London: Bloomsbury, 1994) p. 78.
2. *The Personal Notebooks of Thomas Hardy,* ed. Richard H. Taylor (London: Macmillan, 1978) p. 6 (subsequently cited as *Personal Notebooks*).
3. *The Life and Work of Thomas Hardy, by Thomas Hardy,* ed. Michael Millgate (London: Macmillan, 1984) p. 120 (subsequently cited as *Life*); *Personal Notebooks,* p. 10.
4. Some of these stock Victorian elements were of course used by Hardy in *Desperate Remedies.*
5. Virginia Woolf, *The Common Reader (Second Series)* (London: Hogarth Press, 1932) p. 253 (originally published in *The Times Literary Supplement,* 19 January 1928).
6. Thomas Hardy, *The Hand of Ethelberta,* Ch. 23. Quotations are taken from Macmillan's New Wessex Edition (London: Macmillan, 1975/6). Chapter references for subsequent quotations are given in parentheses in text.
7. *Life,* p. 323.

8. Michael Millgate, *Thomas Hardy: A Biography* (Oxford: Oxford University Press, 1982) p. 174.
9. *Life*, p. 111; p. 106.
10. *Life*, p. 107.
11. *Life*, p. 60.
12. *Personal Notebooks*, p. 5.
13. *Life*, p. 302.
14. D. H. Lawrence, 'Study of Thomas Hardy' (1914). Republished in *Lawrence on Hardy and Painting* (London: Heinemann, 1973) p. 25.
15. 'The most impossible situation in it was said to be that of the heroine sitting at table at a dinner-party of the "best people", at which her father was present by the sideboard as butler. Yet a similar situation has been applauded in a play in recent years by Mr Bernard Shaw, without any sense of improbability.' *Life*, pp. 111/12.
16. David Lodge, 'Thomas Hardy as a Cinematic Novelist', in *Thomas Hardy after Fifty Years*, ed. Lance St John Butler (London: Macmillan, 1977) pp. 78–89.
17. *The Collected Letters of Thomas Hardy*, ed. Richard Little Purdy and Michael Millgate (Oxford: Clarendon Press, 1978) vol. I, p. 37.
18. Thomas Hardy's Will, printed in *Thomas Hardy's Will and other Wills of his Family* (Guernsey: Toucan Press, 1967) p. 3 (Monographs on the Life, Times, and Works of Thomas Hardy, 36).
19. Thomas Hardy, *The Mayor of Casterbridge*, Ch. 14.

Index